Annie's Christmas Wish

Annie's Christmas Wish

Quilts of Lancaster County Series

Barbara Cameron

Abingdon fiction

a novel approach to faith

Annie's Christmas Wish

Copyright © 2013 Barbara Cameron

ISBN: 978-1-4267-3389-5

Published by Abingdon Press, P.O. Box 801, Nashville, TN 37202

www.abingdonpress.com

Published in association with WordServe Literary Group, Ltd.,
10152 S. Knoll Circle, Highlands Ranch, CO 80130

Library of Congress Cataloging-in-Publication Data has been
requested.

Scripture quotations from The Authorized (King James) Version.
Rights in the Authorized Version in the United Kingdom are vested
in the Crown. Reproduced by permission of the Crown's patentee,
Cambridge University Press.

Printed in the United States of America

1 2 3 4 5 6 7 8 9 10 / 18 17 16 15 14 13

For dreamers

Acknowledgments

I have been so blessed by the reaction of so many to Jenny and Matthew's story. Readers have taken them, their *kinner*, and their family and friends to their hearts.

I had no idea what would happen when I turned in *A Time to Love*, the first book in the Quilts of Lancaster County series. It wasn't the usual Amish story.

But readers have been wonderful, writing me e-mails to tell me they've enjoyed each story as it was released. I wish I could meet each one of you in person and thank you!

When the original trilogy I proposed was completed, my editor called to ask for a Christmas story about Jenny and Matthew and their *kinner*. I suggested I write about Annie and I got a yes. I was delighted! Ramona Richards, my wonderful editor, and everyone at Abingdon Press have been so supportive of my books. I'm especially grateful to be able to revisit the Bontragers in this book.

Do you have a special wish for Christmas? Annie has, and it will take a lot to be able to fulfill it. Annie will step into a different world than she knows in Paradise, Pennsylvania. So will Aaron, the man who loves her.

And now, fix yourself a cup of hot chocolate or peppermint tea and find out what Annie's Christmas wish is!

I hope you enjoy this story!

Blessings to you!

Barbara

1

$\mathcal{A}$nnie lay on the quilt-covered bed tucked up in her cozy, tiny attic bedroom. She held up the snow globe and shook it, watching the little snowflakes inside swirl and swirl and then float gently down to cover the skyscrapers of New York City.

It was her favorite Christmas present ever, brought back from the big city by her *mamm* when she went to see her editor years ago. After she'd received the globe with its tiny glimpse of the city, Annie had borrowed books from the library and studied the photos and read everything she could. New York City seemed like such an exciting place, filled with such towering, fancy buildings, its streets lined with so many types of people from so many places. Stories were everywhere, stories of hope and joy and death and loss and—well, her imagination was soaring just thinking about them.

She might be twenty-one now, a woman and not a child, but she was no less interested—some might say obsessed—than she'd been with the city than when she first received the globe. Her one big wish had become to visit New York City, and now it was finally coming true.

Life here in her Plain community of Paradise, Pennsylvania, wasn't boring. Not exactly. She loved everything about it. But she'd always been a seeker, endlessly curious about even the tiniest detail of life. She'd been like that even before her *mamm* had moved here and married her *daed*. Before she became Jenny Bontrager, her mother had been Jenny King, a television news reporter who specialized in traveling around the world and showing people what war did to innocent children.

Annie thought the work sounded amazing. All the travel—it sounded so exciting. Meeting all kinds of people. Telling the stories of people who needed attention to their story to help them. Annie had never lacked for a meal. She'd always had a comfortable bed.

And even though she had lost her mother at a young age, she'd always had so many people around her to love her and make her feel safe and happy. The children her mother had seen overseas in war-torn countries had often lost parents, their homes—even been injured or killed themselves. And sometimes there was little food.

She looked up when there was a knock on the door frame.

"Hi. May I come in?"

"Of course." Annie moved so her mother could sit on the bed with her.

When she saw her mother's gaze go to the snow globe she held, she handed it to her. Jenny shook it and watched the snowflakes settle on the skyscrapers inside just as Annie had done.

"I remember when I gave this to you."

"You came back from a trip there and told us you were going to have a baby."

"Seems like just yesterday."

"Seems like he's been around forever to drive me crazy." She grinned. "Don't worry, I don't mean it. He's a good little brother."

"You mean when he's not being a little terror?"

Annie laughed and nodded. "Right. He's not afraid of anything. Must have some of the adventurer spirit you have inside him."

Her mother glanced down at her traditional Amish dress and laughed self-deprecatingly. "I'm not much of an adventurer now."

"You have a spirit of adventure in your heart," Annie told her.

She studied her mother, who looked so slim and pretty in a dress of deep green; her dark brown hair tucked neatly under her snowy white *kapp* still showed no gray. Jenny never missed the fancy clothes of the *Englisch*—never missed anything from that world from what she said. Annie wondered how she would feel visiting the city she'd made her home base for so many years.

"Getting excited?"

"It's going to be so amazing!" She looked at her mother. "I'm still surprised *Daed* said he wanted to go."

She sat up and hugged her mother. "But I'm glad he did. He's so, so proud of you. We all are."

"I appreciate it," Jenny told her. "But we're not going to the event for them to make a fuss over me. You know that's not our way."

"I know." Annie pretended to roll her eyes. "It's because the organization is helping children. And because your friend, David, is being honored too. "

"Exactly." Jenny paused and grinned. "Of course, it doesn't mean we can't have some fun while we're there."

Annie reached under her pillow and pulled out a handful of brochures. "I sent off for these. Look, the Statue of Liberty, Rockefeller Center, Times Square . . ."

"And the *New York Times*?" Jenny looked over the information packet for the newspaper. "Hardly a tourist attraction."

"Please?" Annie bounced on the bed like a kid. "I want to go so bad. Badly," she corrected herself.

Jenny chuckled. "I guess it *would* be attractive to someone who wants to be a writer."

She glanced over at Annie's small desk. "I remember when you started keeping a word journal. How you loved finding new words to tell us about."

"So this is where you went." Annie's father appeared in the doorway.

He filled the doorway, this tall and handsome father of hers. She and her brothers and sister had gotten their blond hair and blue eyes from him.

"Matthew, look! Annie's gotten all sorts of brochures of places to visit for us to look at before we go to New York City."

"The *New York Times*?" he asked, sounding doubtful. "I'm not sure your brothers and sister are going to be thrilled with going on a tour of a newspaper."

Annie looked imploringly toward her mother.

"Maybe we can think of someplace you and the rest of the family would like to go while Annie and I go on the newspaper tour, maybe the television studio where I used to work," Jenny suggested.

"It's no surprise the two of you would want to go there." He picked up the brochure of the Niagara Falls. "This looks amazing. Amos and Esther went there last year and said the boat ride was exciting. Bet Joshua would love this."

They heard a crash downstairs.

"The Bontrager children are never quiet," Jenny said, sighing. But she wore a smile. "I'd better go see what they're up to."

She patted Matthew's cheek as she passed him. "Supper in ten."

"Smells wonderful."

Laughing, she shook her head. "I'm making baked pork chops."

"One of my favorites."

She glanced back. "And something easy I can't mess up. Well, at least when I set the timer."

Matthew waited until she left the room and then he looked at Annie. They laughed.

"I heard you!" Jenny called back.

He struggled to suppress his grin. "It's still fun to tease her about her cooking."

"You have to stop," she told him sternly.

"You do it too. It's just so easy to tease her when she makes comments first. But she's become a good cook. Not that I'd have been any less happy to be married to her if she hadn't."

Tilting his head, he studied her. "So I guess you're going to miss Aaron while you're gone."

She frowned at him. "Don't tease."

"He's a nice young man."

With a shrug, Annie gathered up the brochures and tucked them under her pillow.

"Annie? Is there a problem?"

"No, of course not."

"We used to be able to talk about everything."

She looked up and felt a stab of guilt. He looked genuinely disappointed.

"He's afraid I'm going to stay there," she blurted out.

Matthew pulled over the chair from the desk and sat down. "You're not, are you?"

She frowned. "Of course not."

But oh, to stay longer than the four or five days they planned to visit. There was so much to see, so much to write about . . .

"*Gut*," he said, looking relieved.

She stood. "I should go down and help *Mamm* with supper."

He nodded. "I'm right behind you. She might need me to get the apple pie I smell baking out of the oven."

"Men!" she said, laughing as she walked from the room. "All you think of is your stomachs."

"Hey, a man works hard, he needs to eat."

When she got downstairs she saw her mother didn't need her help—Mary was visiting and staying for supper. She stood at the counter slicing bread while Johnny set the table. Joshua was no doubt out in the barn finishing his chores. There was nothing he liked better than to feed and water the horses.

She'd known her siblings would be doing their evening chores. But it had been a good excuse for getting out of a discussion of Aaron with her father. She hadn't liked what Aaron said about her going to New York City. And there was no need to be getting into it with her father in any case. Such things weren't discussed with parents until you actually knew you were getting engaged, and right now, she and Aaron were just friends.

It was fun going to singings and church activities and things with him, but she wasn't ready to get married yet. Fortunately, her parents wouldn't dream of pressuring her to do so. Many of her friends were waiting a little longer than their parents had before they married. After all, marriage was forever in her community.

At least, until death did you part.

Annie had been so young when her mother died that Jenny had been the only mother she'd ever known. Although Jenny moved with only a trace of a limp from the car bombing she'd suffered overseas, she'd experienced problems recovering from it that had affected her speech. Annie had bonded with her when her father had offered to drive Jenny to speech therapy on the days Annie went for help with her own childhood speech problem.

But maybe Annie was closer to Jenny, too, because Jenny had lost her mother when she was young and knew how it felt.

Their shared interest in writing came as her mother helped her with schoolwork and found Annie loved to put her active imagination on paper. Now her tiny room was full of boxes of journals and bound collections of poems and short stories.

Annie watched the way her family worked together in the kitchen getting the family meal on the table—especially loving the way her parents got along. Her father had come down the stairs and insisted on checking on the pie. Her mother shooed him away from the oven, insisting it needed five more minutes. She smiled at the way they pretended to argue, all the while teasing each other and loved seeing them occasionally sharing a kiss when they thought their *kinner* weren't watching.

They were different than the parents of most of her friends. Jenny's father had been born Amish but had decided not to join the church, so she was familiar with the Amish ways and had visited her grandmother here for years. Although Jenny and Annie's father had fallen in love as teenagers, Jenny had left one summer to go to college and her father had married Annie's mother some time later.

But then the terrible bombing overseas years later had an amazing result: Jenny's grandmother had invited her to recuperate at her house and Jenny had been reunited with Annie's father. After she joined the church, the two of them had gotten married. So they were different from the parents of her friends in that respect. Annie always wondered if they seemed more in love than other married couples because of all they'd been through. Then again, Amish couples didn't usually indulge in public displays of affection.

"Go tell Phoebe supper's ready," Jenny told her.

It was a simple thing to do—just a few steps across the room and a knock on the door of the *dawdi haus*.

Phoebe opened the door with a smile. "No need to knock, child. Mmm, something smells so good."

"Matthew thinks the pie should come out," Jenny said as Phoebe stepped into the kitchen. "I think it needs five more minutes. You decide."

Phoebe opened the oven door and nodded. "Jenny's right, Matthew. You know you're just impatient to be eating it."

He sighed and pulled out her chair. "You're right."

She patted his cheek before she sat. "Be patient. Even after it's done you'll need to let it cool a little."

Joshua came in from the barn, letting in a cold blast of wind. He took off his jacket, hung it on a peg, and went to wash his hands.

The wind picked up and rattled the kitchen window. "Hope it doesn't snow early this year," Phoebe said. "It'd make travel to the big city hard."

"It wouldn't dare snow and interrupt Annie's trip," Jenny said as the family took their seats at the big wooden kitchen table.

"Annie's trip? I thought it was Jenny's trip," Matthew remarked.

"I think she's even more excited than I am."

She grinned. "You're right."

They were just about to thank God for the meal when they heard a knock on the door.

"We know who it is," Joshua said, rolling his eyes.

"Be nice," Jenny told him with a stern look. But Annie saw the smile playing around her mother's lips.

"I'll get it," Annie said, but there was no need. No one else was getting to their feet.

She opened the door and found Aaron standing there, wearing a big smile and holding his hat in his hands.

"Good evening," he said smiling as he stepped inside and took off his hat. "Sorry I'm late."

❧

Aaron bent his head in prayer with the family and when it was over, he looked up and glanced around the table at Annie's family.

His family, he corrected himself. Each person here—Jenny, Matthew, Joshua, Mary, Johnny—had become so dear to him in these past months he felt they truly were already his family.

He didn't dare say so to Annie just yet. He wasn't a stupid man. He knew she didn't return his feelings yet.

Yet, he told himself. He was a determined man and she was the perfect woman for him, so he'd bide his time and see what happened. When you considered marriage was forever, having to wait months to date and become engaged wasn't so long.

"Aaron? Pork chop?" she asked as she handed him the platter.

He took the platter from her and as he did their eyes met. She smiled at him and he bobbled the fork. It clattered to the floor.

"I'll get a clean one for you," she said and started to rise.

"I can use this one," he told her, bending to lift it.

"Don't you dare!" Jenny cried.

"Your floors are clean," he insisted, but Annie snatched the fork from him and handed him a clean one.

"*Mamm* has better things to do than keep the floors clean enough to eat off of," she told him, frowning.

"I'm sorry," he said quickly. "I didn't mean to offend."

Jenny shook her head and smiled at him. "You didn't. I'm afraid I've been busy with a deadline and just don't have as much time to clean these days."

Aaron found himself glancing at Matthew to see his reaction, but the man was calmly eating his dinner. If he had any feeling his home wasn't up to par he certainly wasn't showing it—or appearing to hide it. Wives in the community often had jobs they performed inside or outside the home, but Aaron didn't know anyone who wrote other than Jenny.

And Annie seemed to want to follow in her mother's footsteps. She wasn't aware of it, but he had watched her daydream when she was supposed to be doing her lessons and had seen her delight in writing exercises. Just how she was going to be doing the writing she spoke of here in their Plain community of Paradise he wasn't sure. He knew Jenny wrote books, but he didn't know if it was something you had to go to college for like Jenny had. And Annie had never said she wanted to go to college, something that wasn't done by the Amish.

He knew Jenny's father had left the Amish community and Jenny had been raised *Englisch* and gone to college. She'd even traveled overseas in countries he hadn't heard of to cover stories for the television. She'd been hurt there, and then she'd come back to heal here. She and Matthew had been attracted to each other as teenagers, but she'd gone off to college and then to her work. When she came to Phoebe's house after her injury in the car bombing, Jenny had been a broken shell of a woman. But she'd recovered, learned to walk again, and ended up walking down the aisle at her wedding.

Aaron glanced over at Annie. He knew not to look at Annie the same way her parents did with each other.

"*Mamm* has an appointment with her editor while we're in New York City," Annie informed him as she passed him a bowl of mashed potatoes. "After, I've been invited to take a tour of the publishing offices."

The mashed potatoes he'd been spooning onto his plate landed with a wet plop on his plate.

"I can't wait," she said, her voice animated. "I'm hoping to talk *Mamm* into going to the *New York Times* building."

He'd never heard of anyone he knew going to visit the *New York Times* or a publishing company. Niagara Falls, some national parks—those were the kinds of places Plain people visited when they took a vacation away from home. He wondered how a building where books or newspapers were published could be interesting.

His own mother had asked him if it was wise to be seeing someone so different from the "usual girl" as she put it. When Aaron had asked her if she didn't like Annie, she'd blustered a bit and then said, of course she liked Annie.

"Jenny keeps to herself a lot," his mother explained. "To do her writing thing. Have you thought about if Annie goes after the same thing how it will affect you?"

He shook his head, as if to clear the thought of that conversation. He couldn't fault his mother—he'd wondered the same thing. But he and Annie had something in common in a way. Some people thought his carpentry was just making things out of wood. They saw him build a cabinet for a kitchen, a dresser to store clothes in. Sometimes they didn't see the workmanship, the way he tried to make something beautiful, not just practical.

Jenny spoke up. "Aaron? You're being quiet tonight."

"Man can't eat and talk at the same time," Matthew said, smiling slightly at him as he buttered a piece of bread.

Aaron nodded. "My *mamm* said don't talk with your mouth full. Especially when you're a guest."

"You're not a guest. You're family," Mary said, brightening. She gave him a gentle smile.

He smiled at her. She was so sweet, but so much quieter than Annie. Maybe it came from being older and married—

and having a husband who had to work long hours in the next town.

"How is *schul* going?" he asked her.

"It's my favorite time to teach," she said. "The Christmas play is coming along so well."

When he glanced at Annie, though, his heart sank. She was frowning.

He wondered if she didn't think of him as family. That hurt more than he thought it would.

"Aaron? Another pork chop?" Jenny asked him.

"No, thanks."

Annie stood, picked up his plate and hers, and took them to the sink. He watched her, admiring how she looked against the fading light coming in the kitchen window. Annie had grown prettier and prettier.

When she turned, he quickly looked away and found himself watched by Matthew.

Aaron's glance slid to Jenny, and he felt a little better when he saw the kindness in her gray eyes. She placed a scoop of vanilla ice cream on a piece of pie on a plate, then, as an afterthought, added another scoop and handed him the plate.

She saw Annie's lips quirk in a sort of smile, but she didn't say anything, just sat and ate her slice of pie. And kept glancing at the clock.

❧

"Thanks for coming. Don't let the door hit you on the way out."

Annie jumped at the sound of her mother's voice at her side. "What?"

"Just an old saying from my *Englisch* days," she responded with a wry smile. "You don't think you hurried Aaron on his way a little abruptly tonight? He barely had a chance to finish his dessert and you were saying we had a lot to do to get ready for the trip."

"We do."

Her mother's lips twitched. "Are we going to do that now?"

Annie tried to come up with a response, but under the steady gaze of her mother, she couldn't.

"I know what you're up to."

She was grown up, but Annie suddenly felt like the little girl she'd been when she first met Jenny. "Where's Johnny?"

"Your father's upstairs letting Johnny read to him. I know a twelve-year-old like Johnny isn't thrilled about doing that, but Mary says it's the only way he's going to improve his reading." She leaned in. "And you're changing the subject. I know that look. You're plotting."

"Plotting?"

"Yes, which story did you get an idea for at supper? I could almost see your brain whirling at the table."

Relieved, Annie leaned against the door. "You made it sound like you thought I was up to something a lot worse."

"Well, you'll never live down some of the wild stories you used to tell. Like the one about the burglars and the chocolate chip cookies that you told me when you were little."

Annie pushed away from the door and started for the kitchen. "It was true."

Now that she was older, Annie was surprised her parents hadn't laughed her out of the room for telling them burglars had broken into the house and eaten all the cookies in the cookie jar. Her father had pointed out nothing else had been stolen. Annie had insisted the burglars weren't interested in anything else once they found out how good her *mamm's* chocolate chip cookies were. Joshua had nodded emphatically, backing her up in her wild tale.

"Right," her mother drawled.

Annie laughed and slipped her arm through her mother's and walked with her into the kitchen. Her father had returned from his bedtime routine with Johnny. He looked up from the cup of coffee he was drinking as he sat at the table.

"What are the two of you up to?"

"She still thinks I'm going to believe the story she and Joshua told about cookies."

Matthew chuckled as he folded the newspaper and stood. "Annie, you didn't even fool me with that story and I always thought you were this sweet little girl who never did anything wrong. Poor Joshua. I think he took the blame for some pranks you pulled."

Annie did her best to look innocent.

Her parents exchanged a look and shook their heads. "One of my *Englisch* friends said I have it lucky because my children are raised Amish. I told her kids are kids wherever they are."

Annie glanced at the sink where the dinner dishes waited, unwashed. "Where's Mary?"

"I sent her up to her old room to lie down. She said she wasn't feeling well."

"Oh, I hope she's not coming down with a cold."

"I don't know. I don't like to ask too many questions. You know." He reddened.

"I'll go check on her."

Annie sighed and rolled up her sleeves. "Guess I'm doing the dishes."

Funny how Joshua was always at the table to eat but managed to vanish when it was time to do the dishes. She was tempted to go get him, but he was probably in the barn and it would just take more time.

"I'll help," her father said. "Wash or dry?"

"I'll wash," she said. "You always dried when we used to do this when I was a little girl, remember? 'Cause I was too short to reach the cabinet to put away the dishes."

His eyes took on a faraway look. "Seems like yesterday."

"You're not going to get all mushy on me, are you?" she asked, pretending to sound exasperated.

"Me? Never."

As much as Annie enjoyed washing the dishes—it was a chore where she could let her mind wander and ideas simmer—she just wanted to be done so she could go to her room. So she washed the dishes quickly, and if her father noticed he didn't say anything. She was relieved a few minutes later when she heard her mother's footsteps descending the stairs.

"Is Mary okay?"

"She's fine. I was afraid she was having cramps—"

"Here," Matthew said, handing Jenny the dish towel. "I'll leave the two of you to your girl talk."

"Honestly, Matthew, you don't need to be embarrassed."

"I'm not. Joshua is still out in the barn. I think I'll see if anything's wrong."

Her mother took his place at the sink but put the dish towel he'd handed her on the counter. "Honestly, you'd think he'd be used to it after having us girls in the house for years." She sighed. "I talked Mary into spending the night. No sense going home to an empty house. Ben will be back tomorrow and he can pick her up then.

"I'll finish. You go write."

"It wouldn't be right," Annie prevaricated. But even she could hear the insincerity in her voice.

Her mother bumped her hip, pushing her out of the way.

Laughing, Annie vacated the space in front of the sink. "Thanks. I'll owe you."

"Don't stay up too late," her mother called as she headed for the stairs. "We have a lot to do for the trip, remember?"

Laughing, Annie climbed the steps two at a time. She paused for a moment to look in on her sister but found she was already asleep. Once inside her own room, she threw herself on the bed. Reaching under the pillow, she pulled out her notebook and began scribbling madly.

2

$\mathcal{A}$nnie had never had enough to drink to get drunk—she'd only tried a beer or two during *rumschpringe* and hated the taste—but she thought maybe she knew what a hangover must feel like. Her head pounded, her eyes felt gritty, and every bone in her body ached.

She opened her eyes and daylight speared into them, making her moan and roll over to bury her head under her pillow. Her fingers encountered paper. She pulled it out and sat up, staring at the notebook in her hand. Page after page was covered with her scrawl. She sat up and squinted at it. Read a page. Then another.

And found herself smiling. Not bad. She'd written for two hours after she'd come upstairs last night, fallen asleep, then woken up at three a.m. to write in a blazing, white hot frenzy until she fell asleep again a couple hours later.

"Annie!"

She collapsed on her bed and pulled the pillow over her head again.

"Annie!"

Johnny tugged on the pillow. "Annie. *Mamm* says time to get up now."

She pulled the pillow off her face and stared at him. "What?"

"*Mamm* says time to get up."

"*Okay*."

He stood there, staring at her.

"You can go now."

He shook his blond head. "*Mamm* says stay here until you get out of bed."

Her mother knew her too well. "Fine." She sat up and swung her legs over the side of the bed. "I'm up. See?"

"'Kay." He started for the door, then turned back. "She said to tell you we're having pancakes."

She nodded, watched him walk out of the room, and immediately fell back onto the bed.

The story unfolded like one of the movies she'd seen. Annie watched her characters come alive like a dream, laughing and crying and acting like real people living real lives. She watched them, fascinated, listening to the dialogue she'd written coming out of their mouths.

"Annie!"

She jerked awake. Her mother's face loomed over her. "Why aren't you up? Aren't you feeling well?"

Sitting up, Annie yawned and shook her head. She held out the notebook. "I tried not to stay up too late, but I woke up with ideas I had to write down."

"Been there, done that." She sighed. "How many times have you and your brothers and sisters come downstairs and found me asleep at the kitchen table? Well, you'd better hurry or you're going to be late for work."

Annie sighed and got to her feet. A day in the life of Annie Bontrager, she thought as she pulled out her clothes and began to dress. She wanted to just stay here in this room and write and not have to go to her day job.

As she walked downstairs, she wondered how often her mother had felt that way. Instead, she not only cheerfully took care of her family responsibilities but also genuinely cared about them. Annie had never once felt she was a "step" kid to Jenny.

She glanced at the clock when she walked into the kitchen and grimaced. "Where is everyone?"

Her mother gave her a look as she piled dirty dishes in the sink. "Off to start the day. There's some oatmeal on the stove for you."

"I thought we were having pancakes."

"You snooze you lose." But her mother sighed and turned back to the stove. "You're lucky. There's just enough batter for two more. Mary couldn't eat much. Said her stomach didn't feel well again."

Annie wrapped her arms around her mother's waist and squeezed her. "Thanks."

Jenny stirred the batter and seemed lost in thought.

"*Mamm?* Something wrong"

She started. "Oh, no. Just daydreaming. You don't suppose . . ."

"What?"

"You don't suppose Mary could be pregnant?"

Annie bobbled the plastic container of lunch meat and cheese she'd just pulled from the refrigerator. She grabbed at it and set it on the counter. "I don't know. Did she say anything?"

Jenny shook her head and poured the batter on the hot griddle. "But they've been married a year now."

"Just can't wait to be a *grossmudder*, can you?" Annie teased as she quickly made herself a sandwich. A few cookies, an apple, and a bottle of juice and she was done.

"No, I can't wait," Jenny admitted softly.

She set the plate of pancakes on the table, poured syrup over them, and began cutting them into pieces. Then she looked up and caught Annie's wry smile. "Just saving you time."

"Okay. Thanks." Annie sat at the table and began shoving the pancakes into her mouth.

Jenny poured coffee into a travel mug, added a little cream and one teaspoon of sugar, and screwed on the top. She set the mug next to Annie's lunch tote, poured herself a mug of coffee, and sat at the table.

"These are good," Annie said between bites.

"They'd be even better if you weren't inhaling them," her mother said mildly.

"Sorry." She finished, wiped her mouth on the napkin, then got up to put her plate in the sink.

She grabbed her jacket, lunch tote, purse, and travel mug, kissed her mother on the cheek and was halfway out the door when her mother called her name.

"What?"

"You forgot your notebook."

Rolling her eyes and shaking her head, Annie dropped everything on the kitchen table.

"Thanks!" she gasped. "Only another writer would think of that!"

She ran up the stairs, taking them two at a time, grabbed the notebook off her bed, then ran back down the stairs. Halfway to the door again, she heard her name called and glanced back to see her mother pointing at her things on the table.

"Honestly, where is my head this morning," Annie said, grabbing them up. She stopped once again to kiss her mother's cheek before dashing out the door.

The day was a little cool for the first week of December, but Annie didn't mind. She walked briskly and felt plenty warm after a few minutes. There was little traffic, but she made sure she stayed to the right.

When she heard the buggy behind her, she didn't bother edging toward the grass at the side of the road. People in her community were careful of pedestrians since they were so often walkers themselves.

"Annie!" a familiar voice called.

She turned and saw Aaron smiling at her from within his buggy.

❧

"Good morning!"

Annie looked up at him, and her big blue eyes were a little unfocused. She blinked and then appeared to recognize him. "Oh, hi."

"You okay?"

She nodded. "I was just thinking about something as I walked."

"Oh. Well, let me give you a ride to work." When she hesitated, he gave her a big smile. "What, you won't take a ride to work?"

After a moment, she climbed inside. "I guess it's silly not to accept a ride."

He wanted to agree with her, but he was feeling good about having Annie sitting in his buggy.

"Beautiful day."

Annie nodded. "You're in a good mood today."

"Why wouldn't I be? Every day is a gift from our Father."

She looked at him, surprised. "Why, Aaron, I've never heard you talk like that."

He felt himself redden. "It's nothing special." He tucked down his chin. "It's not like I can come up with fancy words like you."

"I don't think I come up with fancy words," she said slowly. "I spend a lot of time finding the right word, but it's not always a fancy one—a complicated one."

He shrugged. She'd always seemed to shine at the school they'd attended. He'd wondered if she would follow in her mother's footsteps and go off to get more education after they graduated. Of course, her mother had been *Englisch* then, but still, maybe with Annie's interest in writing she'd want to learn more.

And to learn more she had to leave the community. The day she'd learned she would be going with her family to New York City she'd showed such excitement. He'd blurted out his worry that she might stay, and she'd just dismissed such thoughts.

A car passed them, and a woman leaned out the window to take a photo.

"They're so curious about us," she mused.

"Admit it: you're curious about them."

"Some. But it makes me think. There haven't been a lot of Amish writers who write about our life."

He turned to look at her. "Are you thinking about writing about your life?"

"I think a writer needs to consider all sorts of things. Try all sorts of writing. I've done some fiction, some nonfiction."

"Where do you get your ideas?"

She turned to him and rolled her eyes. "Why do people ask writers that?"

"Do they?"

"Yes. Drives my *mamm* crazy."

"Oh, so what does she tell people?"

She let out an exasperated laugh. "She says writers just see ideas where other people don't because our minds are wired differently. Kind of like the way you see things in a piece of wood, I imagine. Why are you asking?"

"Just trying to understand you, that's all."

"Really?" Her eyes were wide and very blue. "Why?"

How unaware could a woman be? he wondered.

The morning was so quiet the clopping of the hooves of the horse seemed to echo in his head. He wasn't an impulsive person, but maybe it was time he was more direct with her.

He jerked on the reins and signaled to his horse to pull over on the shoulder of the road.

"What are you doing?"

"We need to talk."

"Aaron, what are you thinking? I'll be late to work."

"This'll just take a minute." He turned to her. "Annie, I want to be more than friends with you. I'd like us to date."

Her eyes widened. "You do? You would?"

"Yes, I wouldn't be asking if I didn't."

She pulled her eyes away to look out the window of the buggy for a moment, and then she looked back at him. For the first time since he'd known her, she looked speechless.

"Well," he said. "The fact you're looking so surprised makes me think I haven't been handling this right at all."

He stared ahead, looking for the right words. He wasn't a fumbler with women. Well, it wasn't like he was skilled with them, either. He'd just spent a lot of time training for his trade and he hadn't wanted to rush into things.

Then one day there'd been something that made him take a second look at Annie . . .

She touched his hand, and his gaze shot up as if he'd touched electricity. "Look, don't blame yourself," she said. "I've been kind of preoccupied since I learned about the trip."

The trip. He got this . . . uneasiness every time it came up.

A car drove past and he forced his attention back to the matter at hand. "You need to get to work, and I have a delivery. Could we have supper tonight and talk?"

"Well, it's kind of hard to talk during supper at our house—" she began and then she stopped and shook her head. "Sorry, you meant have supper somewhere."

He laughed. "*Ya*. Like at a restaurant."

She blushed. "Okay, you don't need to make fun of me."

"I'm poking fun at both of us, Annie."

He got the buggy back on the road, and it wasn't long before he was dropping her off at work.

"How about I pick you up after work and we go then?"

She nodded. "I'll call home and let my mother know. I'll be ready to go at five."

He nodded. "Have a good day."

"You too."

He felt a surge of excitement that he'd made a date with her for supper. It was the first step—and wasn't the first step the biggest one in whatever you did in life? You made the decision, stepped out, and started the journey. He'd looked for a trade and given it a lot of thought. His father was a carpenter and he'd always enjoyed watching him build things. In time, since he'd shown an interest, his father gave him his own tools, which he still used today.

There was a lot to do before he returned to pick Annie up. The delivery first, then installation. It would take a big chunk of the day.

Then back home to work on several custom orders. An *Englisch* friend had set up and was running a website for him, so his handiwork was traveling outside the Paradise community. The reputation the Amish had for excellence in carpentry was well-known and Aaron wanted his work to reflect that reputation. It wasn't a question of pride but of value—he wanted those who bought the chests of drawers and bathroom vanities and all the other items he crafted to be valued pieces in their homes.

His business had grown, and he knew he'd be working some long hours to fill new orders. It was one of the toughest things about running his own business—trying to learn how to avoid taking on too much work. Charging too little to cover expenses was also a problem. He'd learned a lot about the business side of carpentry, not just the craft.

He unloaded the kitchen cabinets he'd custom-crafted for a local builder, ran his hand over the cherry wood, and thanked his Maker for giving him the desire to build something that mattered to him. A man's work was a part of his heart.

And the woman God had chosen for him was another.

He hoped he'd know he had found the one when he talked to Annie in the evening, hoped he wasn't listening to his own inner feelings instead of divine guidance.

❧

As jobs went, Annie's wasn't big or exciting. She didn't save lives or anything, although the people she worked for always acted like they didn't know what they'd do without her.

All she did was bookkeeping for a family furniture store. She'd always been good with numbers, not just with writing. Her mother said she was probably whole-brained, which had startled Annie the first time she said it. Didn't everyone have a whole brain? Her mother explained some people were right-brained—they mostly used the side of the brain responsible for creativity, for nurturing, that sort of thing. She'd read a third of people were right-brained like her.

The left side, the logical, scientific side, was the one you used to do math and such. The people who used the left side the most made up another third. And the people who used both sides equally, they were good at math and English.

Her mother knew things like that. It was like she was like a walking encyclopedia. Annie supposed it came from all the education her mother had had. She hadn't been raised Amish, so her father had sent her to college. She'd traveled all over the world, too, and picked up all sorts of things. Stuff about cultures and languages and religions.

It all sounded fascinating to Annie, who had thought about college. She and her parents had even talked about it. But Annie liked figuring out things herself, and so she pursued her own journey of discovery at the library, spending hours there and lugging home books by the dozen until her father teased that she'd read every one the place had to loan.

Of course she hadn't—there were some books she just didn't care to read—but one of the librarians had been delighted in an avid reader and even suggested some books she got through something called an interlibrary loan.

Annie got out the big ledger, a big book that held all the important information about how much money came in and where it went out, and began her work. Time passed quickly in the little office at the rear of the building. Tomorrow, she'd have paychecks ready for the half-dozen carpenters who worked in the back as well as a few who did part-time work. So today, it was important to make sure all bills were paid and there was money in the store checking account for paychecks.

Someone rapped on the door frame, and she looked up, squinting for a minute until her eyes adjusted from little numbers on a page to the woman standing there smiling at her.

"Lunchtime already?" Annie asked her, glancing at the clock.

"Break time," Leila said. "I made tea."

Annie smiled and stood, stretching to unkink muscles tightened a little from sitting too long and working without moving.

"I talked to your mother the other day," Leila told her as she pulled a chair up to Annie's battered desk. "Are you getting excited about your trip?"

"You know I am. Remember how the first couple of days after I found out you'd walk in here and catch me daydreaming."

Leila laughed and nodded. "I was so surprised. You're always this studious little mouse in here working on the books. I walked in here a few times and found you doodling and staring out the window."

Annie took a sip of her tea and carefully set the mug down on the desk. "I'm grateful you and John didn't fire me. I wasn't a good employee."

"Now, now," Leila said and reached across the desk to pat Annie's hand. "Everyone has a little slip now and then. You've been a dependable, hard-working employee for us from the day we hired you. Why, you haven't ever even taken a sick day."

"We need to set some time aside before I leave to show you what will need to be done while I'm gone."

"We'll do that." Leila leaned back in her chair. "So, I saw you got a ride into work today."

Annie felt color flood her face. "Aaron's just a friend."

Leila nodded. "It should start out that way."

"It?"

"Marriage."

"Leila, I don't want to get married for a long time." Annie drained her mug, set it aside, and pulled the ledger toward her, hoping her boss would take it as a sign she needed to get back to work.

The woman stood and collected the mugs. "If you say so."

Annie watched her leave the room and shook her head. *Why did people start trying to plan your life for you just because you got to a certain age?* she wondered. She wasn't the only *maedel* who wasn't rushing to get married. Lots of her friends were getting married later.

She turned her attention back to paying bills, and the next time she glanced at the clock, she saw it was lunchtime. Closing the ledger, she slid it into the drawer of the desk and then reached for her lunch tote. Sometimes, depending on the weather, she ate at one of the wooden picnic tables at the back of the store. Today, though, the sky was overcast, and the wind had been a little chilly on the ride in. So she arranged her lunch on a napkin she'd brought and opened her notebook.

She took a bite of her sandwich, chewed, and began writing her three pages. It was one of the things she'd done ever since she brought home some library books on writing. One had recommended keeping a notebook as a sort of journal entry and sometimes brainstorming place. You were supposed to just write without conscious plan and let your mind flow. What Annie had noticed is she often started out writing about how her day began and what project she was working on— sometimes a problem she was having would emerge on the page and she'd write that she didn't know how to solve it— then, by golly, at the end of the three pages, there would be the solution.

She always let out a happy sigh when that happened.

So today she wrote about how she'd felt a little off-kilter at waking late and then rushing out the door, and suddenly, there had been Aaron asking her if she wanted a ride. And asking if they could date.

She paused and stared at the word *date* on the page. It wasn't as though she hadn't gone out a time or two with a boy before this. Well, she'd mostly just gone to some singings with

Ben Stoltzfus and a picnic and a few church youth activities with Henry Zook. But none of them had come to anything. Those dates felt like going out with a brother. There certainly hadn't been any of the chemistry she'd heard other girls talk about feeling.

Her pencil slowed and she stared down at the last thing she'd written and surprised herself: Aaron Beiler.

Okay, so there was a lot to like about Aaron or she wouldn't be friends with him, wouldn't let him invite himself to supper with her and her family a couple of times a week—yes, she had become aware he was good at charming his way to their supper table. But he was harmless and her family sometimes invited him when she didn't and everyone liked him. So no harm done.

Except now he'd changed things by asking her if they could date.

Annie found herself setting up two columns on the page in front of her: *Pro* on one side, *Con* on the other. Hmm. Doing this was logical, left-brain stuff. Maybe she really wasn't all right-brained? Sure, there were positives to dating Aaron: he was a good friend she could talk to, she'd discovered he loved to read too, and they'd talked at length about books they'd discovered they both liked.

She couldn't come up with any negatives, any reasons she shouldn't at least talk to him about dating.

Except she wanted something more . . . the spark she heard others talk about. The something she saw in her parents . . .

She pushed the pad aside, nowhere near the revelation she often had, the solution to a problem or something bothering her personally or in a writing project.

Thoughtful, she took another bite of her sandwich and chewed it. Clearly, she needed to think about this more.

3

$\mathcal{A}$aron parked and waited for Annie to leave work.

He'd been careful not to show up too early because it might look like he was trying too hard or he was desperate. But in the few minutes he waited, he saw the curious looks of Annie's coworkers as they left the store and headed home.

She emerged from the store carrying her ever-present notebook and her lunch tote. Then she stopped, smacked her forehead with her hand, and went back into the store. When she emerged, she carried her purse as well.

That was Annie . . . just a little absent-minded because her mind seemed to be someplace else some of the time. She reminded him of her mother that way. He wondered if all writers were a little distracted because they were thinking of whatever it was they were writing when they weren't jotting it down.

"Sorry, forgot my purse," Annie said as she climbed into the buggy and set her things on the floorboard. "Second time I forgot something today. I'm not usually this distracted."

She slid a glance at him. "No comment?"

He grinned. "*Nee.* I think I'm learning from watching how your *daed* behaves around your *mamm* about the writing." He got the buggy moving. "Funny, don't you think? She's not your real mother, but you're so much like her."

"Nature versus nurture," she murmured.

"Huh?"

"Oh, some people believe we're more a product of our environment than our genes." She lifted her shoulders and let them fall. "She's the only mother I've known," she said. "My birth mother died when I was so little, so Jenny's the only mother I've *ever* known."

She gazed out the window, and her bonnet hid her face from him. "*Mamm* told me she knew what I was going through—what Joshua, Mary, and I felt because her mother died when she was just a girl."

Silence fell over them, the only sound the clip-clop of the horse's hooves on the road.

A restaurant popular with locals was just up the road. Aaron asked her if she wanted to go there or somewhere fancier.

"That's fine," she told him. "They have good food."

He pulled into the parking lot, and they went inside. The server brought menus followed by their drinks, and soon they were left to themselves.

Silence stretched between them. For all her usual talkativeness, she apparently was leaving the conversational ball in his court.

"This trip. Are you worried your mother will want to stay in New York when you visit?"

She choked on the drink she'd just taken of her iced tea and stared at him with big, round eyes. "Why would you ask?"

Maybe it wasn't the best question. Maybe he should have given it more thought.

"I wonder if she's missed her old life there is all. It's probably more exciting than life here." He spread his napkin on his lap, needing something to do with his hands.

"We're not going to New York City because she misses it," Annie told him. "We're going because some people want to thank her and David for their work to save children."

He felt a bit of tension in the air. He'd obviously overstepped. "I know. You told me."

"Oh." She was silent for a moment. "You just made it sound like she was going there because she didn't want to be here anymore."

"Sorry."

"You don't know my *mamm* very well."

He took a deep breath. "I'd like to know her better."

She turned to look at him. "What?"

"I meant to say, I'd like to get to know her better by getting to know you better."

"I see. Don't you think you've gotten to know me by now? We've known each other for years."

He considered that but shook his head. "We know each other as kids who grew up together, who've attended school and church and activities. But it's not really knowing a person, is it?"

When he glanced at her he saw he had her attention.

"What else do you want to know?"

"Were you as surprised as you seemed by my asking you about dating earlier today?"

She nodded. "I thought you just wanted to be friends."

"I did. Things . . . changed."

"Changed? How?"

Aaron shrugged. "It feels like it's time."

"Time?"

The server appeared with their food and Aaron waited until she left. "I've been working hard to build up my business, to save to have a place of my own."

Annie paused in cutting up her roast beef. "Aaron," she said slowly. "Are saying it's time to start looking for a wife?"

He felt the blood rush to his face. "Well . . . yes."

Her hand flew to her mouth. "Oh, " she managed. "Are you saying you want to marry me?"

Aaron frowned. "Well, maybe."

"Maybe?"

Drawing himself up, he looked at her. "If you're thinking it's a bad idea, I guess not."

"I didn't say that." Her gaze fell to her plate. "I just—well, it's just not something I've thought about."

"Marriage in general or to me?"

"In general. I haven't thought about it much. I mean, I'm only twenty-one."

"Plenty of girls get married at twenty-one."

Annie nodded. "I know a lot of girls think about getting married from the time they're little. But they're not me. You talk about getting your business established. I want to get my own career started before I get married."

"You work as a bookkeeper."

"It's a *job*. It's not a career. I don't want to do that all my life."

"Then why did you take the job?"

"It's just my day job."

"Day job?"

She nodded. "I wanted something to do to make some money, but I want to concentrate on learning how to write."

"You learned how to write in school."

"Not that kind of writing. Not essays. Other things. Articles. Books."

"There's no need to work. You could say home and raise our children."

"Aaron! A woman needs work she enjoys as much as a man does. How would you like it if I said you don't need to work after you marry?"

She tilted her head and waited for him to answer.

He stared at her, at a loss for words. Annie was an easy woman to love, but she sure would be a challenge to live with, that was for sure and for certain.

"Think about it," she said, smiling at him.

⋙∾⋘

"Mmm, something smells good."

Her mother turned from where she stood at the sink and smiled. "You're home. I saved you some meatloaf so you could have it for your lunch tomorrow. "

Annie hugged her mother. "Did you hide it in the fridge?"

Jenny glanced around. "In the secret place," she whispered.

Laughing, Annie went to check. Sure enough, the plastic baggie with two slices of meatloaf was hiding under the salad fixings in the refrigerator.

"What we have to do to keep the men in the house from eating everything," she told her mother. She set her notebook and lunch tote down then took off her jacket and hung it on a peg.

"Want some tea?"

Annie nodded. "I'll make it."

She boiled the water, poured it into mugs, and brought the box of Sleepy Time tea to the table. "Not sure I need this tonight. I kept yawning at supper. I hope Aaron didn't take it personally. I told him I was up late last night. "

"So, a date, huh?"

Annie gave her mother a direct look.

Jenny lifted her hands. "I'm sorry, I know parents usually stay out of this in our community, but it's hard for me. I was *Englisch* before I was Amish, and I was a reporter before I was a parent."

She couldn't help it—the mixture of frustration and embarrassment on her mother's face was priceless. Annie let out a hoot of laughter.

"What's so funny?" her father asked as he walked into the room.

"*Mamm's* having an identity crisis."

He raised his brows as he poured himself a cup of coffee. "Jenny?"

"I know the parents are often the last ones to know couples are dating or getting engaged," she said. "But it just feels unnatural not to—" she stopped, obviously looking for the right word.

"Take an interest?" Matthew put in.

Annie rolled her eyes. "You're just saying so because *you've* tried to talk to me about Aaron."

"Hey," he said, holding up a hand. "I was just expressing a little fatherly interest."

Jenny turned to him. "You never told me you were talking to Annie about Aaron."

"I just said he was a nice young man."

"All I did was ask about her date tonight," she told him.

She turned to Annie. "You know I'm not pressuring you about dating or getting married."

"*Ya*, if she had her way you'd be with us forever," Matthew agreed.

Jenny's jaw dropped. "I don't want that! It wouldn't be good for Annie! Baby birds have to leave the nest sometime."

Annie was enjoying their exchange. "So when *would* I get the boot?" she asked, keeping her tongue firmly in her cheek.

"*Not* funny!" Jenny said, indignant.

"Oh, I'm sorry, but I'm enjoying how you're trying not to pry when you want to so much."

Jenny folded her arms across her chest. "Well. I get laughed at for expressing interest."

Matthew chuckled, and Jenny shot him a censuring look. He strolled over and picked up the box of tea. "Sleepy Time?"

"It's good to relax with at the end of the day. Some of us can't drink caffeine just before bedtime and drop off."

He picked up her cup and took a sip. "Not bad." He frowned. "Tastes familiar." He tilted his head and studied Jenny. "What?"

A giggle escaped her. "Remember last year when you were laid up with the flu?"

"*Ya*," he said, narrowing his eyes. "What about it?"

"You had a little bell you'd ring when you needed something."

"We made about a million trips up and down those stairs," Annie said, remembering.

She watched realization dawn.

"So you made me a cup of this tea," Matthew said slowly, and he shook his head. "Well, aren't you the sly one."

"Men are the worst patients."

"Hey, I was really sick." He picked up the newspaper lying on the table and bent to kiss her cheek. "See you upstairs."

Rounding the table, he hugged Annie and kissed the top of her head before making his way up the steps to the upstairs bedrooms.

Annie propped her chin on her hands, her elbows on the table. She stared into her cup of cooling tea. "What if I don't want to get married?" She looked up at her mother. "What would you think?"

"It doesn't matter what I think," Jenny said slowly. "It's what you think is right for you." She frowned. "Do you not want to get married?"

Annie rubbed her hands over her face. "I don't know. I just don't seem to have this . . . compelling urge like some of my friends do. And Aaron. I like him as a friend, but this thing he has about wanting to date. I don't know."

She got to her feet and paced the kitchen, searching for the words. "He seemed to think I should have known he was interested in dating me."

"You *are* Miss Oblivious. Your father and I both noticed Aaron wanting more than friendship."

"Well, I watched him during supper, and he was so attentive, so much the gentleman." Annie stopped. "But I didn't feel anything."

"Sit down," her mother said. "Come on. Let's talk this out."

She sat as her mother requested, rubbing at one aching temple. The lack of sleep was catching up with her.

"I didn't feel anything," she said, shaking her head. "He did all the right things, but I didn't feel anything."

Her mother reached over and patted her hand. "Don't force it. Just because you know his feelings have changed doesn't mean yours automatically have to flip and match them. Give it some time and see how you feel."

Annie sighed. "You're right."

Jenny rose, rummaged in a cabinet, and found a bottle of ibuprofen. She returned to the table and handed it to Annie. "Let me get you some water."

"I can take it with the tea." She shook two tablets out of the bottle and took them with a swallow of tea, making a face at how cold it had grown.

"You know, just because someone expects something of us doesn't mean we have to give it or be it. Or that we should even try."

"I know. I do." She shook her head. "You're the wisest woman I know."

Jenny glanced at the door to the *dawdi haus* where her grandmother lived. "No, I'm not. That would be Phoebe."

Jenny paused, then sighed and said, "We should get to bed."

Annie nodded. But neither of them moved.

In the silence of the night they heard the tinny sound of a bell. They looked at each other and then they laughed. "I hid that bell," Jenny told her.

"Sounds like he found it."

Jenny put their cups in the sink and turned off the gas lamp. "Well, I'm getting it back from him, and he's not going to find it again."

Annie followed her mother up the steps and walked past her parents' room to her own. She'd said she wasn't sure she wanted to get married, but if she did, she wanted the kind of marriage they had. Otherwise . . . well, she'd rather be an old maid and scribble away in a little place of her own.

⁂

As dates went, the one Aaron had with Annie hadn't gone exactly the way he'd hoped.

Aaron knew Annie was a little untraditional. It was to be expected since her mother hadn't been Amish all her life. And Annie had always been creative. He'd watched her daydream in school, sometimes draw away from the other children and write in a notebook. She had this habit of watching . . . just watching everything. It was like she was always studying life or something.

She never noticed he was watching her watching other people. He thought he was okay with her looking at him as a friend instead of a possible *mann*. The date had been tentative but it was fine. A lifelong commitment was worth spending some time on, and he knew deep inside that relationships that were too passionate . . . too quick . . . could burn out. Better a slow, carefully thought-out plan.

Much like the way he worked. He chose just the right wood for the project, then examined it carefully for structural strength and blemish-free surface. The process, the work, was never rushed.

He glanced up at a knock on the door frame. "Paul! Glad you could stop by."

The other man held up a handful of papers. "Bunch of new orders for you. I don't know how you're going to take care of all these."

"One of my uncles says he can give me some help starting later this week." Aaron took the orders and quickly leafed through them. He looked up and grinned. "I can't tell you how much I appreciate your help with the website. Have a seat and let me get you the check I wrote."

Paul, a lean, rangy *Englischer* Aaron's age, took a seat on one of the newly crafted chairs. "Happy to have the work. Every little bit helps with the family."

Aaron searched his desk drawer for the check he'd made out earlier and handed it over. "How are Susan and the baby?"

"Great, great. You should try married life. I can highly recommend it."

"I'm trying," Aaron muttered, then realized he'd spoken aloud.

Paul perked up. "What? Are you engaged?"

Aaron laughed and shook his head. "Barely dating."

He laid the orders on his desk and returned to the dining table he was building. "I've got some coffee in the thermos if you want it."

"No, thanks, I've had your coffee. I'm used to good coffee now that I'm married."

"Don't rub it in." Aaron frowned as he sanded the top of the table.

"Hey, you sound seriously down."

Aaron stopped and looked at his friend. Their worlds were so different it was a wonder to him sometimes how they had become good friends. The *Englisch* talked of feelings a lot, something not done in the Plain community.

"How did you know Susan was the one for you?"

"We dated for a long time in college."

He fell silent and seemed to look inward. Then he looked at Aaron and shrugged, even looked a little embarrassed. "One day I looked at her and, I don't know, it was like I just knew Susan was the one I wanted to be with the rest of my life."

Aaron continued sanding as he thought about what Paul said. He'd done the same thing with Annie.

"Did you met this girl when you were in school?"

"*Ya*, although it wasn't college. I didn't meet her in medieval literature class." He grinned at Paul . Ever since he'd discovered the man taught such a strange thing, he hadn't been able to resist teasing him about it.

"Hey, some of my students love it. And I almost make a living," he said self-deprecatingly. "I don't make as much as if I taught business classes, but you have to do what you love. God provides. Things come along when there's a need for a little extra money. He introduced you to me and we help each other."

He leaned forward, went through the orders, and plucked one out. "Here, I almost forgot. This order is from me. I want to buy one of those baby cradles. My sister-in-law saw the one you made for us and wants a cradle just like ours. Maybe you can give me a discount?" he joked.

"That makes three sales just from people seeing the cradle I made for you," Aaron said. "Of course, you can have a discount. A big one. And maybe I should be paying Amy a commission."

"She enjoys being a model for you. I brought another picture." He pulled it from his shirt pocket and held it up for Aaron to see.

Aaron leaned over the table and found himself smiling. "She's beautiful."

"She is, isn't she?" Paul said, looking completely goofy as he gazed at the photo. "I mean, people try to be polite when they look at a newborn, but the fact is, many of them look like little pink prunes. Amy? She came out looking so gorgeous. I think she takes after her mother."

"How long did you know her—Susan, I mean, not the baby—before you got married?"

Paul raised his eyebrows. "What a strange question coming from you."

Aaron felt himself redden. "Sorry if it's too personal."

"No, no, it's okay. It's just I've known you for several years and I don't remember you ever asking me a personal question."

He steepled his fingers and looked at Aaron over them. "Like I said, we dated in college for a couple of years. We weren't in a hurry because we wanted to make sure we got our degrees. Got married the week after we graduated."

"So, is that a long time for *Englischers* to know each other before they get married?"

"I dunno what the average is. I heard everyone's waiting to get married later—English *and* Amish." He fell silent for a moment. "Can I ask you a question?"

Aaron bent and blew at the fine dust sandpapering the tabletop had created. "*Schurr*. What do they say—turnabout's fair play?"

"What brought this up? You thinking about getting married? Or is it too personal?"

Shrugging, Aaron turned to get the can of stain and a clean paintbrush. "Maybe," he said finally.

"Don't worry, I won't say anything to anyone."

"Not even Susan?"

"Not even Susan."

Aaron dipped the paintbrush into the can of stain and began spreading it in even strokes along the grain of the tabletop. "It's not like I've planned anything."

"You're just private about things."

Nodding, Aaron set the can down, laying the brush atop it, and used a rag to wipe at the excess stain. He nodded in satisfaction. The wood nearly glowed with the color. Picking the can and brush back up, he continued working. "I've known this girl since we were both children."

Glancing up, he grinned. "She's a bookkeeper for a furniture store. You'd like her. She's smart. Oh, I don't mean about the numbers she adds. She's the first person to tell you it's her 'day job' as she calls it. She wants to be a writer like her *mamm*."

"Are you talking about Annie Bontrager?"

Aaron nearly bobbled the can of stain. "You know Annie?"

Paul shook his head. "I've just heard about her mother. Jenny Bontrager. She's going into New York City later this month to be recognized for her work about children, right?"

There it went, Aaron thought. He felt his heart plummet right into his stomach at the mention of Annie venturing into the big city.

"*Ya*," he mumbled. "I wish—"

"Aaron!" a female voice called.

He sighed. "Back here!" he hollered. Then he glanced at Paul. "Don't say anything. You're about to meet my mother."

4

Annie jumped at the knock on her bedroom door. "Who is it?"

"It's me, Mom."

"Come in!" She watched her mother enter the room, and after a quick glance behind her, she shut the door without Annie asking.

"What's in the bag?"

"Promise you won't laugh?" Jenny sat down on the bed clutching a bag with the Stitches in Time logo to her chest.

"Okay."

Jenny reached into the bag and then paused. "It's such a beginner's work."

"Come on, it can't be that bad."

"Anna says it's coming along well, but I don't know." She sighed, then pulled out a muffler in shades of gray wool. "You promised not to laugh."

Annie reached out and stroked the muffler. "It's beautiful. Why would you think it looks like a beginner's?"

Jenny bit her lip. "You think it's okay?"

"Yes. *Daed* will love it."

"I took the knitting class almost as a joke. I went into Stitches in Time one day needing some thread and Anna was teaching this knitting class. It just looked so relaxing, you know? So, I go whenever I have time. This month we're making gifts for Christmas."

"You need something to help you relax."

Jenny shrugged. "I know. And I like the idea of making the gifts we exchange. Makes the holiday so much less commercial."

Annie had heard her mother talk about how much she preferred the holiday here in the community over her past life living in New York City. There, people apparently bought and bought and bought.

"So, you're working on a Christmas gift, too, huh?"

Annie opened her eyes wide and pretended innocence. "No, I'm making notes . . ." she drifted off when her mother reached over and touched the cuff of the man's shirt peeking out from under Annie's pillow.

"Now it's your turn not to laugh," Annie warned as she pulled it out. "I'm working on a shirt for *Daed*."

She sighed. "I wish I were good at sewing like my mother was." She stroked the quilt she sat upon. "She made each of us a quilt before she died. Look how small and neat her stitches are, how she made something so beautiful out of scraps of material."

Jenny leaned forward and examined it, then the shirt Annie was sewing. "Oh, you're doing a wonderful job. Remember, your mother had been sewing for a lot longer by the time she did your quilt. You'll get better if you keep sewing.

"I just don't have the patience to do this hand stitching." She stroked the shirt. "So soft. And I love the color. It's just the color of his blue eyes." She looked at Annie. "And yours and the rest of the children." She grinned. "Even Johnny got the blue eyes, not my gray which I always thought were boring."

"Yours are pretty too," Annie said sincerely. "And Johnny might not have gray eyes, but he looks like you." When her mother just continued to look at her, she grinned. "Well, no, he looks like the rest of us. Maybe if you have another baby, he or she will look like you."

"I think those days are over," Jenny said with a sigh. "I DID tell God I'd be happy if I had just one baby of my own." A look of consternation came over her face. "Oh, I don't want you to think I didn't always think of you children as mine—"

Annie patted her hand. "Don't worry. I know. I never felt like you were my stepmother. You've always been my *mamm*." She knotted her thread, clipped it, and threaded her needle.

"Matter of fact, I thought you were only my *mamm*," she said. "Not Joshua's. Not Mary's. You were just for me."

"Not their *mamm* at all?"

She shook her head. "We bonded, remember? Both of us had trouble talking, and we had to go to speech therapy." She stopped sewing for a minute. "Kids can be so mean. I remember getting teased about my speech problem. You understood because you had the same problem. Not for the same reason. But you understood."

Then she cringed. "I'm so sorry. I didn't mean to remind you about the awful bombing—"

Jenny leaned forward to pat her hand. "You know you don't have to walk on eggshells around me. I have scars on my body, so it's not like I don't have reminders every day," she said quietly.

She glanced at the window, and Annie's gaze followed hers. The trees were bare of leaves, outlined against the fading light.

"It was this time of the year when I came back here," she said softly, her expression becoming reflective. "I thought I'd recuperate, get over the last operation I had to fix me. Instead, I got a husband and a family."

Annie grinned. "I thought you were marrying me, not *Daed*. That's how mixed up I was."

"You were just a little girl. A precious little girl I fell in love with before I fell in love with her father." She grinned at Annie.

"It was all about me." She picked up her needle again. "I think I could be described as egocentric." When her mother raised her eyebrows, she laughed. "I know, there I go using one of those words I used to like to write down in my notebook."

She spread the shirt out on her lap and looked it over.

"The shirt looks wonderful. Why are you frowning?"

"I was just thinking about Aaron. I just don't understand why he's interested in me. We're so different." She looked at her mother. "I know people say opposites attract, but doesn't it get hard to be around each other?"

Jenny shrugged. "I suppose it depends on what kind of things you're looking at when you talk about differences."

"He works with his hands and I work with words."

"So far you could be describing your father and me."

Annie blinked. "But you haven't heard all of it. He said I could stay home and raise children and not work."

"Well," her mother said slowly. "I had no idea Aaron felt that way."

"I'm not sure he's thought so far ahead. Or," she muttered, "if he's thinking at all. I can't imagine not working."

"Well, if you're a mother you're going to be working. It's a twenty-four-hour-a-day job."

"Of course, I've watched you. But you know what I mean. I want to have a family, but I want to do something—have work I enjoy—too. Children do grow up, you know."

"I've heard," her mother said dryly.

Annie stared at her and then laughed. "Yeah, and I heard some of them actually leave home."

She found herself hugged. "I know we were joking about this the other day, but Annie, don't you dare think I want you leaving the nest before you're ready. Don't you dare. Promise me."

Tears rushed into her eyes. "I won't. I promise."

▬

"Hey, I'm here. Ready to get those packages out?"

Aaron looked up. "Paul. You're sure you don't mind?"

"Nope. We're off for winter break." He held up a sheaf of papers. "Printed out what I think are the last orders we'll get before Christmas. I wanted to make sure you got them before Susan and I left to see her parents."

"Great, thanks."

Aaron took the stack of orders and sent up a silent prayer of thanks to God for the abundance He was sending.

"And these are the last of the orders to get mailed out so they reach the customers in time for gifts," Aaron told him, waving his arm at a pile of small and medium boxes stacked in the corner. "I have some bigger local pieces Tom Baylor is helping deliver later in the week."

"This one has Amy's name on it," Paul said when he lifted it and read the name written on the box.

"I did that so I wouldn't forget," Aaron told him. "It's one of the wooden duck pull toys I make."

Paul grinned. "She'll love it. We got a lot of orders for those handmade toys. Grandparents seem to love to buy them. I guess they make people feel like they're something they played with when they were little."

The two of them carried boxes out to Paul's pickup truck and soon had all the boxes loaded.

Paul slapped his hand on the truck's side before they climbed in and headed off. "I'm going to miss her. Got a buyer for her, a man who's getting it for his son for Christmas."

"What will you do without it?"

"We're going to try being a one-car household. Susan wants to be a stay-at-home mom for a while, so we don't think we need two cars. It'll cut down on expenses."

"What does she do?"

"She's a kindergarten teacher. It'll be a good schedule for her one day when she goes back to work. The kids'll be enrolled in the school where she teaches, and when they're out for the summer she can be home with them. Sometimes I get a month or so off during summer. I'll probably ask for a couple classes this summer to take up the slack of losing her income."

He drummed his fingers on the steering wheel. "I'm hoping to get a promotion this year. Did all the paperwork for tenure."

"Tenure?"

"It's something you earn when you work at a college or university. Job protection. It'll mean more money and some job security."

"I hope you get it. Do a lot of students take your medieval literature class?"

"It's a pretty popular course, especially with female students. They're interested in that time of history, when courtly love existed."

"Courtly love?"

"You know, knights rescuing damsels in distress, that sort of thing."

"Sounds like something Annie would like to read."

"Is she a romantic?"

"I know when she was younger she liked reading fairy tales."

"I'm talking about does she like stories about knights and princesses and adventure? People think the Amish are practical people, but I know a lot of Amish, and they love to read all kinds of stories."

Aaron thought about it and remembered seeing her carrying home some of those books. He'd noticed she read nearly everything.

"Women love romantic gestures," Paul told him.

Shrugging, Aaron looked out the window. So far he hadn't felt successful in pursuing Annie. He turned to look at Paul. "So what kind of romantic gestures are you talking about?"

"You know, anything that makes them feel cared for. Special. Like opening a door or bringing flowers. I'm not saying they can't do those things for themselves, but it's nice when we show them we're thinking of them. Men were protective of women back then and looked out for them."

"Annie's pretty independent," Aaron said.

"Susan is too. But she likes my being protective of her. It doesn't mean I try to tell her what to do."

"Kind of like being head of the household doesn't mean we're controlling our wives."

"Exactly."

Paul parked and they began carrying the packages inside the post office. The line was long but not as bad as Aaron had feared. After he mailed the last of them off, he took the receipts, folded them, and shoved them into his jacket pocket. The feel of the papers made him think about how his job wasn't complete just because the work shipped out.

He and Paul climbed into the pickup truck and started the trip back to Aaron's workshop.

"You don't suppose Susan would like a small part-time job, something she can do at home?"

Paul took his eyes off the road to glance at Aaron. "Like what?"

"I'm getting overwhelmed with all the paperwork. By the time I'm finished work for the day, paperwork's the last thing I want to deal with."

"I'll ask her."

"I was thinking I could get one of the stories you talked about for Annie. Maybe give it to her for a Christmas present. I've already made a present for her, but she does love to read."

"Sounds good. I'll write down some titles for you."

"We had this joke back when I was in school," Aaron said. "What do you call a person who keeps on talking when people are no longer interested?"

Paul shook his head. "What?"

"A teacher."

"Ha ha," said Paul. "Very funny."

∼❧∼

Annie spotted the new list on the refrigerator and slanted a look at her mother. "Another one?"

"We've never taken a big trip like this as a family," Jenny said, unperturbed by Annie's look. "I'm determined it goes well."

"It's going to go well," her father said as he hung his jacket on a peg.

"Where's Joshua?"

Matthew glanced at the back door. "Right behind me."

Jenny smiled. "You know Joshua and his horse. Who knows when he'll come in."

"My brother never misses a meal." Annie grabbed a shawl from a peg. "I'll go ring the bell."

"I want to ring it!" Johnny cried. He slid down from his chair. "Can I ring it?"

"Sure," Annie told him. She tossed him his jacket and once he'd pulled it on, they went out onto the back porch. He rang the bell, but Joshua didn't come out of the barn.

"Can we go get him?"

"Okay."

They walked to the barn and Johnny called Joshua's name when they pushed open the door. Annie heard a moan and her heart stopped, then started beating fast. She rushed inside, looking around frantically, then heard the moan again.

Joshua lay on the ground, unconscious. Blood spurted from a wound on his thigh.

"Joshua!"

She knelt beside him, pulling off her shawl and tying it in a tourniquet above the wound. The bleeding slowed, then stopped.

"Get *Mamm* or *Daed* to call 911. Tell them Joshua's bleeding."

He ran out of the barn, and she heard him yelling all the way to the house. Turning back to Joshua, she patted his cheeks and called his name, hoping he'd wake.

It felt like hours before her father rushed into the barn, but she knew it was probably just minutes. He fell to his knees beside her, calling Joshua's name as she'd done.

"What happened?"

Annie pointed to the trail of blood from one of the horse stalls. "Pilot must have kicked Joshua. The bleeding's slowed a lot, but look how much he lost." She felt faintly nauseous, but she was determined to help her brother however she could.

Her mother came running into the barn next and joined them in kneeling beside Joshua. "The dispatcher said paramedics are on the way." She glanced at the blood and back at Joshua. "I can't believe Pilot hurt him."

"Something must have spooked him," Matthew said, shaking his head.

They all looked up when they heard sirens approaching. When paramedics entered the barn, Annie and her parents stood and moved out of the way.

"Looks like a nicked artery," one of them said as he pushed the shawl a few inches away and blood began spurting again. "Who did the tourniquet?"

"I did." Annie stepped forward. "I hope I didn't make things worse."

He pulled a piece of rubber tubing from his medical bag, tied it around Joshua's thigh, then pulled away the shawl and threw it on the floor. "You probably saved his life."

"Where'd you learn that?" her father asked.

She shrugged. "Writers know a little about a lot of things. I don't remember where I learned it."

They checked Joshua over and loaded him onto a gurney. "He'll need the artery stitched and they'll check him for a concussion. One of you can ride with us to the hospital."

"You go," Jenny told Matthew. "I'll get a ride and meet you there as soon as I can."

Annie stood watching the gurney being loaded into the back of the ambulance. Joshua never opened his eyes. Her hands felt sticky and when she looked, she saw all the blood covering them. She shuddered, thinking of how much he'd lost.

She felt her mother wrap her arm around her waist. "You okay?"

"Yeah."

"I don't think so. You're shaking."

"It's cold," Annie said, but she didn't move.

They watched the ambulance move down the drive, turn onto the road, and head in the direction of the hospital.

"Come on, let's see about getting me a ride to the hospital."

They walked into the kitchen and found Phoebe talking quietly with Johnny. The food on their plates had barely been touched.

"Is Joshua going to be okay?" Johnny asked. His eyes widened when he saw the blood on her hands.

Annie saw the fear in his eyes and saw his lips trembling. Her grandmother looked tense too, her lined face pinched with worry.

Jenny bent to hug him. "Yes, sweetheart. They had to take him to the hospital so they can fix his leg. I'm going to go call for a ride and go there to be with him."

"I want to go."

Jenny hugged him tighter. "I know. Maybe later." She pulled her jacket on and went out to use the phone in the shanty.

Phoebe walked over and rubbed Annie's back. "I'll fix you some tea. Then try and eat."

Annie still felt shaky and a little nauseous. But she washed her hands, sat down at the table, and looked at Johnny. "You need to eat."

Phoebe set a cup of tea in front of Annie. "I put the food in the oven to keep it warm," she said. She took out the pot roast and vegetables and fixed a plate.

Annie thanked her and began eating mechanically.

Jenny walked into the room. "Someone will be here in a few minutes."

"Eat something before you go," Phoebe said. "You don't know how long you'll be at the hospital."

Looking distracted, Jenny walked over, rummaged in a cupboard, and pulled out a travel mug. "I'll take some coffee with me. I couldn't eat now."

She poured coffee into the mug, added milk and sugar, and set it beside her purse. Then she paced, looking out the window for the ride she'd called.

Phoebe took the plate of bread to the counter, sliced some of the pot roast, made sandwiches, and wrapped them in foil. She tucked them into Jenny's voluminous purse. "In case you're there awhile and you get hungry. You never know if the cafeteria will be open at the hospital."

"My ride's here!" Jenny picked up her purse and started to walk away without her mug.

"*Mamm!*" Annie touched her arm and Jenny turned back. She handed her the mug.

Jenny impulsively hugged Annie, then rushed over to do the same to Johnny and Phoebe. "Sorry, I almost forgot. I'll be back soon." Then she rushed from the room.

Annie stood with Johnny at the front window and watched their mother climb into the van.

"*Kumm*," said Phoebe, gesturing at them. "Let's pray for Joshua and then the two of you should be getting to bed."

"I don't want to sleep until we hear about Joshua," Johnny told her.

Phoebe gave him a gentle smile. "I'm sure it's going to be a while before we hear anything."

They prayed for Joshua and sent Johnny upstairs to bed. Annie and Phoebe did the dishes and cleaned up the kitchen.

Then Phoebe turned to Annie. "You look worried. Do you want to talk?"

Annie shook her head. "I'll be all right. You go on to bed. I'll let you know if I hear anything."

Phoebe hugged her and went to her bed in the *dawdi haus*.

Long after the house became quiet, Annie sat in the kitchen and listened to the sound of time ticking on.

5

Someone was knocking at the front door.

Annie sat up and realized she'd fallen asleep on the living room sofa while she was waiting for her parents to come home from the hospital. She got to her feet, straightening her dress and smoothing back her hair.

She opened the door and blinked in surprise. "Aaron! What are you doing here?"

"I heard Joshua got hurt."

"Who's at the door, Annie?" her grandmother called from the kitchen.

"Aaron."

"Well, invite him in. No need to stand there letting in the cold."

Annie held the door wider, and Aaron walked in and took off his hat. "*Guder mariye*, Phoebe."

"*Guder mariye*, Aaron. I just made coffee."

He walked into the kitchen, and Annie trailed behind him tucking her hair under her *kapp*. Who knew how wrinkled it had gotten sleeping on the sofa in it.

"How did you hear about Joshua?"

"One of my nephews was in the emergency room for an earache. My brother saw the ambulance bring Joshua in."

Phoebe set a cup of coffee on the table, and Aaron sat.

"I thought I'd come see what I could do to help."

Annie glanced at the kitchen window. Dawn was just breaking.

"Figured your *daed* and Joshua wouldn't be here for morning chores."

"That's very thoughtful," Phoebe said, giving Annie a look.

"*Danki*, Aaron," she said, feeling chastened. But she was barely awake, she wanted to say.

"I'm not sure it's a good idea to get around the horse that kicked Joshua."

"Show me which one it was, and I'll be careful." Aaron took a last swallow of coffee and stood.

"Do you think it's a good idea?" Phoebe asked, looking doubtful.

"Who knows when *Daed* will be home," Annie said as she grabbed her jacket and pulled it on. No need to comb her hair or fuss with her appearance to work in the barn. "Don't worry, we'll be careful. I think Pilot may have kicked Joshua because Joshua was treating his foreleg injury. We're not going near it. I'll call the vet when we come back in."

Phoebe nodded. "*Allrecht*. I'll have breakfast ready."

Feeding the horses was a pleasure. Cleaning up what came out the other end wasn't. Annie wasn't fond of the work, but it couldn't be helped. As soon as she thought Leila, her boss, had opened the store, she'd call and tell her she'd be late coming in.

"You okay?"

"What?"

"Are you okay?" he asked quietly, his eyes searching hers.

Annie felt her stomach turn at the sight of the blood-soaked hay near the stall. "I was so scared when I saw him," she admitted, forcing herself to look away. "He was unconscious, and there was so much blood." She sighed. "I wonder how much longer it'll be before we hear something."

She dug a shovelful of hay and tossed it in the wheelbarrow.

They worked in silence, the only sound their shoveling and their labored breath, the horses snuffling in their feed troughs. She glanced at him, then away when he looked up and saw she was staring at him.

"I'm sorry I should have thanked you when you said you came to help," Annie told him.

"I'd do anything for you," he said quietly.

That touched her so much. Uncomfortable with the feelings suddenly rushing up inside her, she turned and awkwardly added another shovel of manure and hay to the wheelbarrow.

"Annie?"

He waited until she looked up.

"It's okay. You don't need to thank me for helping. Besides, you have a lot on your mind, I'm sure." He grasped the handles of the wheelbarrow. "Be right back."

Annie leaned the shovel against the wall and flexed her shoulders. This wasn't her usual kind of work, and her muscles were aching. Although Aaron seemed fit because he worked with his hands on building furniture and hanging kitchen cabinets, she sensed the work had been strenuous for him as well.

They walked back to the house, and when they entered the kitchen, her heart beat faster. Her *mamm* and *daed* sat at the table tiredly eating breakfast.

"You're back!" Annie cried. "How is Joshua?"

Her father looked past her to Aaron, acknowledging him with a nod, and then he looked back at Annie. "He woke up in the emergency room. No concussion. The doctors think he passed out from blood loss—not because he hurt his head.

They rushed him into surgery and repaired the artery in his leg. They think he can come home in a couple of days."

"It's wonderful news," Annie said as she felt tears rush into her eyes. "I—I'll be right back."

She rushed out of the room, shut herself into the downstairs bathroom, and scrubbed at her hands. Only then could she use a tissue to wipe her cheeks.

Taking a deep breath, she opened the door and saw Aaron leaned against the hall wall.

"No need to worry," he told her quietly.

She nodded. "I know." She took a deep breath. "Wash your hands and come eat. You must be starving."

He nodded and went into the bathroom. She walked back to the kitchen and took a seat at the table.

"We were surprised to see him here so early," her father said.

"Matthew," her mother said, giving him a warning look.

His jaw tightened. "Just thinking about what it looks like."

"I told you, I was up, and they went out to the barn to do chores," Phoebe told him, refilling his coffee cup. "But Aaron isn't the type to take advantage of Annie."

"All young men are," he muttered.

"*Daed!* Even if he is, I wouldn't let him. I'm a grown woman and I can take care of myself."

"I know what young men are like, especially in a barn," he said, but he subsided when Jenny elbowed him as Aaron came into the room.

"Aaron, sit down and have something to eat," Jenny said warmly. She gestured at the chair next to her. "It was nice of you to come and help."

"I'm happy to for as long as you need me," he told her. "Even after Joshua comes home I'm sure he won't be able to do chores for a while."

Phoebe slid a plate filled with bacon and eggs in front of him.

Jenny pushed her plate away. "I'm worried he'll get an infection," she said, her lips trembling. "A horse's hooves are dirty, and the barn floor isn't much better."

Phoebe patted her shoulder. "Let's not worry —"

"Because worry's arrogant," Jenny said, trying to smile. "I remember you telling me that when I first came here after my accident. You're always saying it's arrogant to worry because God knows what He's doing."

"He does," Phoebe said simply. She set a plate of food in front of Annie.

Annie looked up when she heard feet hit the floor above her head. Johnny. She could tell from the direction of his footsteps that he ran into Joshua's room, then Mary's old room. Then she heard footsteps clattering down the stairs. A moment later, Johnny rushed into the kitchen. He looked around and then, as he realized Joshua wasn't there, his face fell.

Johnny's lips trembled. "Joshua's not—he's not—"

Jenny jumped up from the table and hugged him. "Joshua's okay. He just can't come home for a few days. Tell you what. We're going to take a nap, and then when you come home from school we'll all go see him. How about it?"

"Let's go now," Johnny said.

She tousled his hair. "No. School first. Then we'll go. Now, go get dressed."

"Do you want us to pick you up from work?" Matthew asked Annie.

"Yes, please."

"I'll give you a ride into work after you clean up," Aaron said. "If you want."

Annie started to refuse because he'd already done so much for her and her family. But when she looked into his eyes and remembered the connection she'd felt when they worked in the barn she didn't want to refuse him.

"*Danki*, I'd appreciate it," she said. "If you have the time."

"I have the time," he told her. Matthew cleared his throat, and Aaron jumped and blinked at him for a moment, as if he'd forgotten the other man was in the room. "Matthew, I'd like to talk to you about Pilot while Annie's getting cleaned up. Can you give me a minute out in the barn?"

Matthew took a last swallow of coffee and stood.

"Don't be long," Jenny called after them. "You need to get some sleep!"

"I'll make sure he comes right back in," Aaron promised her, and then he drew back when Matthew turned and looked at him. "Uh, well, I just meant it wouldn't take long and I know you want to get some rest so I won't keep you—"

Jenny patted his shoulder. "He knows what you meant, Aaron. Don't let him intimidate you."

Annie hid her smile as she walked past them to go upstairs. Her father was sweet, but he was being so predictable. She wondered if all fathers behaved this way and decided she'd have to ask some of her friends.

⊷୨ର

The elevator pinged, and the doors slid open. Johnny's eyes were wide as he stepped out, followed by Mary, Annie, and their parents.

"Wow," he said as he gazed around him. "The box carried us up here?"

Annie smiled down at him. "Right. It's an elevator. We'll be using them a lot when we go to New York City."

Her mother shook her head and seemed to be sending some silent message to her. Annie lifted her eyebrows in question, but Jenny continued to shake her head as she jerked her head toward Johnny.

"*Mamm?*"

"We'll talk later," Jenny whispered. "Johnny? Help me find Room 202."

He studied the room numbers as they walked along the corridor. "This is it!"

"Sssh," she cautioned. "Indoor voice. Joshua might be sleeping."

Joshua was awake, looking wan and in pain, his injured leg propped up on the bed. The family filed into the room, giving him careful hugs.

"*Aenti* Hannah, *Onkel* Chris, and Jonah were just here with Phoebe."

"*Gut,*" said Matthew. "They said they were coming by."

"How are you feeling?" Jenny asked him, leaning over him to stroke the hair from his forehead.

Annie frowned when he didn't try to fidget away from their mother's hand. He loved her, but he had always acted like he was too manly, too grown up to tolerate such affectionate behavior. The fact he was so passive scared her.

"Doctor said I can't go home for a couple of days," he complained. "*Daed,* can you talk to him, tell him I want to go home now?"

"I did talk to him before we went home for a while this morning, *sohn,*" Matthew told him. "He has good reason to keep you here."

"But the horses—"

"Aaron helped me with them this morning," Annie spoke up.

"You?"

She made a face at him. "I might not be as good with them as you and *Daed,* but I can do what needs to be done."

"And how sore are you tonight?" he teased. "You don't have muscles like me."

"Thank goodness," she retorted. "What woman wants muscles?"

Mary moved closer to his bed. "Johnny and I brought you something."

She reached into the tote bag she carried and handed Johnny an envelope. He held it out to his brother.

Joshua smiled at him as he opened the card, then he held up it up for them all to see. Johnny, a budding artist, had drawn pictures of horses in charcoal.

"I love it," he told Johnny. "Can I have a hug?"

"Careful!" Jenny warned.

Johnny wrapped his arms around his brother's neck and squeezed. Joshua winced a little and Jenny took Johnny's shoulders and guided him away from the bed.

"I brought your horse books so you could read," Mary told Joshua. She pulled them from her tote bag and set them on the table next to the bed.

"*Danki*," he said. "It'll give me something to do." His lips trembled. He looked at his parents, blinking hard as if he were trying to hold back tears. "Can't you please talk to the doctor again? I want to go home."

Matthew dug in his pocket and handed Mary some change. "Why don't you take Johnny to the vending machines and get a snack."

Experienced with her younger brother's high energy, Mary caught him by the jacket sleeve as he dashed toward the door.

"I'm going to go talk to the nurse," Jenny said and left the room.

Matthew pulled up a chair for Annie, then one for himself. He sat down heavily and reached for Joshua's hand lying on top of the blanket. "We would take you home if we could," he told him. "But you don't just have a little cut on your leg. They had to stitch the artery—the big vein in your leg. Now I know you know about anatomy because you've studied it to be able to know what to do for the horses. Right?"

Joshua nodded—if a bit grudgingly.

"And the barn full of bacteria. So the doctor's started you on antibiotics, which is what that fluid bag has in it. We have to be patient and make sure you're ready to come home. *Allrecht?*"

"I guess," Joshua said. Then he sighed and nodded.

Jenny walked back into the room. "Your nurse says you can have some more pain medicine and something to help you sleep," she told him. "Then we need to go, so you can get some rest."

Annie watched her brother and saw how his eyelids were already drooping. He brightened up a little when Mary and Johnny walked in and put a package of peanut M & M's—his favorite—in his hand.

"Let's pray together before we leave," Matthew said, and the family linked hands and bent their heads.

The drive home was silent, the adults tired and lost in their own thoughts.

A buggy was in their drive. "I didn't know Chris and Hannah were coming over," Annie said.

"Chris offered to help with chores," Matthew said.

"But I was going to help," Annie told him.

"There'll be plenty to do for all of us. And I didn't know how long we'd be at the hospital today."

The van pulled into the drive, and everyone got out. Mary and Johnny went into the house.

"What didn't you want me to say earlier?" Annie asked her mother as they walked up the drive.

Jenny bit her lip, then she sighed. "I didn't want you to say anything about the trip. I think we're going to have to cancel it."

Annie gasped. "Oh no, why?" Then she clapped a hand over her mouth. "I'm sorry. You're afraid Joshua won't be well enough to go."

"We don't know yet," her father said as he came up behind them. "Let's give it a day or two. Jenny, I'll be in the barn with Chris for a while."

"Okay." She looked at Annie. "I could use a cup of tea. What about you?"

"I'd like to say hi to Chris first."

"Okay."

Her father stopped so abruptly Annie nearly walked into him. He looked at her, then Jenny, and she'd have sworn he seemed uncomfortable. "I'll be sure to bring him in before he goes home. I think your mother needs your help. Don't you need her help, Jenny?"

Jenny narrowed her eyes and then she nodded and pressed her lips together as if she were trying to hold back a laugh. "Yes, I do. Annie, I just remembered I need your help in the house."

"But—" Annie began. Then she shook her head. Ever the dutiful daughter, she followed her mother inside, mystified at the exchange that had just taken place. Parents. Sometimes there was no understanding them.

They walked into the kitchen and Annie was pleasantly surprised to see her *Aenti* Hannah, Chris's wife, sitting at the kitchen table visiting with Phoebe.

The women hugged, and then Annie went to make the tea, insisting her mother sit down.

"Joshua was pretty sleepy when we stopped by earlier today," Hannah said, taking Jenny's hand and squeezing it. "How was he when you visited?"

"He stayed awake during our visit, but he was having a bit more pain," Jenny told her. "They gave him something to help him sleep."

"*Mamm*, what did you want me to help with?" Annie asked her as she set a mug of water before her.

Her mother straightened and some of the tiredness and worry left her face. She glanced over at Hannah and smiled at her. "Hannah, Annie was going to say hello to Chris, but Matthew said I needed help in the house," she said conversationally as she dunked her teabag in the hot water. "I think he just didn't want her out in the barn. Wonder why?"

Hannah blushed. "Don't tease." She turned and glared at Phoebe when the older woman laughed.

Annie looked at each of them. "Tease? What's going on?"

Lifting her chin, Hannah smiled at Annie. "Everyone still seems to think they need to tease me about Matthew walking in on Chris and me in the barn the first day we met."

"Oh?" Annie looked from her mother to Hannah and back again.

"Nothing happened!" Hannah insisted.

"Nothing?" Jenny asked.

Hannah glared at her. "My big brother seemed to think he had to defend my honor."

"*Daed?* He was going to fight *Onkel* Chris?"

"You can't blame him," Jenny told Hannah. "After all, he caught both of you up in the loft."

"*Caught* is not the right word!" She looked at Annie. "Chris actually came looking for your mother."

Annie raised her eyebrows at her mother. Jenny frowned at Hannah, but the other woman just laughed, saying, "Turnabout's fair play."

"Chris and I met when I went for an appointment at a veteran's hospital," Jenny told her. "We'd both been wounded overseas. After he was released from the hospital, he decided to look me up when he visited the area. He didn't know he was going to meet Hannah here."

"The woman who hasn't let me have a minute of peace since," Chris said.

Startled, Hannah looked up at him. "I didn't hear you come in."

He grinned. "I heard my name mentioned and decided to see what was being said."

Phoebe hugged him. "You know what they say. Eavesdroppers never hear anything good."

Matthew stepped into the room behind him. "What's going on?"

"I was just telling Annie how Hannah and Chris met," Jenny told him.

He gave her a telling look. "And you wonder why I made the remark about not trusting Annie and Aaron in the barn."

All eyes turned to Annie and she blushed. "What?"

"Matthew!" Jenny sighed. "Annie, your overprotective father just said he didn't trust any young man to be alone with his daughter."

Chris grinned at Hannah as he passed her on the way to wash his hands. "Did you tell Annie my intentions toward you were honorable?"

She shook her head. "Jenny was having too much fun making her think something happened in the loft."

Stopping, Chris glanced back at Annie. "I fell asleep waiting to talk to your mother," he told her. "Hannah walked into the barn and heard a noise. She climbed the ladder, and I don't know who was more surprised."

"I was so surprised to see someone up there I started to fall," Hannah explained. "He kept me from falling," Hannah said, looking up at him, love shining from her eyes.

"I think I fell in love with you that day," he said quietly. "You saved my life."

Then, as if a little embarrassed at what he'd said, he looked at his dirty hands. "Gotta get washed up."

Wow, thought Annie, watching him leave the room. She'd heard her parents' love story but not her aunt and uncle's.

As if she were aware of Annie's gaze on her, Hannah looked at her and smiled. "Guess you never thought of the barn as being a romantic place, did you?"

Annie felt the color rushing into her cheeks. "No," she said. "Maybe it was for you and Chris, but Aaron and I were mucking out stalls."

"I see," Hannah said, nodding.

Hearing movement, Annie dared to look at her father and was relieved to see he had his back to her as he poured himself a cup of coffee. But when she looked back at her mother, she saw her gazing thoughtfully in her direction.

6

$\mathcal{A}$nnie was tired, but she couldn't sleep.

Maybe she should have drawn her curtains. A full moon beamed its light into her room and made it seem almost as bright as dawn.

The light wasn't the only thing keeping her awake. Her mind just wouldn't shut off. She'd been surprised by the teasing about Aaron earlier in the evening. It had only been family, and she knew they meant well. They loved her and just wanted her to find love as they had.

Maybe it wouldn't have unnerved her if it hadn't come just hours after she and Aaron had looked at each other in the barn and seemed to see something different than they ever had.

She sighed and leaned over to put her arms on the window-sill and gaze out at the moon. Did Aaron lie awake and look at the same moon and think of her as she did him? She sighed and shook her head. No, probably only a woman did things like look at the moon and think of a man who acted interested in her.

Until today, she'd thought he was just a friend. Until today, she'd thought she was too practical a woman to engage in thinking about anything but the work she hoped to establish herself in. Until tonight, she hadn't thought of him at night when she lay all alone in her narrow bed and the silvery light of the moon filled her room.

She frowned. She should be thinking about her brother, not herself and some romantic notions. He'd been badly hurt and could have even died. Yet her own mother had thought she was disappointed she might not get to go on the trip, that it meant so much to her that she'd even been thinking about it at a time like this.

Well, she was ashamed to say she had just blithely thought life would go on and, of course, her precious trip would still take place.

The light fell on her snow globe, making the tiny snow-flakes inside it glisten. She rolled over. What was the point of looking at it? The trip was probably off.

She lay there, trying to turn her mind off. Sleep refused to come. And it was like ignoring the snow globe just made it worse. She rolled over, reached over to pick it up, and shook it. Snowflakes rained down gently on the skyscrapers of New York City inside it. The scene never changed. She sighed. Life sure did.

She'd been looking forward to the trip for weeks, ever since her mother had told the family about it and they had talked about whether they should go. But in one split second, Joshua's horse kicking him had changed everything. It was so unfair.

She sat up, put the snow globe back on her nightstand, and looked out the window, hoping that her brother wasn't wide awake and restless like her, looking out at the same moon. She hoped he wasn't in pain the way he'd been when she'd seen him earlier.

And she hoped the infection her parents and his doctor were concerned might be lurking would never happen.

When her mother died, she'd thought it was the worst thing that could happen to her, and for years and years, it was. And then this happened and made her remember just how fragile life could be, how God could have a different plan than she did for the way her life went.

Reaching for her robe, she pushed her feet into slippers and padded downstairs, not needing a light because she'd taken them so many times. Someone else couldn't sleep, either. Halfway down, she could see a light on in the kitchen.

Her mother sat at the kitchen table with Phoebe. Both had been drinking tea. The delicate scent of chamomile, favorite herb of the insomniac, drifted toward her.

"Can't sleep?" her mother asked. "The water's still hot if you want some tea."

Annie fixed herself a cup of tea and sat at the table.

Her mother reached over and touched her hand. "I'm sorry. I hope you weren't upset about the teasing earlier. I should have stopped them."

She shrugged. "It's okay. It was just family. Joshua teases me all the time. I'm used to it."

Phoebe reached over and hugged her. "In my day, no one knew we were seeing the man we were interested in until we announced the engagement."

"Some of my friends keep it a secret. But Aaron hasn't asked me to marry him."

"You'd tell me, wouldn't you?" her mother asked her, staring at her intently.

"Jenny!" Phoebe exclaimed.

She frowned. "But a mother deserves to know."

A mother. Annie impulsively hugged her. She had two friends whose widowed fathers had remarried and they hadn't been so lucky with their new mothers, who'd treated them as stepchildren.

"You'll be the first to know."

Her mother gave her a misty smile. "Aaron is a special young man, and he looks at you the way any mother would want one to look at her daughter. But it's for you to decide."

"If he's the one God set aside for her, she'll know," Phoebe said confidently.

"I did," Jenny said as she looked at her grandmother. "Who knew I'd find him living right next door to my grandmother."

"Think you can sleep now?" Phoebe asked her.

"In a minute."

"Your mother is worried about her children," Phoebe told Annie.

"*Mamm?*"

"Mary's still not feeling well. She promised to go see the doctor later this week."

"It's probably just a bug going around."

"I know. I'm probably just anxious since one of my children is in the hospital."

"She's talking again about canceling the trip," Phoebe said. "I think I convinced her to go ahead with it, though."

Annie's heart leaped. "You mean it?"

Phoebe nodded. "We talked to Joshua today, and he doesn't want his being hurt to keep the family from going."

"I don't think he wanted to be away from his horses even before the accident," Jenny said, looking thoughtfully into the depths of her cup of tea. "Just like Mary didn't want to leave her students and go with us."

"I can't say I'm enthusiastic about going into the city at this time of year," Phoebe admitted. "I was there when you had your surgery, and while I'd like to attend the dinner, I think it makes much more sense if I stay behind and take care of Joshua while the family goes on the trip."

Jenny shook her head. "I couldn't ask you to take care of him—"

"Of course you could," Phoebe said firmly. "Matthew and his children were dear to me before you ever met them and they became family."

"But I want both of you to go," Annie said. She couldn't imagine leaving Phoebe and Joshua behind.

"I think the trip would be too strenuous for him." Phoebe looked at Jenny. "Why not just let him stay home and be with his horses?"

"You wouldn't let him sleep in the barn?" Jenny asked her. "You know it's where he'd be if we allowed it."

Phoebe laughed. "You know I won't let him sleep in the barn."

Annie watched her mother with bated breath. Was she considering letting Joshua stay home if Phoebe cared for him—and kept him out of the barn?

She sipped her tea and tried not to show her excitement. She cared for her brother and didn't want the fact she longed to go on the trip be more important than his health.

"I'm still not sure," Jenny said as she rubbed her temples with the tips of her fingers. "I'll talk to Matthew about it again in the morning."

She looked at Annie. "I'm sorry. I know you've been looking forward to seeing New York City."

Annie suddenly felt so guilty. There her mother sat, obviously so worried about Joshua she couldn't sleep, and she was thinking of how disappointed Annie was about the trip.

She leaned over and hugged her mother. "I did look forward to it. But all we need to think about is Joshua getting well. I want my big brother back here where he belongs."

Phoebe covered her mouth as she yawned.

Jenny patted Annie's hand and stood. "We should try to get some sleep. Morning comes early around here."

"Try to sleep in a little in the morning," Phoebe said as she got to her feet. "I'll get Johnny off to school."

"You need sleep too."

"Less as I get older," she said with a shrug. "See you in the morning."

Annie climbed the stairs with her mother, and they hugged before they went into their rooms.

Once inside her room, Annie took off her robe and tossed it on the end of her bed. She kicked off her slippers and climbed under the covers. But sleep still remained elusive.

She sat up, reached for her notebook and pen, and began writing a note to her brother:

> *Dear Joshua,*
>
> *I was so scared when I found you hurt in the barn. You're my big brother, and you've always looked out for me. There was blood everywhere. I didn't know if I could do anything to help you.*
>
> *I know you don't like being in the hospital, but you need to be there so they can help you get better. I love you, and I don't know what I'd do if I didn't have you in my life.*
>
> *I know you will be home soon. In the meantime, everyone is taking care of the horses—especially Pilot—and you're not to worry.*
>
> *I will say a prayer for you every day and know God is watching over my big brother.*
>
> *Love you,*
> *Annie*

She folded the note, found an envelope in her desk drawer, and slid it inside. Tomorrow—today, actually, seeing as how the clock said it was morning—she'd take it to the hospital when she saw Joshua.

A big yawn overtook her as she tucked the note inside her purse. She climbed back into bed. She thought she could sleep now.

⤳⤳

Aaron heard the sound of laughter as he approached Joshua's hospital room.

Annie sat in a chair beside her brother's bed, and both of them were chuckling over something. It was good to see her happy. She'd looked so worried since Joshua had been hurt.

He stopped for a moment and just watched them. No one could mistake them for being anything other than brother and sister. They had the same blond hair and blue eyes, although Annie's features were more delicate. Usually Joshua towered over his sister, but somehow, lying in bed, he seemed smaller than she was. They looked up when he knocked on the door frame.

"Aaron! Are you playing hooky?"

He was embarrassed at the reason he'd had to take off a little early but kept it to himself. "Just thought I'd see how you were doing." He walked into the room and pulled up a chair next to Annie. "What's so funny?"

They looked at each other as if deciding what to say. "Joshua was complaining about the food, and I reminded him of *Mamm*'s cooking," Annie said.

"She's a wonderful cook!" Aaron protested.

"Now," said Joshua. "Not when we first met her." He looked at Annie. "Klunk!" and they both laughed.

"Her biscuits," said Joshua, shaking his head. "I dropped one on a plate and wasn't sure if it might break."

"The biscuit or the plate?"

"Either!" Annie told him, wiping a tear from her eye. "When she heard it and realized we were all trying to be polite she took them and threw them out the front door. We felt sorry for the animals that might come along and eat them."

"Well, she's gotten a lot better since then."

Joshua sighed and pushed the tray on his bedside table away. "I miss her cooking. The food here is awful."

"Tell you what—I'll ask her to bring you something when she comes to visit."

Joshua grinned. "Great." Then his face fell. "'Course, it would mean I'd have to stay here longer." He folded his arms across his chest and stared at his leg propped up in the bed.

"When we started to complain when we were sick my *mamm* used to say we were getting better," Aaron said. "It was back to school the next day."

"I want to get out of here, but I have to stay for another day."

"Joshua, that's great news! Just one more day?" Annie nearly bounced in her seat she looked so excited.

He shrugged. "I guess it is. I just want it to be today."

A nurse came in, looked at the tray, and raised her eyebrows at her patient. "Sorry, I wasn't hungry," he said politely.

"I know it's wrong to lie," he told Annie after the nurse left with the tray. "But I didn't want to hurt her feelings." He looked hopefully at her purse and lunch tote. "I don't suppose you have any lunch left?"

"No," she said. "And if I did, it wouldn't be good for you. It's been hours since I ate."

"We could go get something from the hospital cafeteria for you."

Surprised, Annie stared at Aaron. "It's very nice of you, but—"

"It's probably the same as the stuff they just brought me," Joshua said.

Aaron shook his head. "Two of my sisters had babies here. I've eaten in the cafeteria, and the cheeseburgers and French fries are pretty good."

"Cheeseburgers?" Joshua sat up straighter in bed.

"You're speaking his language," Annie told Aaron with a laugh. "Okay, we'll go get you a cheeseburger."

"And fries."

"And fries."

"And a Coke?"

"A Coke too. A big one."

Laughing, Annie shook her head as she walked out of the room. "You're right, he must be better."

Her smile faded as they walked down the hospital hallway. "Are you okay?"

She glanced at him. "I just want him to be better and come home."

They stopped at an elevator. Aaron pressed the button. "It won't be much longer."

The elevator opened, and they stepped inside. The space seemed small and intimate. Aaron caught the scent of flowers over the antiseptic smell of the hospital and realized it was probably Annie's shampoo.

He was relieved when the doors opened on the cafeteria floor.

"It smells good," Annie said.

"Are you hungry? We could get something before we take Joshua's food up to him."

Annie shook her head. "I'm expected home for supper."

"Maybe some coffee? We have to wait for the cheeseburger to be cooked anyway."

"You're right."

They got their coffee. Annie gave the order for Joshua's food, but before she could pay, Aaron was handing the cashier some bills.

He saw Annie's gaze go to the small hand brace covering his hand.

They found a table and sat down. Annie stirred some sugar into her coffee and took a sip, then looked at him.

"What happened to your hand?"

He looked at it and frowned. "Doc said I 'overused' it. How do you overuse a hand? Its job is to work, I told him. But apparently, I've been working too much lately. Christmas rush."

She nodded. "We've been busier at the store this season than last year." She leaned back in her chair and sighed. "It'll be nice to have some time off soon."

They sat and talked quietly and had finished their coffee when Joshua's food was delivered to their table.

"Smells good," she said, lifting the lid on the to-go box and checking out the contents. "I think we should make sure the fries are okay."

He grinned as she took one and ate it. "How are they?"

"I think you should weigh in on this."

She leaned across the table, and he let her feed it to him. He felt the brush of her fingers against his mouth and watched her eyes widen at the contact.

"They're good," he said.

"We—we should go before the food gets cold," she said quickly, snapping the lid closed and standing.

They didn't talk as they walked back to Joshua's room. Aaron was glad he'd suggested the food when he saw Joshua's eyes light up as they walked in and Annie set it on his bedside tray.

"I better be going," Annie told her brother. She stood, pulled a note out of her purse, and placed it on the table next to his food.

"What is it?"

"Just something I wrote you. Read it after you eat."

"Okay."

"I'll see you tomorrow."

"Here's hoping I'll be home," he said.

"If it's God's will."

He nodded and popped a French fry into his mouth. He looped his arm around her waist when she bent to kiss his cheek and squeezed it. "*Danki.*"

"Don't thank me," she told him. "Aaron insisted on paying."

"Well, then, thank you," Joshua said.

"You're welcome. If you don't mind, I'll go so I can give Annie a ride home."

"Since he has his cheeseburger, he won't miss us," Annie told Aaron.

"Yes, I will," he disagreed as he picked up the sandwich.

But when they got to the doorway and looked back, Joshua was eating it with gusto and not looking in their direction at all.

Annie laughed and looked at Aaron. They stood there in the doorway for a moment, not paying attention to anyone or anything but each other until someone walked past and broke the spell of the moment.

❧

"I'm going to see if your father needs any help," Aaron said as he got out of his buggy at her house.

"It's very nice of you, but what about your hand?"

He glanced down at the brace and shrugged. "I can still do, long as I'm careful."

"I don't know," she said doubtfully. "But I'll let *Daed* and you decide. There's no reasoning with men sometimes."

He laughed. "It's more like there's no reasoning with women. I should know with four sisters."

They walked into the kitchen and found her parents and Johnny finishing supper. He was invited to join them, as he always was, and he watched as Annie insisted her mother keep eating while she fixed plates for Aaron and herself.

"We're having an early supper," Jenny told her. "Phoebe's next door with Hannah, Chris, and Jonah."

"I get to go to the hospital to see Joshua," Johnny said.

"We went to see him," Annie told her parents as she placed a plate before Aaron.

"We?" her father asked, looking pointedly at Aaron.

"I went to see him, and Annie was there." He lifted his fork and felt a twinge.

"What did you do to your hand?" Jenny asked.

"I hurt it," Aaron told him.

"How?"

"I just did something to it working a lot." He didn't know how to explain overusing his hand. Fact was, it didn't make sense to him, and he'd had a doctor explaining it to him.

"My *daed* works a lot," Johnny said.

"I know." Aaron looked at Matthew. The older man looked tired and seemed quieter than usual. "Is there anything I can help with?"

"No, but thank you," Matthew said. He pushed his plate aside and wrapped his hands around his mug of coffee. "Chris came over and helped with the horses. We have to be grateful Joshua's injury happened in the winter instead of a busy time like planting or harvesting."

"I'll just be happy when he's home safe and sound," Jenny said. "I spoke with the doctor earlier and she thinks he can come home in the morning."

Aaron watched a smile bloom on Annie's face. "Oh, he'll be so happy. He was a little grumpy earlier. He misses your cooking."

"He misses his horse," Jenny said, smiling.

"No, he hates the food, so Aaron bought him a cheeseburger."

"That was kind of you," Jenny told him. "Annie, I spoke with your father today, and we're going to take the trip after all. But Joshua will stay home with Phoebe."

"Oh." Annie set her fork down on her plate and her shoulders slumped. "I guess it's good news, bad news."

"Huh?" Johnny looked from one to another.

"Good news because I want us to go on the trip, but bad news because Joshua and Phoebe aren't going," Annie explained.

Johnny speared a bite of meatloaf on his fork and looked at Aaron. "Maybe since Joshua's not going, Aaron can go with us?"

7

$\mathcal{A}$nnie nearly choked on the mouthful of iced tea she'd just sipped.

She looked at her mother and wondered if she looked just as surprised as she felt.

"Well, I imagine Aaron will want to do things with his family since Christmas is coming soon," Jenny said, looking at him.

"But we're like fam'ly to him, right? He's here eating supper with us a lot," Johnny pointed out. "We're like fam'ly to him. He helped when Joshua got hurt."

Annie tried to suppress her smile, but when she cast a furtive glance at Aaron she saw she must not have been successful. She saw him studying her and wondered what he was thinking.

Aaron grinned at Johnny. "I do eat here a lot, don't I? Your family has been very generous inviting me to join you for supper."

She watched him as he put another bite of meatloaf into his mouth. He'd been a friend and the invitation was often casual. But things were changing, and whatever was happening didn't feel so casual any more.

"It's our first vacation," Johnny said as he speared a green bean. "We never been on a vacation."

"*We've* never been," Jenny corrected.

"Yeah, that's what I said." He put his elbow on the table, propped his chin in his hand and studied Aaron. "Have you ever been on a vacation?"

"No. Annie's been telling me about the one you have planned. It sounds very interesting."

Annie raised her brows. Aaron had listened to her talk, but she didn't think he'd actually thought the places she mentioned them visiting had been interesting to him.

"What place sounded the most interesting to you?" she asked him as she casually buttered a piece of bread.

"Oh, uh, well, all of them."

"But which one would you want to see if you could?"

Aaron finished the food on his plate and shook his head when Jenny asked if he wanted more meatloaf.

"Yes, Aaron, which thing interested you the most in the rather long list of things that must be seen in the big city?" Matthew asked.

Annie saw a glint of mischief in his eyes. So, he'd picked up on her question and decided to put the younger man on the spot.

Aaron thought for a long moment. "Not a specific place. I'd just want a tour, see all the people, wonder why they wanted to be squashed together in one small space."

"Come on, a place," said Annie.

"Okay, maybe the Empire State Building."

Annie leaned forward. "Why there?"

"I kind of doubt he wants to see the *New York Times* like we do," Jenny said. "It's something you and I want to do because we're writers. Your father and Johnny are going to find something else to do then, remember?"

Annie nodded. Her father didn't share an interest in writing with her mother and they still had a great relationship. He supported what she did and that was what was important.

"So, Aaron, why the Empire State Building?" Matthew asked him.

He shrugged. "Once I thought about building—not just being a carpenter making furniture."

Annie remembered. He'd gone through a period in school when he liked reading books on buildings and construction. These days, he was always the first to show up at a barn raising and climb around on the structure like a monkey.

She watched him fidget with the brace on his hand. "So what did the doctor tell you about working with your hand?"

He shook his head. "I have to give it a rest for a couple of weeks. He thinks with the pills he gave me and some rest it'll be fine." He looked at Jenny. "Joshua said he's missing your cooking. Annie promised him she'd ask you to bring him something when you visit."

"How about a meatloaf sandwich and one or two of the whoopie pies we made yesterday?" Annie asked her mother.

"Good idea," Jenny agreed.

Annie took the plate of sliced bread and the meatloaf platter to the counter and began making the sandwich.

She wrapped the sandwich and a whoopie pie, then on second thought, added a second whoopie pie to the brown paper sack. When she finished, she saw Aaron was watching her. And her father was watching Aaron.

She looked at her mother and, ever observant, Jenny nodded. "Well, we should get going if we're seeing Joshua. Johnny, put your jacket on."

Matthew rose, plucked his son's jacket off the peg, and tossed it to him. He pulled on his own jacket and started for the back door. "I'll go hitch up the buggy."

"I'll help," Aaron said, getting to his feet.

"Could you help *Mamm* clear the table?" Annie asked him. "I'd like to talk to *Daed* for a moment." She smiled at him.

"I—uh, sure," he said.

Annie grabbed her shawl and hurried after her father. She closed the back door behind her, turned, and found him standing there on the back porch, his arms folded across his chest, a knowing expression on his face.

"Just what is it you want from me, little one?" he asked. "And don't be giving me the smile you just gave Aaron. You can't wrap me around your little finger anymore, like you did when you were a *kind*."

She tucked her arm in his and began walking with him toward the barn. He was her dear, dear *Daed* and she knew very well she could.

"You're going where?"

"New York City." Aaron eyed the stack of pants he'd tried to fold neatly. He counted them and wondered if he had enough.

"This is all so sudden." His mother stood in the doorway of his room, her hands on her hips. "Or have you known and you're just thinking to say something now?"

She hadn't been blunt with him in years. He met her piercing gaze and remembered how often she'd pinned him with it like this when he was younger—when she'd caught him in some mischief. He hadn't grown up to be honest on his own; Vera was determined he and all her six *kinner* would be.

"Matthew just asked me tonight. Joshua isn't going, and he and Jenny thought I might like to go along."

She watched him try to fold a pair of pants, then made a clucking noise with her tongue and elbowed him aside. "You'll look like a wrinkled mess folding them like that."

He cradled his aching wrist in his other hand. "Did the best I could."

"Well, it's not good enough." She got to work refolding them and then started on his shirts.

"So you're getting serious about Annie after all this time?"

He must not have answered her fast enough because she plucked at his sleeve. "Aaron. Did you ask Annie to marry you?"

"No."

"But you're thinking on it? You've said something to her? I can't imagine a father would ask you to join a family trip if he thought you were just a friend."

He paused in his study of his shirts. Maybe she was right. Maybe Annie had asked her father to invite him along. He hadn't thought to ask—he'd been surprised but not so surprised he hadn't said yes immediately.

He didn't care about seeing New York City. He'd jumped at the chance to go on the trip so he could spend some time with Annie.

"Aaron!"

"What?"

Turning, he looked down at her. His *mamm* was a small woman, just five feet. He'd gotten his height from his *dat*— well, he'd surpassed his father's six foot two inches by two more.

She shook her head. "It's like you already left. Just like your *dat* when he's getting ready for a hunting trip with his friends. His mind just wanders off before his body does."

"Sorry."

"So when are you leaving?"

"Day after tomorrow."

"Not much notice."

"They just found out Joshua can't go. Phoebe's staying back to take care of him."

"Joshua's not worse?"

Aaron shook his head. "Doctor just said he needed to rest more than he would on a trip."

He thought about how Johnny had brought up the idea of him taking the trip when they were at the supper table last night. It must have given Annie the idea to ask her father because, shortly after, she'd gone off with him as he went out to the barn.

Such a nice *kind*, that Johnny.

"What's going on?" his father asked. "Timer's going off on the stove when I walk in and you're up here?"

"My pie!" his mother exclaimed, and she rushed out of the room.

"I pulled it out and put it on top of the stove," he called after her, but they could hear her continue to descend the steps to the kitchen.

Aaron fingered his Sunday shirt. It was looking a little worn.

"You moving out?"

He turned. "No. You wanting me to?"

"*Nee*. Might be another mouth to feed, but it's another set of hands to help."

Since his father's eyes were scanning the piles of clothing on the bed, Aaron answered the unspoken question and told him about the trip.

"Seems like the Bontragers are welcoming you into the family, taking you along on a trip."

His mother had asked him a question. His father made a statement.

"Haven't asked her yet. But I'm hoping we're headed in that direction."

Isaac nodded. "'Bout time."

"The trip will give me some time to spend with Annie and get to know her better."

"Seems like you should know all about her. You grew up with her, went to church and such with her."

Aaron shrugged. "Annie's different. She's more . . . complicated than some of the girls I know. I think the time will be good for us."

"Sounds like this could be a *gut* idea then." With that, he headed downstairs.

A few minutes later, Aaron heard his mother call him for supper.

Supper at the Beiler supper table was quiet compared to the Bontrager one. Aaron and his younger sister, Rebecca, were the last left at home. Tonight, her place was empty.

"Off spending the night with your sister, Katie," his mother told him as Aaron gave her a questioning look.

His father passed the platter of fried chicken to him and he chose a thigh and a leg. A bowl of mashed potatoes followed, topped by browned butter. Aaron sighed in satisfaction as he helped himself to a large portion. Nothing better than his *mamm's* mashed potatoes.

"Christmas," his mother said suddenly.

"I'll be back before then."

She nodded. "It's as it should be. Family should be together at Christmas."

"So is there anything you need to take?" Vera asked. "Don't want you going looking less than you should."

"I'm thinking I need a new Sunday shirt," he told her, stabbing a carrot glazed with brown sugar. "There's some fancy event Jenny's going to, although I'm not sure if I'm invited. I talked to a friend and he's going to loan me his suitcase."

"I have some nice fabric," she mused. "You and your father do the dishes after supper and I can get a start on it, have it ready for you tomorrow."

His father stopped eating. "Just give him one of mine. You just made me a new one last month."

"Now you know it won't fit Aaron," she told him. "He's bigger than you."

"Maybe he wouldn't be if he didn't eat so much," Isaac said.

Looking up from his third piece of chicken, Aaron grinned. "I'm just a growing boy."

Isaac grunted. "Eating me out of house and home. Good thing you'll be leaving soon."

Aaron saw the glint of amusement in his father's eyes. "If I have my way," he said easily. "And how many pieces of chicken is that for you?"

"Gotta let your mother know I appreciate her cooking."

"Sure. And we'll show it when we wash the dishes and clean up the kitchen after. Right?"

He laughed when his father scowled. Nothing his father hated worse than kitchen work. But he pitched in without complaint as his wife started on Aaron's new shirt.

❧

Annie watched from the barn as Joshua came home with her parents.

The van driver drove all the way up to a few feet from the barn and stopped.

"Come on, Pilot," she said, leading him out by his bridle.

Her father stepped out of the van and left the door open. When Joshua saw the horse, his face lit up. Annie walked him up to the open van, and Pilot stuck his head in and let Joshua stroke his nose.

She smiled reassuringly at the driver, who'd edged back a little in his seat as he watched. "Thank you," she mouthed and he nodded and smiled.

Joshua turned to his mother. "Back when I had my concussion you let me sit on the porch and you brought Pilot up to it so I could spend time with him . . ."

She laughed and shook her head. "Maybe tomorrow. This is as good as you get today."

He leaned forward and kissed the horse's nose. "See you tomorrow."

Annie wondered if her brother would ever look at a woman the same way he looked at his horse. "Come on," she told the horse. "You guys can see each other tomorrow."

Was it her imagination or did the horse seemed reluctant to return to the barn? She pulled an apple she'd tucked in the pocket of her dress ahead of time. "Got this for you if you go back in your stall for me. That's right, you get the apple."

She guided him to his stall and, once he was inside, gave him the apple. Then she made sure all was secure before she left the barn and hurried to the house.

"Why can't I go to my own room?" she heard Joshua ask as she walked down the hall to the downstairs bedroom.

"The doctor doesn't want you going up and down stairs for a while," her mother said. She tucked a quilt around him.

"Let your mother fuss," Matthew told him. "She's happy to have you home."

"Even I'm happy to have you home," Annie spoke up as she handed him a package.

"What's this?"

"Something Johnny and I got you so you'll stay in bed and rest."

Joshua pulled the wrapping off a book about horses. "Thanks. I've wanted this one. He's my favorite author." Joshua flipped the cover open and started to read, then caught himself and put the book down. "I'll start it after supper."

"You're welcome," Annie said wryly.

She heard a knock on the front door and went to answer it. "Aaron!"

"I wanted to see if Joshua was able to come home from the hospital today."

"He sure was. He's been complaining about what *Mamm* won't let him do." She held open the door. "Come on in. I'm sure he'd love a visit."

"Thanks."

She felt his hand on her arm as she started to walk away, so she turned and looked at him.

"I came to talk to you too."

"What about?"

"Aaron! Good to see you!" Jenny said. "Are you staying for supper?"

He looked at Annie. "I came to see Joshua—"

"Stay for supper," Jenny said. "You'll deserve it after talking to Mr. Grump. Right, Annie?" She headed for the kitchen.

"Rhetorical question," Annie told Aaron. "Come on, Joshua's in the downstairs bedroom." After showing him to Joshua's temporary room, she went to help her mother in the kitchen.

Jenny looked up from stirring a pot on the stove. "Didn't know Aaron was stopping by."

"I didn't, either. Says he came to see Joshua and he wants to talk to me." She pulled plates from a cupboard and began setting the table. "I wonder if he's changed his mind about going on the trip."

"Why would he do that?"

Annie shrugged. "I don't know."

"He's crazy about you," Jenny said softly. "He'd follow you all the way to New York City just to spend time with you. Doesn't that reassure you?"

She set the last plate down on the table, the one at the usual spot where he sat when he came for supper. "I guess. This is all sort of new to me. Until recently I hadn't thought about him being more than a friend. Hadn't thought about marriage at all."

"I know."

"What do you think?" Annie asked as she came to stand near the stove.

"I think I like what this famous man once said about parental advice. He said he went to his parents one day wanting to ask their advice and they refused to give it. They said if he listened to them too much he'd only be getting the benefit of their experience. He needed to get some of his own."

Annie considered and nodded. "I guess that's wise."

"You want to go give the ten-minute warning for supper? It's almost ready. Oh, and tell Joshua he's getting his on a tray in his room."

She nodded and went to do so only to turn at the doorway. "By the way, who was the man?"

"Stephen Spielberg."

"Should I know him?"

"Director."

When Annie still looked vague, Jenny laughed. "Your brothers might have heard of him. *Raiders of the Lost Ark.*"

"Oh, a movie."

Jenny laughed. "Only you could dismiss it as a movie."

Annie ran into Aaron in the hallway as he came out of Joshua's temporary room.

"Can we talk now?" he asked.

"We have ten minutes to supper."

"It'll be long enough."

"Let me grab my jacket and we'll talk on the porch."

She found him pacing the porch when she returned.

"You sure it's not too cold out here for you?"

"You said it wouldn't take long."

"Right." He looked out at the road, then back at her. "Annie, I just want to make sure you want me to come on the trip. I didn't think your father would ask if you hadn't asked him, but I wanted to make sure."

"I bet you were surprised when he asked you, weren't you?"

"Shocked would be a better word," he admitted with a laugh. Then his expression became serious and he reached for her hand. "Annie, does this mean what I think it does? Are you ready to start thinking of us as . . . us?"

He was a lot like her father, a man of few words. One who preferred to let his actions speak for him. But "us." Such a simple but powerful word.

She looked down at his hand holding hers, then up at him and nodded slowly. "Yes."

8

"We need to talk about staring," Jenny said.

"You worry too much," Annie told her as she gazed out the window of the van. "We get stared at all the time."

Jenny smiled. "No, I'm talking about all of you not staring. There are going to be some . . . unusual sights. Not just places but people you haven't seen before."

"*Mamm*, you're talking like we're going to visit a zoo."

"I want to go to the zoo!" Johnny spoke up.

"It's on our list," she assured him. "The Central Park Zoo. But that's not what I'm talking about. We're going to be seeing a lot of people who are different from those we see in Lancaster County."

Annie knew that. She'd studied the photographs in the books about New York City she'd borrowed from the library. People from all walks of life, from all sorts of cultures and countries lived in the city. Diversity, they called it. Why, they even had the Statue of Liberty greeting people coming to the country, and so many different people had come to the country it was called a melting pot. Annie thought it was a weird term and wanted to ask her mother about it when she had a minute.

It was certainly going to be a different sort of place than Lancaster County. And it was exactly what Annie had decided she was going to love about it.

She glanced over at Aaron. He wasn't a talkative man, but today he was very quiet. Maybe it hadn't been the best idea for him to be seated next to her father in the van. She wondered if Aaron felt a little uncomfortable around him . . . since she'd let her father know she and Aaron were getting "comfortable with each other."

"We're on our way," she told her mother.

Jenny sighed as she looked out the window. "I didn't think it was going to happen. I still feel guilty leaving Joshua with Phoebe."

Matthew reached over and took her hand. "You know Phoebe will take good care of him."

She nodded. "I also know Joshua will be doing anything he can to be up and in the barn with his horses."

"Phoebe knows. He won't get past her."

"Back when I was a teenager, I got past her—" Jenny stopped when all eyes turned to her. "Look, there's Naomi Lapp! Everyone wave!"

"Nice save," Annie heard her father murmur.

She turned to him. "Did you remember to bring—"

"*Ya.*"

"You don't even know what I was going to say."

He squeezed her hand. "I used the list you gave me. And the second one."

Annie tried to suppress her smile, but her mother caught her.

"Oh, so you think my lists are funny."

"I believe you're what the *Englisch* call OCD."

"OCD? What's that?" Matthew wanted to know.

Annie looked at her mother, then her father. She was getting to go on the trip. Maybe she should be diplomatic. "You've lived it," Annie told him. "Amazingly organized, capable of multitasking, keeper of lists extraordinaire."

"My daughter, the vocabulary queen," Matthew told Aaron. "I think she was born with a dictionary in her hand."

"Words are my life," Annie said with satisfaction.

She turned to her mother. "I can't wait to see where you came from."

"Well, I wasn't born in New York City," Jenny told her. "I actually came from a small town in upstate New York. But to do the work I wanted to do, I had to move to the big city. I was thrilled. It had always been a place I thought of as kind of magical." She grimaced. "Well, once I got there I discovered it's a kind of gritty magical in some places."

She turned to Annie. "You'll see what I mean when we get there. I hope you haven't over-romanticized it."

"But isn't New York City supposed to be magical and romantic during the Christmas holiday?"

Jenny smiled and Annie thought her smile seemed a little nostalgic. "Yes, it is."

Matthew leaned to look out the window at a barren field, waiting for the spring planting.

"We'll be back before you know it," Jenny whispered to him.

He turned and covered her hand with his. "I know. I am so looking forward to the trip."

Annie found herself studying the two of them. She knew her father hadn't been interested in going to New York City, and he, like her brother, preferred the simple comfort of home. Even though more Amish were traveling for work and vacation, he'd never felt the urge. But he'd made the effort for her mother and she loved him even more because of it. She was old enough to know how much her mother did for the family, what sacrifices she made—although her mother would deny she'd sacrificed. She loved her family, she loved what she did for them, and that was that.

How nice they would all be together when her mother was honored for her work writing about children living in terrible conditions around the world. She knew her as *Mamm*. Others knew her for her work in a world beyond her small Amish community.

Her mother made a tiny grimace as she shifted in her seat. Although she tried to hide her movement, Annie saw her father glance at her and frown in concern.

"It's okay. I just overdid a little getting ready for the trip. I'll be fine."

Annie had been a young girl when her mother had several surgeries to repair damage from being hurt in the bombing overseas. She knew surgery had repaired much of the damage, but there were times, like now when she'd overdone, when she would experience some discomfort.

Annie would make sure once they were in their rooms that her mother rested while Annie unpacked.

"How long will it take to get there?" Aaron asked.

"Didn't Annie tell you?"

She grinned. "I did. He probably tuned me out."

"I would never—" he spluttered and his face turned red.

"Relax," Jenny told him. "We wouldn't tease if you weren't considered part of the family."

There it was again, thought Annie. He'd been teased at the supper table not long ago and Mary had said he was part of the family.

Annie wondered if Aaron had listened to other important details of the trip. When the van pulled into the entrance of the airport, she saw his shoulders tense and knew he'd remembered this one. He swallowed, and his Adam's apple bobbled.

When he turned, though, and saw her looking at him, he quickly changed his expression.

The pasty color of his skin betrayed him.

A quick retort came to her lips but, when she saw her father watching her, she held it back. Her father had come because it was important to her mother; like him, Aaron had said he'd come because this trip was important to her.

"I heard flying's just like sitting in a car," she told Aaron as they climbed out of the van. "You don't even feel any different."

Annie saw him adjust the brace on his hand and wondered if it was paining him or if it was from nerves. "And it's a quick trip. *Mamm's* friend arranged for this private plane. We'll be there in practically no time."

⌘

"Annie, are you okay?"

She nodded, but she didn't look okay. Her face was white, she was breathing fast, and her hands were shaking.

They'd been flying for a short time and she'd seemed to be enjoying herself. The pilot had just announced they'd reached a certain altitude. Annie leaned to look out the window and exclaimed over the beauty of the clouds. Then she'd suddenly gone quiet—something unusual for Annie—and Aaron had become concerned.

"Annie, maybe you shouldn't be looking out the window."

"I'm fine." Then she turned and pressed a hand to her mouth. "Oh."

"Push her head down on her knees," he heard Jenny saying. She thrust a bag in his hands and he saw it was labeled "air sickness bag." "Air sickness?" He'd never heard of such a thing. How could anyone be sick of air?

"Annie, are you going to throw up?" her mother asked as she leaned over Aaron. "Use the bag if you need to. I'll go ask the flight attendant for some ginger ale."

"No, I'm not going to throw up," Annie mumbled, her voice faint from her face pressing up against her skirt. "I don't think so."

After a moment, she lifted her head and sat up. "It wasn't supposed to be like this," she told Aaron, sounding annoyed. "I thought you were the one who'd get sick sitting next to the window."

"You're the one who hates heights. You've always tried to hide it, but it's nothing to be ashamed of." He unbuckled his seatbelt. "Here, I'll change seats with you."

"No, I'll be fine. I just won't look out the window anymore."

"Here, drink some ginger ale," Jenny said, handing Annie a plastic cup. She looked at Aaron. "Do you want to trade seats with me and I'll take care of her?"

He shook his head, then glanced at Annie. "Not unless you want me to?"

She met his gaze and after a moment, she shook her head. "No, I want to you to stay here."

Aaron smiled at her. He knew she was independent and didn't like to admit to weakness of any kind. But she was letting him take care of her in a small way and it felt good.

"I saw the Empire State Building on your mother's list," he said quietly. "I've been meaning to ask what you're going to do about that?"

She grinned, looking more like herself as she sipped the ginger ale. "I was going to sit in the lobby and people watch. Or go up, but stay far back from the railing."

"We can sit in the lobby and people watch together."

"But I don't want you to miss the view. It's supposed to be wonderful."

"I won't miss it," he said and watched her blush.

She glanced away and watched Johnny bouncing in his seat as he looked out his window at the clouds. Her mother appeared to be enjoying herself. Her father sat next to her and seemed to be taking it all in with his usual equanimity.

Annie spent the rest of the flight talking with Aaron about all her mother had planned.

"I'm glad you have a chance to see the city since you've always wanted to," he told her.

"I have," she said slowly as she gazed at her mother sitting in the opposite row. After rushing around preparing for the trip, missing sleep over Joshua, her mother had finally wound down and slept, her cheek pressed against her husband's shoulder.

"But part of it is I want to understand *Mamm* better. She's had a foot in each world—the Amish and the *Englisch*—and I always wanted to know more about her before she became my mother."

She looked up at Aaron. "Does that make any sense?"

He thought for a minute and said, "I never thought about it. I mean, my mother's my mother. What is there to understand?"

"But she was born Amish, was raised Amish. She's never been outside the community. *Mamm* lived a different life before she became part of my family." She smiled and sighed. "She gave up her life because she loved my father. I guess I always wanted to know how she did it."

Nodding, he glanced over at Jenny, then back at Annie. "You can't explain love. It just is." When she stared at him, her brows drawn in a frown, he grew concerned. "What, did I say something wrong?"

"No," she said at last. "Sometimes you say just the right thing."

Thank You, God, he couldn't help thinking. Navigating his way around this relationship wasn't as easy as he'd just made it sound. He wanted no other woman but Annie and felt she was the one God had chosen for him. But sometimes he didn't feel as articulate as she was, didn't feel as if he knew as much even though they'd gone to the same *schul*. He guessed it was all the reading and writing she did.

He leaned back in his seat and relaxed as the pilot began talking about approaching the city of Annie's dreams.

⌒◞

Annie saw the sparkle of lights on the periphery of her vision and just had to look out the window.

This time, she was relieved she didn't feel the rolling nausea she had before. Did the fact that night had fallen and she couldn't see how far up they were keep her from getting sick? The tall buildings below seemed magical, lit with thousands of twinkling lights. She'd seen a picture of New York City at night, but nothing had prepared her for the wonder of the scene they were now flying over.

"Should you be looking out the window again?" she heard Aaron asking.

Turning, she waved her hand at him, almost speechless with excitement. "Look! Look!" She glanced over at her mother and saw she'd woken up. "*Mamm*! It's amazing!"

"So many lights!" Aaron murmured.

"I know. It's like they're fairy mountains."

The pilot talked about their approach to the city and how soon they would land. The family dutifully buckled their seatbelts and began chattering about getting off the plane and getting started with their adventure.

"Are we staying with David and Joy?" Johnny asked.

"No, we're going to be in a big hotel, remember?" Jenny made sure his seatbelt was secure. "They're coming to the hotel and bringing their children tomorrow morning."

"Now I remember," he said, nodding.

"I hope I didn't inconvenience your parents coming along," Aaron said in a low voice. "I offered to pay for my room, but your father wouldn't let me. I'm going to insist on paying for my meals."

"You're taking Joshua's place so you're not costing anything extra," Annie told him. "If you want to pay for a meal now and then I'm sure it'll be fine. But don't worry about it. You've eaten supper with us so you know how much Joshua eats."

She grinned at him. "You'll be saving *Daed* money."

The family got their carry-on luggage out of the overhead bins. Annie watched Aaron like a hawk, concerned about him hurting his hand. But he lifted his luggage carefully and used his left hand to guide his rolling suitcase as they filed off the plane.

Jenny went to inquire about their transportation to the hotel. When she returned, she frowned.

"There was some miscommunication," she said. "The hotel's not sending someone to drive us there. We'll have to get other transportation."

"Don't worry," Matthew said. "I made sure to bring extra money for changes in plans."

"Money's not a concern right now," she said. Straightening, she fixed a bright smile on her face. "I'd just rather take a limo instead of a van or taxi into New York City."

"We've taken vans and taxis before," Johnny reminded her.

"There's no comparison to what we have back in Paradise," Jenny whispered to Annie as she moved to her side. "How's the nausea?"

"Long gone."

"I hope so."

A van pulled into line and Jenny shepherded them inside. Jenny leaned forward and gave the driver the name of their hotel and the vehicle lurched out into traffic.

As Johnny had said, they'd taken van and taxi rides back home. But Annie had never been in a vehicle that darted and dashed and sped along the crowded city streets at a breakneck speed.

Annie was amazed and appalled and suddenly realized why her mother had asked if she was feeling okay before they climbed inside the van.

"Mr. Toad's Wild Ride," her mother muttered, clutching Johnny.

"What?" Annie asked.

"Used to be a ride at Disney World."

Matthew leaned forward. "Sir, could you slow down a little?"

The driver said something in a foreign language.

"What?" Matthew asked.

Jenny patted his knee. "Don't worry, we're almost there."

"Not soon enough," he said between clenched teeth.

Annie glanced at Aaron, but he paid no attention, staring wide-eyed at the canyons of glass and steel rising up on each side of the street, at the people moving with purpose on the sidewalks.

The van screeched to a stop in front of one of the biggest buildings Annie had ever seen. A man with a fancy scarlet military-looking coat with epaulets on the shoulders opened the taxi door with a flourish and a tip of his hat. Annie saw mild curiosity in his eyes, but he was faultlessly polite.

Another man retrieved their luggage from the trunk, piled it on a cart, and pushed it inside the hotel. Annie overheard her mother reassuring her father it was the man's job.

"Tip?" he whispered and she told him what to slip the man.

Matthew liked to do things himself, but he nodded.

Rules of behavior, thought Annie. They existed in so many ways, so many places, not just in her community.

The massive lobby had a huge Christmas tree and arrangements of poinsettias.

"We've been expecting you," the man behind a shiny wood counter told Jenny. "I am so sorry there was a mix-up in your transportation. We will, of course, reimburse you for your expense. Did you save your receipt for the transportation by any chance?"

"Yes, I did. We took a van," Jenny said as she signed some paper the man handed her. "It was quite the experience for my family."

"Ah, it's not a trip to New York City without a wild ride," he said, nodding, a mischievous glint in his eyes. "It was something, wasn't it?"

"*Mamm* called it Mr. Toad's Wild Ride," Johnny said, chuckling. "How silly. The man didn't look like a toad."

"John Gabriel Bontrager, go stand by the elevator and wait for it," Jenny told him. She rolled her eyes as he scurried over to stand where she gestured.

The man smiled. "Kids will be kids."

Jenny laughed. "So true."

Johnny looked fascinated by the elevator, so much fancier than the one at the hospital where Joshua had stayed. Once they piled inside, he got to press the button to their floor. When they began ascending, he looked nervously at his feet.

The man who took them to their rooms called it a suite, and he opened the door with a card of plastic instead of a key. Another man followed with a cart loaded with their luggage.

Annie's eyes widened as they walked into a huge room with doors leading off it. One bedroom would be for Aaron and Johnny, another, Annie's. And the biggest room would be for their parents. The man with the cart quickly distributed luggage to the proper rooms, then hurried out of the room—but not before Jenny touched Matthew's arm and once again, his hand disappeared into his pocket, reappearing with folded bills for a tip.

Even though her mother had told her things were expensive in the big city, Annie couldn't help thinking they'd already spent a LOT of money.

The suite looked huge. Two families could have stayed here and there would still be room, she thought, gazing in wonder as the man opened the doors to an armoire and revealed a large television he called a flat screen. A little refrigerator held soft drinks and bottles of water that Jenny warned with a shake of her head wouldn't be for them. "Too expensive," she whispered as the man walked on to open the curtains, revealing the view.

Annie approached the window cautiously since they were so high up. The stores in the buildings opposite the hotel had closed. Despite this, people—so many people—still hurried about on the sidewalks, looking like purposeful ants from up here.

Her father handed over another tip and the man left, closing the door quietly behind him.

Johnny jumped up and down. "Now what are we going to do?"

Jenny groaned and slumped into a chair.

Annie pressed a hand on top of her brother's head as if he was a spring she could stop. "We're going to go to bed," she told him, taking him by the shoulders and gently guiding him in the direction of his bedroom. "Then we can get a nice early start on our day."

"Awww," he complained. "I'm not tired."

"But everyone else is," she told him. She lifted his suitcase onto the bed, unzipped it, and took out his pajamas. "Put these on and then go brush your teeth. Then climb into bed and go to sleep. *Mamm* needs to lie down. I think her back is bothering her."

"But I want to read a story."

She pulled a book from the suitcase. Her mother remembered everything. "Here you go."

His bottom lip jutted out. "*Mamm* or *Daed* always helps me with my reading."

"How about I do that tonight?" Aaron asked from the doorway. "That book has one of my favorites when I was a *kind*."

Johnny looked at him, narrowing his eyes as he studied him. "Really?"

"Yes. I never had a younger brother I could help. I'm the baby of the family."

"Baby!" Johnny thought that was funny. He scooped up his pajamas and raced to the bathroom. "Be right back."

Annie patted Aaron's arm. "You have a good time, big brother."

He grinned and leaned forward. "I'm not your big brother," he teased, and there was a glint in his eyes that made her heart race.

They were just inches apart when Annie heard a noise and spun around to find her father glaring at Aaron.

"I'm going to go see how *Mamm*'s doing," she said and escaped.

It was chicken of her to leave Aaron alone to face her father. She could practically hear clucking in her ears as she did. At the same time, she felt herself grinning. Their vacation was just starting and she was already having such fun.

9

Annie knew she was fidgeting like a little kid, but she couldn't help it.

Yes, the dining room in the hotel looked like nothing she'd ever seen: a huge room filled with cloth-covered tables, fine china, and the fanciest knives, forks, and spoons she'd ever eaten out of. A waiter even stood nearby, never leaving them in case they needed anything.

An envelope lay just inside their door. True to his word, the man who had checked them in had sent them a paper crediting them for the transportation and provided tickets for them to eat free at the hotel's breakfast buffet to make up for their inconvenience.

Breakfast was a meal Annie had always loved, but she grew impatient with how long her family was taking to look over the contents of the buffet and eat. Yes, the food looked lovely and was clearly an expensive treat she didn't want the family to miss. But she wanted to get going. *Patience*, she told herself as she chose a few items quickly and sat down to eat.

Johnny grinned as he showed his mother his plate. "The man with the hat said these fishes are kippers," he said. "Do I like kippers?"

Annie watched her mother struggle to suppress a smile. "You've never had them, but I bet you'll like them."

He took his seat, put a bite of the fish into his mouth, and chewed. He made a face, but then, under the stern eye of his mother, finished the kipper, scrambled eggs, and a big bagel. The Bontragers didn't believe in wasting food.

Aaron and her father opted for eggs, bacon, and toast, but then, just as Annie thought they had finished, they went back for enormous waffles made on the spot.

Honestly, where did men put away all the food they ate, she wondered. When they nodded to having their coffee cups refilled for the third time, only the fact that *she* received her mother's stern eye this time made her subside.

Jenny finished her breakfast and pulled a list from her purse. She handed it to Annie. "Here's our itinerary for the day."

"Itin—itin—" Johnny struggled with the word.

"Itinerary," his father said. "A plan."

Annie wasn't surprised her father knew the word. He might not have gone to college like her mother, but he loved to read.

She studied the list: Macy's. Bloomingdale's. Barney's.

"Stores?" Annie said. "We're going shopping?" The day she'd looked forward to for so long was rapidly going downhill.

When her mother just looked at her, Annie felt a twinge of guilt. "I'm sorry. We're here for you."

Jenny just smiled. "We're here for all of us. I have it planned so everyone's going to get to enjoy something of the city."

She smiled at her husband. "Even you."

Annie wondered if there was something Aaron would enjoy but figured he'd been invited to join them too late to have some place special picked for him. She looked at the rest of the list. Staten Island Ferry. Statue of Liberty. Ellis Island. Times Square. Central Park. Subway.

Why would they want to get a sub sandwich? she wondered. *Hmm.* Maybe it was a place her mother liked to eat lunch in the city. *Oh, wait a minute. The* subway. *Hmm. It could be interesting.* She wasn't sure how her father would feel about it—she'd heard subways were very fast, and he'd tried to get the driver to slow down last night . . .

"Annie? Thought you wanted to get going?"

Lost in thought, she hadn't realized everyone was getting up. She jumped to her feet, nearly knocking over her chair.

"And she's off," Jenny murmured behind her.

Cold air with the faint scent of exhaust fumes hit her the minute she walked outside. And in her rush she almost got run over by several people walking past on the sidewalk.

"Sorry!" she stammered and resolved to be more careful.

This time they were more prepared for the crazy dart through traffic. The van Jenny had hired deposited them in front of a huge department store.

"It always seemed like the holidays started when Macy's revealed their Christmas window display," Jenny told them as they gathered in front of the first window.

Inside it, animated figures dressed in costumes from the early part of the century gathered in front of a fireplace decorated with stockings and admired their Christmas tree. Each window featured another scene representing some depiction of an *Englisch* family celebrating the holiday.

"Before she died, my mother used to bring me here each year when I was a little girl," Jenny said, raising her voice over the traffic noise. "It was something just the two of us did. After, we'd go have tea with little sandwiches and fancy cakes and cookies at one of the big hotels." She grinned. "Don't worry, I'm not going to make you do that."

"We can do that," Johnny said, looking up at her. "I like sandwiches and cookies and stuff."

Jenny bent and kissed his nose. "Thank you. But I have a more fun lunch planned for us."

She stood and Annie saw her father slip his arm around her mother's waist. He didn't often make a public display of affection. She knew her mother hadn't had her own mother for many years before she died, and her father had been so devastated he hadn't been as much of an emotional support as she'd needed. Even with a father who genuinely tried to help, as her own father had been, Annie knew no one could ever be everything a child needed when she lost a parent.

She slipped her hand in her mother's and squeezed it, and her mother glanced at her and smiled.

They strolled along and watched the characters in the window, and when they were on the 34th Street side, Jenny told them about her favorite Christmas movie.

Johnny listened but seemed confused. Amish children weren't encouraged to believe in Santa, so he didn't understand why *Englisch* children were.

"People just believe in different things," he was told.

"But you said the movie was about a miracle," he said. "And look at him." He pointed at a Santa standing beside a Salvation Army bucket nearby. "Doesn't that mean Santa is religious?"

Annie had seldom witnessed her mother looking speechless, but she surely was this time. Jenny bent down and looked at her son. "Tell you what. I'll get a copy of the movie and we'll watch it later. Then you'll understand."

"Okay." Johnny turned his attention to the last window.

"We used to get hot roasted chestnuts back then," Jenny told Matthew. "I wonder if they're still sold by one of the sidewalk vendors."

She took them to see the windows of two other big stores, and it seemed to Annie that each of them tried to outdo the others with the sheer grandeur of their windows.

Annie noticed they were the object of attention, but she didn't mind. She was busy observing people herself. It seemed New Yorkers were in such a hurry, rushing to wherever they were going. Even the people who were clearly tourists rushed as if they had to see everything in one day.

Jenny sighed. "I enjoyed it, but I don't think it was as interesting for our men," she told Annie. "I think our next stop will be a lot more interesting."

❧

The ferry ride was like nothing Annie had ever experienced.

Annie stood at the railing watching the play of emotions on Aaron's face and saw he was enjoying it.

A brisk wind tossed the water into peaked waves that slapped at the ferry and sent spray flying into their faces every so often. But it felt exhilarating. Annie had never been on a boat of any kind and didn't even mind getting cold since it was such an exciting adventure.

They weren't the only ones braving the chill on the decks. Others crowded around them, many of them looking curiously at the family.

"What's that big house over there?" Johnny asked, pointing at the structure as it came into view on its own island.

"Ellis Island," Jenny told them. "It was an immigration center. Where people who wanted to live in this country had to be cleared first."

"Did we have to go through there?"

Matthew picked him up and held him so he could see easier. "You know you were born in Paradise."

"Then did Phoebe come through here?"

Jenny laughed and shook her head. "The Amish came to this country hundreds of years ago, way before the time I'm talking about."

"Oh."

"Annie, the island was called the Island of Tears or Heartbreak Island. Do you know why?"

She shook her head. "Why?"

"You love to look things up. I'll let you do that."

"Okay," she said slowly, tilting her head and studying her mother.

"Might be something you want to write about. Forty percent of the people in this country came through there or had a relative pass through Ellis Island. They came for the American Dream. Braved dangerous ocean crossings and sickness and fear. All for a chance to live and work and love here."

Jenny leaned on the railing and gazed out at the island. "Or maybe you might like to write about where you came from."

"I'm from Paradise, just like Johnny."

"I'm talking about your ancestors. People are so interested in the Amish these days. You might want to write about it."

Hmm, thought Annie. She'd hoped to learn more about her mother by seeing where she'd come from here in this big city. Now her mother was telling her perhaps she'd like to find out more about her Amish ancestors.

"There's a lady with a crown," Johnny piped up.

"The Statue of Liberty," Aaron said. "There was a picture of it in one of those books you got from the library."

She stared at him. "How do you know?"

He shrugged. "I looked through some of them. Wanted to see what you were so interested in."

"So why is there a big lady with a crown?" Johnny wanted to know.

"That's Lady Liberty," Jenny said. "She was given to us by some people from France. They were impressed about us celebrating one hundred years of freedom as a country. She's been standing here for a long time as a symbol of freedom, welcoming immigrants to the country. There's a saying at the base that says, "Give me your tired, your poor, / Your huddled masses yearning to breathe free, / The wretched refuse of your teeming shore.— "

"Send these, Send these, the homeless, tempest-tost to me. / I lift my lamp beside the golden door," an elderly woman chanted behind her.

They turned and she smiled, her face creasing into many wrinkles. "Sorry. I just couldn't help finishing it. It's our story, the story of America."

"Exactly," Jenny said, beaming at her. "I came here with a group of kids from school several years ago and we climbed all the steps up and up and up to the top."

"Can we climb up it?" Johnny asked.

"I don't think we'll have time," Jenny said. "But we're going way, way up to the top of the Empire State Building later and it's even bigger."

"You're quite the tour guide. Maybe you'll want to help Nick with his tour business back home," Matthew teased.

"Nothing a New Yorker loves more than to show off her city. Well, a former New Yorker."

"Let's find a place to thaw out and get some lunch," Jenny suggested when they were back on land. "I'm frozen."

Then she tilted her head and grinned. "Say, do you know I even know a place where we can get frozen hot chocolate?" She glanced at Annie. "Oxymoron, right?"

Annie nodded.

"How is that possible?" Matthew asked Jenny with an indulgent smile.

"Anything is possible in New York City," she said.

They made the trip to Serendipity 3, a cozy little restaurant decorated with a whimsical touch. Jenny said she'd been there many times, and as they pored over the large menu, she made recommendations. Annie went with a corn chowder soup to warm up and the frozen hot chocolate for dessert.

Waiters carried tray after tray of ice cream delights to diners in the restaurant. The frozen hot chocolate seemed to be a favorite. It was a luscious cold chocolate concoction large enough to share. After they had warmed up and stuffed themselves with lunch and dessert, Annie used some of the money she'd saved for the trip to buy a few packages of the "frrrozen hot chocolate mix" to take home.

"For Joshua and Phoebe and Mary," she told her mother as she tucked her change in her purse.

Jenny bit her lip and looked worried. "I want to call them when we get back to the hotel later."

"What's next on our itinerary?" Aaron asked and Annie saw the mischievous twinkle in his eyes. "My word for the day," he told her.

"Central Park," Jenny said. "Then I thought we'd go back to the hotel to rest a little before we meet David and Joy for dinner."

❦

Aaron watched Annie watching people in Central Park.

What a surprise it had been to find a park in the middle of all the big buildings. He noticed Annie was fascinated, sitting beside him on the bench like an alert little bird, eyes bright, body tensed for quick movement. In fact, she was so interested in others she didn't notice they'd become the object of stares themselves.

A woman stood snapping photos of them with her camera phone. It wasn't the first time it had happened to either of them, of course. So many people came to Lancaster County as tourists and did the same thing.

When he started to his feet to say something to her, Annie put her hand on his arm. "Leave it alone," she said. "It's okay."

He subsided and leaned back on the bench. "We should probably have gone with your parents. I don't want another of those looks from your father."

"I think he's been pretty good considering he caught us nearly kissing last night."

Aaron looked down at her. "Is that what we were doing? Nearly kissing?"

She blushed. "You know we were."

"And what would you have done, Annie Bontrager, if I'd kissed you?"

"It's not like you haven't done it before," she told him, sounding a little cross. "Or have you forgotten?"

"I haven't forgotten," he said slowly. "I wasn't sure if you had."

"Stop looking at me like that," she hissed. "We don't know when they'll be back."

Aaron looked out at the people walking past. Running past. Bicycling past. Everyone seemed in perpetual motion here.

It was a beautiful day, even if a cool wind occasionally swept through the bare tree branches and a cloud would obscure the sun. Maybe it was because he was in such a good mood being here with her, watching her fascination with everything.

But as much as he didn't want to, he felt he had to talk to her about something he'd noticed.

"Speaking of your father."

"Were we?"

"I noticed a couple of times today he hasn't looked happy."

"Oh?"

Aaron hesitated, then plunged ahead. If they were going to have the kind of relationship he hoped for, it had to be one of complete honesty and openness.

"Sometimes when he looks at you he frowns and looks worried." He paused. "I think he's concerned you're going to like it here too much."

"Too much? How can it be a problem?"

He sighed and shook his head. "Isn't it obvious? You're already following in your mother's footsteps with the writing. Maybe he's worried you'll follow those footsteps right here to where she lived."

"Why, Aaron! I thought I was the one with the imagination."

"Just think about it for a minute."

She crossed her arms over her chest and stared off into the distance.

The longer she sat there, frowning and silent, the more he wondered if he'd been right to speak up.

"I'm not trying to make you think badly about your father."

"I know." Her words were grudging, but when she exchanged a look with him he saw she wasn't upset with him.

"We passed a cart with hot chocolate and coffee. Want some?"

"Coffee would be nice. Thank you."

"Don't go anywhere," he said as he got to his feet. "And don't talk to strangers."

She laughed. "Honestly, I'm not a child."

"You are in this place. We all are," he told her.

"Cryptic, aren't you?"

When he returned, her parents and Johnny joined him.

"We saw more statues," Johnny told her. "Guys on huge horses. And a big dog took medicine to sick people. What was his name, *Mamm*?"

"Balto."

"And Alice in Wonderland and some soldiers and oh, oh, Annie, they have a zoo here. *Mamm* says maybe we might get to come back if we have time later."

"Later in the week, not later today," she corrected. "And speaking of later, we should be getting back to the hotel."

Aaron handed Annie her coffee and she sipped it as they walked out of the park.

They heard a commotion up ahead and people were running toward it. "I wonder what's going on?" Jenny said. "Must be an accident or something."

"Somebody call 911!" a woman yelled.

Matthew grabbed Jenny's arm. "Where are you going?"

"I'm sorry, old habit," she told him and she sighed. "Reporters and photographers run toward the action, not away from it." A cloud passed over her face. "Until the last time, that is."

The crowd shifted and parted and Aaron saw one of the horses that pulled a carriage lay sprawled in the street, eyes rolling wildly, lungs heaving. Its driver and another man were arguing about how to get the horse back on its feet while bystanders were yelling about the horse being abused.

"Let's see if we can help," Matthew told Aaron. He turned to Jenny. "Promise me you'll stay right here, so I don't worry about you."

"That sounds sexist, but I'll ignore it," she told him, gathering Johnny closer to her.

Aaron and Matthew approached the horse cautiously and offered their help to the driver. The four men arranged themselves around the horse, and with some considerable exertion, they got it to its feet. Someone offered a bottle of water and Matthew poured it over the head of the horse. He spoke quietly to it and the horse calmed a little.

"Shameful, just shameful!" a woman standing nearby said. "They need to get these poor horses off city streets before more of them collapse like this."

There were some muttered comments. A police car pulled up, lights flashing, and two officers got out. They got the crowd moving and then turned their attention to getting the horse to the stables to rest.

Aaron looked at Matthew. "I think we've done everything we can do."

"Thanks, guys," the driver said.

"You're welcome." They walked back to the women.

"Good job," Annie told Aaron.

He shrugged and tried not to let on his injured hand was protesting the exertion. "Who knew there'd be a horse we could help in the middle of New York City."

"They're talking about getting them banned," a woman near them said. "It's just not a good idea with all our traffic. Replace them with electric cars." She eyed their clothes. "Amish, huh? Guess you wouldn't know about electric cars."

Aaron tried not to grin. "No, ma'am. Wouldn't know about those."

10

$\mathcal{A}$aron recognized David the minute he walked into the hotel lobby.

He hadn't met the man before, but even without Annie's powers of observation, it was easy to recognize a man who held power in the *Englisch* world. The man strode with such confidence through the people milling about through the lobby, and they seemed to part like the Red Sea, many of them staring at him as they recognized him. News was of huge importance to the *Englisch*—especially, it seemed, in this city.

He ignored the people staring at him and focused all his attention on greeting Jenny with a big hug, then welcomed Annie and Johnny. He shook Matthew's hand, then turned to Aaron.

"So glad you could come, Aaron," he said. The man didn't do manual labor like Aaron and Matthew, but his handshake was firm.

"Joy's waiting in the limo with the kids. We should go."

"Limo? I thought you didn't believe in them," Jenny said.

He shrugged. "Boss insisted on it. Said it would make it easier for all of us to get around tonight."

Joy, David's wife, jumped out of the limo when they approached and hugged Jenny. Aaron was surprised when Joy gave him a quick hug after the introductions.

"Sam!" Johnny cried and hustled to sit next to him. They'd always enjoyed visits when the family got together. Annie was delighted to see Emily Ann, the daughter David and Joy had adopted. She was a petite and pretty pre-teen with the same Eurasian delicate looks as her mother. Annie felt a little old next to her; she could remember when the family first brought her to the farm as a baby.

"Honey, we're holding up traffic," David cautioned, so they piled into the limo and it pulled away from the curb.

"Oh, I've missed you! I'm so glad you finally came to see us!" Joy exclaimed.

"Me too," Jenny said.

"I thought we'd take a drive through Times Square and then go to dinner."

"That sounds great. Matthew called me a tour guide earlier," Jenny told Joy. "I said New Yorkers love to show off their city. Even us past New Yorkers."

"Once a New Yorker, always a New Yorker," David said.

Aaron watched Annie press her nose to the limo window as the vehicle drove slowly down the street. The square exploded in a kaleidoscope of colored lights and sound. Huge screens mounted on skyscrapers advertised everything from Broadway shows to the latest technology.

And all the people. He'd never seen so many people moving about in one place in his entire life. At a time when everyone would have been settling in for the night back home, it seemed the night was just beginning here.

He glanced at Matthew and found him watching his daughter's reaction to the scene outside with a troubled frown.

"This is where the ball drops on New Year's Eve," Sam told Johnny.

"A ball?"

"A big ball made of lights falls to announce the New Year. It's cool. I guess you don't watch it on New Year's Eve since you don't have a TV."

Johnny shook his head. "We don't stay up late, either."

"I don't either, much. Except on New Year's Eve."

"Don't let him fool you," said Joy. "He fell asleep before the eleven o'clock news last year."

Sam made a face and then he laughed. "Busted."

"So, Jenny, how does it feel to be back on your old stomping grounds?"

She laughed. "Old stomping grounds?" Tilting her head, she looked out the car window, then back at him. "If you'll remember, I didn't spend much time here. I think I spent more time flying back and forth for assignments overseas than I did in my apartment."

Jenny smoothed her dress over her knees. "We're going to go by there this week. Annie's curious about where I lived."

"So, Aaron, tell us about yourself," Joy invited.

He shrugged, uncomfortable with talking about himself. "I'm a carpenter."

"Aaron makes the most beautiful furniture." Annie smiled at him.

"I thought it would be fun to eat in Chinatown," Joy told Jenny. "We used to get Chinese takeout a lot when you lived here, and I figured you probably don't get it often in Lancaster County."

Jenny laughed. "No, can't say we do." She glanced at Matthew. "What do you say? Are you ready for some adventure?"

"It's been an adventure ever since I married you," he said.

"Mostly an adventure eating my cooking."

"I didn't say that."

She patted his knee. "No, you're too smart to say it."

⎯⎯⎯

Exotic smells. Strange-looking food. A restaurant decorated with bright red walls and kimonos framed on the walls. The music had an unfamiliar, almost dissonant quality yet was oddly soothing.

People who looked so different from any ethnic group she'd ever met. Annie couldn't have been more fascinated.

Her mother, David, and Joy helped Annie, Aaron, and Matthew go over the menu, but in the end the group ordered a vast array of appetizers and entrees so there'd be a little of everything to try.

"You can use a fork if you want," Emily Ann told Annie as they waited for the food to arrive. "But try the chopsticks. They're fun!"

They talked about a little of everything. Emily Ann didn't like school much but had joined the drama club. She wanted to date, but her father had forbidden it until her grades improved. Annie watched as Emily Ann got a text from a boy and answered it without her father being aware.

Or so she thought. A few moments later, her father word-lessly caught her attention and he frowned at her. Emily Ann sighed and put the cell phone away.

When the food arrived, Emily Ann showed Annie how to work the wooden sticks to pick up a piece of sweet and sour chicken. She watched it plop back on the plate.

Aaron wasn't having much better luck with the chopsticks and something called General Tso's chicken. *Who was General*

Tso and why was this dish named after him? she wondered. Aaron looked at her as he dropped another piece of chicken on his plate, and they burst out laughing.

Johnny had better luck getting food into his mouth because he didn't worry about if he was doing it right: he used the tips of the sticks to shovel food into his mouth. Which, when she thought about it, wasn't much different from the way he ate with a fork back home. His favorite seemed to be the little steamed dumplings—maybe because they were easy to transport into his mouth.

Her father gamely tried the chopsticks but quickly picked up his fork to try some lo mein. He loved homemade noodles, and after the first bite he nodded and began eating with enthusiasm. Annie noticed David and his family used chopsticks easily and naturally. She guessed they must eat with them a lot to be so experienced.

Jenny served herself some cashew chicken and passed the dish to Annie. "Try this, it's my favorite."

She turned to David and Joy. "Tell me what you've been up to since the last time we talked."

"Everyone's looking forward to your visiting tomorrow," David told her.

"I can't wait to see where *Mamm* worked." Annie put her fork down and leaned her elbows on the table. "Where you work."

"Your mother tells me you're interested in being a writer."

She nodded. "I'm trying all sorts of things right now. Non-fiction, some things about being Amish. Even some fiction. You know, to see what my interest is. What I'm good at."

David paused, his chopsticks halfway to his mouth. He looked at Jenny. "I don't suppose she could ever do an internship."

Annie watched her mother glance at her father and her gaze followed. Her father was frowning. She felt the hair on the back of her neck stand up. Something was going on here. Aaron had told her he thought her father hadn't looked happy the past two days . . .

"It's not something we've talked about." Her mother seemed uncomfortable.

"Internship?" Annie came to attention. "Is that like an apprenticeship?"

"Yeah," David said. "Sometimes people—usually students—do one at a place they think they'd like to work. Then they get to know what the job entails. They see if it's something they really want to do."

"I hadn't thought about it," Annie said slowly.

"Matthew, what are you, Aaron, and Johnny doing tomorrow?" Joy asked.

"He said he'd take me to the Central Park Zoo," Johnny said before his father could. "Aaron's going with us. We've never been to a zoo. They've got all these animals there." He jumped up and down in his chair until he got a stern look from his father. "I want to see a zebra. I saw a picture of them in a book once."

Another round of dishes the likes of which she'd never experienced were brought by their waitress.

"No like?" the woman asked Matthew, gesturing at his nearly full plate.

"It's delicious," he said quickly, picking up his fork and eating again.

"Try something else if you don't like the lo mein," Jenny told him after the woman left. "You don't have to eat it. Johnny will finish it for you."

"It's fine," he repeated in a firmer tone.

Jenny bit her lip and stared at her plate for a moment, and then she looked up and smiled. Annie couldn't help staring. Something was going on.

"Anyway, you can get a feel for things when you visit the network tomorrow," David said. "And your mother tells me you're going to take a tour of the *New York Times* tomorrow after you visit us."

Joy murmured his name and he looked at her, raising his eyebrows in question. She shook her head—it was an action so subtle Annie might have missed it if she hadn't been trying to figure out what was going on—and after a quick glance at her he picked up a plate of egg rolls the waitress had just delivered to the table and held it out to Matthew. "You have to try these," he said. "They're one of my favorites."

"Thanks." Matthew took one and bit into it, then stared at it. "What's in it?"

"Pork or chicken, shredded cabbage, carrots, some bamboo shoots."

"Bamboo shoots?" Johnny said, looking dubiously at the egg roll in his hand. He bit into it, examined the contents that were revealed, and munched.

"We haven't found any food he doesn't like," Jenny told them. "Well, except maybe kippers."

"Johnny, did you know pandas love bamboo shoots?" Sam asked him.

"Should I save this egg roll to give it to one tomorrow?"

"No, they eat raw bamboo. The zoo has stuff you can buy to feed some of the animals."

Annie watched how excited her brother was and turned to look at Aaron. He was busy working his way through a little of each dish they'd been brought.

"Are you sure you want to go to the zoo? You can always change your mind and go with *Mamm* and me."

Aaron swallowed and took a sip of iced tea. "No, the zoo sounds more interesting to me." He stopped as if he realized what he'd just said. "I'll enjoy hearing about what you saw, but I'd like to see the zoo."

"Even if it means being with my father for the day?" she whispered, and she watched his expression.

Aaron paled a little and darted a nervous look at Matthew, but then he straightened. "I'm sure we'll have a good time. And it'll give us a chance to get to know each other better."

She decided she'd ask her brother some careful questions tomorrow evening to find out how things had gone.

The waitress brought a plate of fortune cookies to the table. Annie broke hers open and read the message inside: "You will live a long and interesting life," she read.

Well, of course it would be interesting, she thought. *God had made such an amazing world for them to live in, hadn't he?* She slipped the message into her pocket to save in her notebook as a memento of the trip.

"Well, this has been great," David said, tucking his credit card and receipt in his wallet. He'd insisted dinner was on him since they were his guests. "I'll be by at nine to pick you and Annie up," he told Jenny.

She stood and hugged him, then Joy and their kids. "I'm looking forward to it. Too bad my old boss retired. I'd love to have seen him again."

"Yes, too bad," David agreed. "I hear he's having a great time writing his memoir and fishing at the lake."

They drove back to the hotel and said goodbye. As Annie walked to her room she wondered if she was too excited about what she was going to get to do the next day to sleep. All the green tea she'd drunk at dinner wasn't helping, either.

She climbed into bed, wrote in her journal for a while, and finally felt she could sleep. An hour later, though, she lay awake, worrying about why her father wasn't happy with the way things were going on the trip.

⊷❧

Annie woke early, dressed, and was waiting in the living room of the suite the next morning.

She had the television turned on, the sound low so she wouldn't wake anyone, and was watching a morning news program when she became aware of voices. Her parents were talking about something. She couldn't tell what, but neither of them sounded happy.

For a moment, she debated returning to her room so they wouldn't walk out of theirs and think she'd been listening to them.

She didn't like the idea of them having an upsetting discussion. It had never happened before. Oh, there was a period some time back when it seemed like something was a little . . . off. *When was that?* she wondered. She thought for a moment. Just before Jenny had announced she was going to have a baby—Johnny. Annie thought maybe she imagined a little distance between her parents and decided later maybe her mother just wasn't feeling well and that was what was wrong.

Because her parents loved each other. There was no doubt.

The voices behind the door grew louder, and she heard her name. Sighing, she raised the volume on the television, figuring she needn't worry about waking anyone—they all needed to be up and starting their day if they wanted to eat together before David came.

The bedroom door opened and her mother walked out, then stopped when she saw Annie. "Oh, you're up."

Annie nodded. "Do you want me to get Johnny up?"

Her mother glanced back and then shook her head. "I will." She hurried to the bedroom he and Aaron were sharing and knocked on the door. "Johnny? Aaron? Time to get up."

Her father emerged from his room a few moments later. "Did you get any sleep at all last night?"

"I did." She took a deep breath. Best to just ask and get it over with. "*Daed*, did you change your mind about me going with *Mamm* to the network and the newspaper today?"

"Why would you think so?"

She shrugged. "I don't know. Something seems different. You seem different."

He walked over and sat on the sofa beside her. For a long moment he watched the program she had on and then he stood. "Come on, let's take a walk. Tell your mother we'll meet her at the restaurant downstairs."

Frowning, wondering what she'd done that might have displeased him, Annie went to get her jacket and purse.

Aaron walked out of his room, dressed for the day, and smiled at Jenny and Annie. "Johnny is in the bathroom brushing his teeth," he told Jenny.

"Without being nagged?"

"I think he can't wait to get to the zoo."

"*Mamm, Daed* and I are going downstairs. He says we'll wait for you there." She touched her mother's arm. "I think the two of us need to talk."

"Okay," Jenny said slowly. "We won't be long. I just need to call home. "

"I'll go watch television with Johnny," Aaron offered. He waited for her to go into the room for her call and turned to Annie. "Anything wrong?"

"I don't know. He just said he wants to talk."

"If he's upset with me in any way, I—"

"I'm sure it's not that," she told him quickly. "He'd tell you if he had a problem with you."

"But if he's got a problem with you—"

"Then it would be my problem," she said firmly. "He's my father, Aaron."

Sighing, he nodded. "See you in a few minutes."

Annie met up with her father at the elevator. The doors slid open, revealing a number of people. Annie looked away from their curiosity and stepped inside. The doors shut and the car descended. Her father didn't speak. He wouldn't, too private a man to have a personal conversation with her in public.

When the elevator doors opened, he gestured at several chairs grouped together in one side of the lobby. "Let's sit over there."

Annie loved the festive atmosphere of people coming and going, their arms full of gaily wrapped packages and shopping bags. Everyone seemed in such a happy mood.

They took their seats and he sat motionless, his hands resting on his knees for a long moment. She wanted to know what was wrong, wanted to get going with her day. But she knew not to rush him. Her father was a calm, deliberate man who always took his time thinking over what he wanted to say. She thought the world could use a few more people like him.

"So are you enjoying the trip? Has it been everything you hoped it would be?"

She nodded vigorously.

He smiled slightly. "You've been looking forward to coming here since you were a little girl, ever since your mother brought you the snow globe."

Annie smiled. "I almost brought it to compare it with the real scene, just to see if it's the same. But I figure I've looked at the globe a million times over the years."

"Your mother doesn't think I've been supportive—"

"That's not true!" she broke in. "You didn't have to agree to let us come here at all. Other fathers might not have."

He held up his hand. "Your mother is right. I said we'd come, but since we've been here I've been—" he paused, clearly searching for words, "quiet and unsupportive. I've been a wet blanket."

She'd have laughed at her father using such a term, but he looked so serious, so sorry that she just couldn't.

"Aaron noticed," Annie began slowly. "I hadn't." She tilted her head and studied him. "I'm sorry you're not having fun."

"It's more than that." He got to his feet and paced, something he'd never done except for the time in the hospital waiting room after Joshua had been hurt . . . when they were afraid they might lose him.

Her hand flew to her mouth and her eyes went wide. "Oh," she whispered. "*Daed*! Are you afraid I'll want to stay here?"

Emotions warred on his face. "*Ya*," he said quietly, so quietly she almost missed what he'd said.

"Why didn't you say something?"

He sank into his chair. "I don't want to hold you back. And it would seem like I don't trust God. Maybe this is part of His plan for you, this internship thing David spoke of."

"The one David brought up last night? It's the first I heard of it."

"But you're so interested in writing. It would be a wonderful opportunity."

Impulsively she reached for his hand. "*Daed*, I love my life, and I have no desire to leave home. Even for writing."

"You can't be sure—" he stopped. "I'm sorry. I didn't mean to say that. I have to have some trust in Him here."

Annie smiled slowly. "Yes, *Daed*. You do. About this and about Aaron." She laughed when he made a face. "You know he's a good man. I think he's the one."

When he sighed, she laughed again and patted his hand. "He'll grow on you. He did on me. Come on, everything's going to be fine. Look, there's *Mamm* getting off the elevator. Let's go have breakfast so we can get started on our adventures today."

11

It was a wonder no one could hear Annie's heart nearly beating out of her chest. She glanced down at her chest, convinced she'd see the visitor's badge bouncing up and down to the beat of her heart.

She sent up a prayer of thanks as she, her mother, and David walked into the network building. A quick ride up the elevator took them to one of the newsrooms filled with people frenetically moving around desks loaded with computers, iPads, tape recorders, and other technology. A bank of television screens filled one wall, multiple news programs on each of them.

David's face loomed large on several big screens. A couple of people were viewing his broadcast from the night before.

He turned and rolled his eyes. "Guess I'm going to hear about the pronunciation mistake I made last night when we have our meeting this afternoon."

"You didn't say 'Ourkansas,' did you?"

He laughed. "Annie, that line came from a TV comedy about a clueless television news announcer."

"Oh," she said. "Arkansas, right?"

"Bright kid," he told Jenny.

"Too bright for her own good sometimes," Jenny joked.

Annie started to ask how you could be too bright, but David was leading them down a corridor and she turned her thoughts to where they were going.

He spent the next hour showing Annie every aspect of the network, from people editing film to on-air personalities going over their notes to getting hair and makeup done. The building was full of so many people hurrying around doing their jobs—all to create news and entertainment on a screen for others to watch.

Here and there, Annie saw she and her mother were the objects of curiosity. Sometimes a man or woman would recognize her mother and smile and wave or rush over to hug her. Annie's heart warmed at how they remembered her and viewed her with such affection even though she'd been gone for a long time.

David stopped before a door with a huge sign that said taping was going on. She knew it meant they were filming a show to broadcast it later. He ushered them inside, holding a finger to his lips in a signal for Annie to be quiet, and she nodded. They watched as an attractive woman dressed in a blue suit interviewed a woman who was talking about parenting.

So many people worked on the set, moving about quietly to work the cameras, to fuss with makeup when they went to commercial breaks, to adjust lighting, and on and on. All of it to get the image of one show host and her guest into the box called television.

The taping came to a close, and the woman jumped up, took off her microphone, and ran around her desk to throw her arms around Jenny.

"I didn't believe it when David said you were coming for a visit today!" the woman exclaimed. "You know what a jokester he is!"

"I do indeed," Jenny agreed. "I remember his practical jokes all too well."

David frowned at them. "I haven't played one in years."

"Which makes us all worry you're overdue," the woman said. "So are you Annie?" When she nodded, the woman extended her hand. "I'm Marla Black. Your mother and I worked together here." She shot Jenny a look. "Don't you dare call me an old friend."

"Wouldn't dream of it," Jenny responded. "It would make me old too."

Marla turned to David. "So, ready?"

When he nodded, she slipped her arm through Jenny's and began walking with her out of the room. "So how's your handsome hubby? And the other kids?"

Annie couldn't hear her mother's response because suddenly a door was thrown open and dozens of people were calling out, "Surprise!"

A big banner stretched across the room with a "Welcome back, Jenny!" message. People milled around helping themselves to food spread out on two tables.

Marla invited Annie to get some food and then dragged Jenny off to talk to some people. She sat watching everything and felt proud her mother was receiving such a warm welcome.

She was finishing a piece of cake when a man approached her table.

"So have you been enjoying the tour?"

Annie looked up at the man and smiled politely. He was late joining the party, but everyone greeted him as if they were truly glad he'd arrived. "Very much."

"May I join you?" he asked, and when she nodded he took a seat.

He was a distinguished-looking man, dressed in what seemed to be an expensive suit, and from the way a waiter came quickly to pour him a cup of coffee and offer him food, she thought he must be an important man here as well.

"I'm Gordon Manning," he said. "And you're Annie Bontrager."

"How did you know my name?"

"I make it my business to know such things." He sipped his coffee. "What did you enjoy the most about your tour?"

"Talking to one of the writers," she said immediately. "It made it feel possible that I can do something with my own writing."

"What was the writer's name?"

"Tony."

"His last name?"

She thought about it for a moment. "I'm sorry, I don't remember."

Gordon pulled a cell phone from his jacket pocket, texted, then returned his attention to Annie. "What's next on your agenda?"

"We're going to see the *New York Times* building."

"It won't be as exciting as this place," he said with an air of utter confidence.

Annie stared at him. Had she offended? Before she could say anything, Tony appeared at their table. He was breathing hard, and perspiration dotted his upper lip.

"Tony! Annie here says she enjoyed talking to you about writing for the network."

He glanced at Annie and appeared at a loss for words for a moment. "I—uh, that's nice. Sir."

"Maybe you can talk to her more about your work while I chat with her mother." Gordon stood and gestured at his chair.

Tony nodded and bumped the table with his hip as he came around to take a seat.

"Well, uh, what else would you like to know?" Tony asked her. When a waiter brought him a cup of coffee, he nodded and took a sip.

Annie shrugged. "I don't know. I was just telling Gordon I enjoyed talking to you. Then all of a sudden you were here."

Tony coughed and sounded like he was choking. Annie reached over and thumped on his back until he recovered.

"Gordon? You're on a first name basis with him?"

"It's what he said his name is."

Tony used the back of his hand to wipe his lip. "Yes, well, I've been here five years and I've never been told to call him by his first name." He took another sip of coffee, and Annie noticed his hand wasn't quite steady. "But my supervisor was just called and told to send me up here stat to talk to you."

"Stat?"

"Fast."

"Oh." She frowned as she watched Gordon talking to her mother. "Wonder what they're talking about?"

"*Time* magazine called him the most ambitious network CEO of all time," Tony said. "People are so interested in the Amish these days. I wouldn't be surprised if he's hoping he can talk your mother into doing a special for the network—" He stopped and flushed. "Listen, forget I said anything. I shouldn't be talking about the boss.

"So," he said, giving her a charming grin, "I was told you wanted to talk more about what I do here. I'm all yours. Fire away."

"This is gonna be fun!"

Aaron looked down at Johnny, then at Matthew. "Yes, just us guys today."

They walked through Central Park to visit the zoo. Just like last time, people everywhere were enjoying running, walking, or just sitting on benches relaxing.

Johnny eyed a pedicab going past them and his eyes grew big. "Can we?"

Matthew shook his head. "We're getting there on our own two feet."

Aaron figured it hadn't been a desire to avoid walking but rather a curiosity about a man propelling a cab.

When a horse-drawn carriage passed them with passengers avidly taking photos, Aaron and Matthew exchanged glances. "Wonder how the injured horse is doing?"

A few minutes later, they came upon a carriage driver watering his horse. He nodded when he saw them approach. "You fellas visiting the big city, huh? Want a ride?"

Then, before they could answer, he narrowed his eyes. "Say, are you the two Amish dudes who helped one of the drivers with his horse when it collapsed yesterday?"

Aaron had never heard himself called an "Amish dude," but he nodded.

The man grinned and extended his hand. "Ronald was saying he was so upset about his horse he wasn't sure he thanked you enough."

"No thanks needed," Matthew said. "Is the horse going to be all right?"

"Yup. Say, we don't see many Amish in the city. Cousin says they like to go to Niagara Falls, but not so many come to the Big Apple." He shrugged. "Guess it's a little bit of culture clash, but there are some good, God-fearing people in these parts."

"I'm sure there are," Matthew said, nodding. "My wife used to live here before she moved to our community. Maybe you knew her? Back then her name was Jenny King."

The man shook his head. "Nope, it's a big city." Then he frowned and appeared to reconsider. "Wait a minute, was she the young woman who used to report on children in war zones for the TV? Got hurt in a car bombing?"

Aaron watched Matthew's face light up. "That's her."

"Well, I'll be! Small world. She doing okay?" He looked around.

"She's doing well. Over visiting the network today."

"Seems it was in the newspaper she and the network anchor guy are being honored at some big banquet this week. Guess that's why you're in town."

"And we're going to the zoo!" Johnny spoke up.

"Well, you have a wonderful time, young man!" the driver said, tipping his hat.

They walked on and Aaron couldn't help wondering, as he had several times, how Jenny had gone from being someone who was well-known in the *Englisch* world to the quieter, humbler life in their Plain community. And he wondered how her visit to the place she used to work was going.

Even more important, he wondered what Annie was doing there today. Annie, who so loved learning about writing and people and places . . . there were no coincidences. God had a plan for her just as he did all His children. He could have gone along and known for himself, but Aaron wanted her to enjoy herself, and besides, he didn't think he'd fit in there, a man like himself who worked with his hands and led a simple life.

"What animal are we going to see first?" Johnny said, interrupting Aaron's thoughts.

"I don't know," his father said. "Which one do you want to see first?"

"The penguins. I like the way they look like they're dressed up like the waiters at the hotel."

Matthew laughed. "They do look pretty fancy when they serve a meal. The waiters, not the penguins."

"And giraffes. They have such long necks." He stretched his as much as he could. "Why are they so long?"

"To reach the leaves in the trees."

Johnny looked up. "There aren't any leaves in the trees right now."

"I know. But there are most of the time."

"So what do they eat now?"

"Why don't we wait and see? I'm sure someone there will tell us."

It seemed to Aaron the zoo was in an unusual place—right in the middle of this modern glass and steel city. The colorful brochure they picked up at the entrance told the history of the zoo. Apparently, it had come about because some city residents had dropped off animals they no longer wanted.

Aaron didn't understand the reference to alligators and sewer systems and started to ask Matthew if he did, but Johnny tugged at his sleeve.

Aaron had never been to a zoo, but growing up, he'd seen photos of penguins in books. Seeing them in person awed him with their ability to dive into water and swim so quickly, jumping back up onto the snowy banks and then diving back into the water to swim around and around. They flapped their wings and chattered at each other in a language only they understood and made their crowd of onlookers laugh.

Enthralled, Johnny stood there staring, his eyes round with wonder.

"There are more animals to see," Matthew reminded him.

"In a minute. Please?"

Matthew glanced over at Aaron. "Are you wishing you'd gone with Annie and Jenny?" he asked with a grin.

Aaron shook his head. "This is fun. And we've only started." He was relieved. Whatever Annie and Matthew had talked about had changed things. Matthew looked relaxed and himself again—not distracted and worried the way he had earlier.

‎ *❧*

"I warned you it would look different."

Annie glanced at her mother as they stood on the sidewalk outside of the *New York Times.*

"I hope you won't be disappointed."

This wasn't the building forever trapped in the snow globe she'd left back home. "It's amazing," Annie breathed, overwhelmed by the glass and steel building as it loomed over them.

They walked inside where visitor badges awaited them, arranged by David, along with a special tour guide. Men like David got special privileges. The guide led them through the lobby garden that reminded Annie of how Central Park existed like a jewel in the midst of glass and steel buildings in the middle of the city.

"The building is just six years old," the guide said, as they were led through the lobby garden featuring seven tall trees with white bark giving the glass-walled garden a sort of fairy tale feel.

"The trees are paper birches," he said. They were an apt choice when you thought about it, Annie mused.

"We had some of those near my house when I was growing up," Jenny said softly. "I used to love to pull a piece off and write on it."

A modern art exhibit called Moveable Type gave visitors a visual of constantly changing images of the paper and the news of today and the past. The small digital screens fascinated

Annie, who wanted to examine all of them before her mother gently urged her along.

An open area filled with reporters manning desks and working at computers on the news of the day was a kaleidoscope of color and movement.

Both the network and the newspaper had a compelling intensity about them. They moved up one floor, then another, through the huge, open structure, and as they did, the windows seemed to get bigger and bigger until it seemed the city was a part of the building as much as the building was a part of the city. Annie even saw the big electric signs of Times Square flashing at one level.

They ended up in the cafeteria at big, round tables with a view of the city. The guide left them to eat a light lunch and promised to be back in half an hour.

"I hope your father and Aaron aren't letting Johnny eat a bunch of junk while they're at the zoo," Jenny said. "But I sure wouldn't mind having a hot dog right about now. Nothing better than a hot dog from a New York City street vendor. We'll get one before we leave and you'll see what I mean."

Annie loved food as much as anyone, but she was enjoying watching a table full of men and women her age engage in a vigorous discussion. It was rude to eavesdrop, but she wished she could hear what they were talking about.

She looked around. "Well, the network was a little more interesting when they were taping a show and things like that, but Gordon wouldn't like to hear I think this building is more amazing than the network one."

"Well, the paper has been around for a long time." Jenny finished her sandwich and sipped at her tea.

"What was he talking to you about before we left?"

Her mother shrugged. "Nothing much. He wanted to know what we were doing before the big dinner. Speaking of dinner,

I thought it might be nice to go to this little Italian place in my old neighborhood."

Annie blinked at the sudden change of topic and wondered if Tony was right—if Gordon had been talking with her mother about her working for the network on a project again.

Before she could ask, the guide showed up again, bringing the managing editor, who said he wanted to meet Jenny. Although he and David were friends, he and Jenny had never met, and they talked about her impression of the city after years away.

He tried to persuade Jenny to be interviewed right then, but there wasn't time before she and Annie were expected back at the hotel to meet the rest of the family. They left him with the promise that a reporter could do an interview after the big dinner later in the week.

Their driver smiled at them and opened the door to the limo when they walked out of the building. "Did you have a nice time, ma'am?"

"It was wonderful. But it's been a long day."

She climbed inside the limo with Annie and sank back against the seat. "You know what I'd like to do?" she said to the driver. "I'd like to find a video of *The Miracle on 34th Street* and share it with my family, maybe eat some popcorn tonight."

"There's a store on our way where you can find it," the driver told them as he pulled out into traffic. "Shall I stop there before I pick up the rest of your family?"

"Yes, thank you."

Annie had gone to some movies with her friends but hadn't seen the one her mother mentioned. Her mother told her the setting for the movie was the Macy's store they'd visited the first day and Santa, such an important figure in the Christmas holiday for *Englischers*, played a big part. Annie was intrigued, but her mother said she had to wait to see the movie and wouldn't tell her more.

Sure enough, the store the driver took them to had the movie and bags of popcorn and boxes of candy like those sold in movie theaters. They loaded up on goodies and walked outside to find the limo wasn't by the sidewalk.

"He probably had to move," Jenny said. "He'll be back for us." She stood there, tapping her foot, then suddenly she straightened. "Oh, why didn't I get *A Christmas Carol?* Your father loves that book and he's never seen the movie! Here, can you hold these?" she asked, pushing the bags she carried into Annie's arms. "I'll be right back."

She started into the store, then turned back. "And don't move!"

Snowflakes began falling—when Annie looked up they drifted down between the steel spears of skyscrapers, reminding her of the swirl of flakes inside her snow globe. She'd hoped it would snow while they were here.

She felt more than saw something move out of the corner of her eye and glanced over. A teenager stood in the doorway of the next store. She looked thin—except for the rounded tummy that told Annie she was pregnant. When she saw Annie staring in her direction, she drew her thin jacket closer and shrugged.

A clerk came out of the store and approached the pregnant teen. "Uh, lady? My boss says you can't stand here anymore. You gotta move on."

"Tell him I just need a few more minutes. Someone's coming to meet me."

The clerk went back inside.

"That wasn't very nice," Annie said. "They don't like people standing in doorways here?"

The woman bent her head, and when she looked up Annie thought she saw a tear running down her cheek. "Not if you do it for a long time." She shivered and tried to button her jacket but couldn't. "Oh great, now it's snowing."

"Are you okay?"

"Me? Oh, I'm great, just great." As if to challenge what she said, more tears slipped down her cheeks.

"Look, there's a coffee shop right there, just a little ways from here," Annie pointed out. "You can get inside and stay warm while you wait."

"They won't let me. I don't have—" she stopped and reddened.

Annie reached into her jacket pocket and pressed the two twenties she'd pulled out to pay for the movie into the girl's hand. She was glad now her mother hadn't let her pay, so that she had it for this. "Have some hot chocolate and get warm. My name's Annie. What's yours?"

"Melissa. Look, I'll get this back to you," the girl promised, wiping away her tears with the heels of her hands. "As soon as Jason gets here, we'll bring it to you. Where are you staying?"

"You don't have to—" Annie began.

"I won't take it, if you won't let us return it."

Annie told her the name of the hotel and turned as noise spilled out of the store behind her when the door opened. Her mother emerged, a bag in hand.

When Annie turned back, the girl had slipped away.

"Who was that?"

"Just a girl I was talking to. *Mamm*, I think she needs help. I think she's homeless."

Jenny looked around. "I don't see her."

"I told her to go get warm in the coffee shop."

"Then we'll look there."

But the girl was nowhere to be seen. Disappointed, Annie walked with her mother to the curb where they waited for the limo to return.

12

"They say you can't go home again."

Annie glanced at her mother as the family stood before the brownstone building. "'They'?"

"Well, it's a quote from Thomas Wolfe, a famous writer, but a lot of people have said something similar. Things just aren't the same."

"But the building hasn't changed, has it?"

"You mean it's not a new building like the *New York Times* today? No, it's the same building. The neighborhood is even still pretty good. It hasn't run down. But honey, it doesn't feel like home here to me. It didn't ever feel that way when I lived in an apartment upstairs. I wasn't here very much since I worked overseas."

She turned to Matthew. "Remember how little I brought to my grandmother's?"

"Six boxes. I counted them."

Jenny shrugged. "I never much cared for things."

"Except for books. Four of those boxes were filled with books."

"The essentials." She turned to Annie. "So I said I'd take you to where I used to live."

"We can't go inside?"

"The apartment belongs to someone else."

"We could at least walk inside the building, couldn't we?"

"I suppose." She turned to Matthew. "She is the most curious child."

"Got it from you. Didn't you say once environment is more important than genes?"

She stared at him. "I didn't think you were listening when I talked about that."

"I always listen to you. You're the smartest woman I know."

"I don't know what to say. I'm speechless."

Matthew turned to Annie. "An historic occasion. Record the time and date."

Laughing, Jenny opened the front door and they filed inside.

"It's smaller than I thought it would be," Annie told Aaron as they walked down the hallway. "I figured *Mamm* would live in a bigger place like David."

"He always made a lot more money as the network anchor than I did," Jenny said, startling Annie. She had thought her mother was way behind her and couldn't hear her. "I was just a lowly overseas correspondent."

She stopped in front of an apartment and sniffed. "Mrs. Pulaski was always making potato or cabbage soup. When she saw me she'd invite me in and give me some. Said I needed to eat more."

"Are you going to say hello?"

Jenny gazed at the door and shook her head. "She was old then. I doubt she's still alive." Taking a deep breath, she knocked.

A man opened the door and frowned at them. "Yeah?"

"I'm sorry, I was looking for Mrs. Pulaski?"

"Oh, she moved down the hall to a smaller place last year," the man said. He shut the door.

They walked in the direction he'd indicated and this time, when Jenny knocked on the door an elderly woman opened it and her face lit up. "Jenny King! I always hoped you'd come by your old place!"

Annie watched her mother get enfolded in a hug.

"It's Jenny Bontrager now," she told the woman. She introduced them and the woman stared up at Matthew.

"Well, aren't you a tall, handsome one," Mrs. Pulaski said with a twinkle in her eye. "Always hoped she'd find a nice young man and have a family. She didn't need to be traipsing all over putting herself in harm's way."

"No, ma'am," Matthew said, reddening under her scrutiny.

"I'd invite you in, but I've gotten a few more cats since you lived here." She held the door open so they could see a half-dozen sprawled on the sofa. "They're watching Animal Planet with me."

"We need to be getting some supper anyway," Jenny said. "I just wanted to stop and say hi."

"Let me know ahead of time next time you're in town and I'll make you some soup."

"I sure will." Jenny stepped forward, hugged her again, and turned to leave.

Aaron bent and snatched up a cat that tried an escape and handed it, hissing, back to its owner.

Then they walked to a restaurant Jenny said had been a favorite. "I hope it's still here."

She fell silent and after watching her for a few moments, Annie reached for her hand. Her mother looked over at her, her eyebrows raised in question.

"You look sad."

Jenny shrugged. "A little. Mrs. Pulaski was a good friend. I should have done more than send her some Christmas cards over the years."

"I saw those cards sitting on her mantel while you talked to her," Annie told her. "I think they meant a lot to her."

Jenny squeezed her hand. "You really notice things, don't you?"

"I guess." But she knew she did.

"Here we are," Jenny announced as they approached a little Italian restaurant tucked in between two shops.

"Something smells good," Matthew said.

"The owner used to make the most amazing chicken piccata." Jenny paused with her hand on the door. She opened it and Annie was reminded of a little Italian place back in Lancaster County.

They sat at a table with a checkered cloth and a straw-wrapped bottle of Chianti. The family was much more familiar with Italian food than with the Chinese dishes they'd eaten earlier in the week, so they ordered quickly.

A man began singing in the kitchen, his voice a rich baritone. Annie didn't understand the Italian aria, but it seemed to her it had something to do with love lost.

She jumped a little when she felt a hand touch hers and then realized Aaron had reached under the table to hold hands with her. They exchanged a glance and she smiled at him, then sneaked a look at her father. Fortunately, he was giving his order to their server.

Johnny noticed and, with a gleam in his eye, opened his mouth. With a speed born of practice with similar incidents, she grabbed a breadstick with her free hand and shoved it into his mouth. He made a face at her but crunched on the breadstick anyway.

Annie glanced up, wondering if either of her parents had noticed her evasive action and saw tears were running down her mother's cheeks. "*Mamm?*"

Jenny glanced over. "It's okay. I'm just remembering. Sal, the owner, used to sing sometimes when I was here eating dinner."

"Sal? You know Sal?" the server asked as she set a plate of antipasto on the table. "He's my father-in-law. That's his son singing."

"Oh. I guess that means . . ." Jenny trailed off.

The server stared at her for a long moment and then she realized what Jenny meant. "Oh, Sal and Marie are retired and enjoying living in Boca Raton."

Looking relieved, Jenny smiled. "Good. They used to work so hard."

"Tell me about it," the woman said, nodding as a customer signaled for attention. "I'm already looking forward to retirement, and I've only been doing this for five years."

"You sure things haven't been too much?" Matthew asked her.

"I'm sure." Jenny traced a finger in the condensation on the side of her glass of water. "I have to admit I was wishing my old boss was at the network today."

"Didn't David say he's fishing at some lake and writing his memoir?"

"Yes." She sighed. "I didn't expect things to be the same. Things change more in my old world than they do in Paradise."

A big, burly man appeared at their table. He wore an apron with tomato stains and rested his hands on his hips as he regarded Jenny. "Tiffany says you knew my pop." He peered closer at her. "We got a picture of you in the back with Mom and Pop. You worked at the network. I remember you."

"And I remember you."

"Chicken piccata, right?"

Jenny's eyes widened. "You remembered."

"You ate in here a lot. Made Pop proud some bigwig liked his food."

"I wasn't a bigwig," she said modestly.

"You were on the television, you were a bigwig to me and the parents." He straightened. "You up for some chicken piccata? Bet mine's better than Pop's." He looked around. "Not that you should say so to his face, you understand."

"I understand," she said, laughing. "And yes, I'm up for some chicken piccata."

Nodding, he strolled off toward the kitchen, singing an aria from *La Traviata* at the top of his lungs.

Annie's heart warmed as her mother smiled.

❧

The desk clerk looked up as the family returned to the hotel. "Miss Bontrager, someone just dropped something off for you. She waited here for a while and then left." He reached under the counter and handed an envelope to Annie.

"You just missed her."

Annie glanced back, then started for the front door.

"Where are you going?" her father called after her.

"I just want to make sure Melissa's okay."

"I'm going with you," Aaron said, already at her side because of his long strides. "Who's Melissa?"

"A girl I met. I think she's homeless."

The doorman swept open the front door with a big smile and a tip of his hat.

Annie looked in one direction, then the other. She turned to the doorman. "A girl just left. Did you see which way she went?"

"That way," he pointed.

"Melissa!"

The girl stopped and turned.

Annie rushed to her. "I'm sorry I missed you!"

"It's okay. Did you get the money?"

She held up the envelope. "The desk clerk just gave it to me. You didn't have to return it. Did your boyfriend show up?"

The girl bit her lip and shook her head. "I shouldn't have believed he'd come. He's just like my parents—" she stopped. "Anyway, thanks. I only spent five dollars on some hot chocolate and a doughnut. If you give me your address I'll send it to you as soon as I can."

"Where are you going now?"

The girl shrugged.

Annie gave Aaron a desperate look. Do something! she seemed to say.

"Can I call you a taxi?" he asked her. "It's cold and getting late."

She shook her head. "I don't have any place to go."

"Let us help you," Annie said. "There must be something we can do. My *mamm* used to live in this city. She'll know what to do."

The girl looked startled and her hand flew to her stomach. Aaron knew he should look away, but the look of wonder on her face mesmerized him. He remembered seeing the same look on the faces of his older sisters when they were expecting a child. The baby must have moved at that moment.

It was then he knew how he could persuade her to let them help. "You need to keep safe for the baby's sake," he said. "I've heard about crime in the city."

"I can take care of myself," Melissa insisted, lifting her chin. "I lived in the Bronx."

"What if you catch cold?" he asked quietly. "It won't be good for the baby."

Melissa closed her eyes, then opened them. Aaron saw the tears she was fighting to hold back.

"Why do you guys care? You don't even know me."

"We're supposed to help each other," Annie said quietly. "If I were in the same situation you'd help me, wouldn't you?"

After a long moment, the girl nodded.

So the three of them walked back into the hotel, Annie telling Melissa again her mother would know what to do—how to find a place for Melissa to sleep tonight and find her more help the next day when social services or something was open.

"How's your family going to feel with me barging in on your vacation with my problems?" Melissa asked, looking nervous.

Aaron thought about how generous Annie's family had been inviting him along on the trip, refusing to let him pay for things. He'd worked so hard the past couple of months . . .

"They'll want to help," he assured her. "Let me go see if they have a room for you for tonight," he said. "Then Jenny can figure out what to do tomorrow."

Annie gave him a grateful look.

"You sure you can afford it?" the girl asked nervously. "Hotel rooms are expensive."

"I'm sure I can manage," he said with more confidence than he felt. He had no idea how much hotel rooms were. But if he didn't have enough cash he had his debit card with him.

"I have to go to the ladies room," she said when they walked into the hotel. "I'll be back in a minute."

Aaron felt himself pale when he heard how much the hotel room was, but he didn't let Annie know. He paid the money, signed a form, and turned to Annie. "You want to make sure she's okay?"

"I guess I should." She looked at the room number on the key card. "Why don't you go to the hotel gift shop and get her a toothbrush? When we get to the room we can order room service for her before we go back to the suite."

He nodded and took off to do what she said. Annie and Melissa had just joined him in the room when a knock sounded on the door.

When Aaron opened it, Jenny and Matthew stood there.

"Where's my daughter?" Matthew demanded, stepping forward with an angry scowl on his face.

❧

"*Daed?*" Annie pushed past Aaron. "I'm right here."

"Matthew!" Jenny grabbed at his arm, but she was no match for his strength.

"This is how you betray our trust?" her father shouted in Aaron's face. "You get a room right under our noses?"

Annie slipped between the two men and hoped her father wouldn't throw a punch. "*Daed!* We didn't get the room for us! We got it for Melissa!"

"Who's Melissa?" Matthew demanded.

"I am."

She stepped forward, her bottom lip quivering. "I didn't mean to cause a problem. It's all I seem to be doing, causing problems."

Annie saw her look toward the door. "No more running away. It won't help anything."

"What's going on here, Annie?" her mother asked, moving quietly in front of the door.

"Melissa, if you haven't guessed, these are my parents, Jenny and Matthew. *Mamm,* Melissa's parents threw her out when they found out she's pregnant. We got her a room for tonight and we were going to ask you to help us find out what we can do for her tomorrow."

Jenny held out her hand. "Nice to meet you, Melissa. I'm sorry to hear that about your parents."

She looked pointedly in Matthew's direction, and he nodded and extended his hand. "You have to excuse Matthew's excitement," Jenny told Melissa. "We didn't know what had happened to Annie and Aaron."

"How did you find out we were here?" Annie asked her.

"Front desk called us," Matthew said bluntly. "Thought we'd want to know the two of you got a room."

"What?" Annie spluttered. "We're adults!"

Her father shot her a look and she subsided.

"It's my fault," Aaron said. "We should have talked to you first."

"We were going to ask you to help Melissa in the morning," Annie told her mother.

"Well, let's see what we can do," Jenny said briskly. "Matthew, would you go back to our room and make sure Johnny's okay?"

She looked at Aaron, then Matthew. "Do you think the two of you will be all right up there together?"

Matthew slapped Aaron's shoulder. "Sorry I overreacted."

"Don't blame you," Aaron mumbled as the two men left the room.

"First things first," Jenny said. "You're sure you shouldn't call your parents and let them know where you are?"

Melissa shook her head. "They want nothing to do with me. Boyfriend said he'd help me, but he didn't show up."

"It's got to be hard," Jenny said softly. "But you've got a warm place to sleep tonight and—oh, when's the last time you ate?"

Annie watched the war of emotions on the girl's face. "You need to think about your baby. If you haven't eaten, he hasn't."

"I had a breakfast biscuit this morning," she said. "And hot chocolate and a doughnut with the money Annie gave me."

Jenny crossed the room, picked up a room service menu, and handed it to her. "Let's get you something to eat. Pick out a sandwich and maybe some hot soup? With a glass of milk?"

Melissa nodded. "It would be nice if it's not too much trouble. Maybe the tuna melt and chicken noodle soup? If it's not too much trouble."

"It's not too much trouble." Jenny picked up the phone and gave the order to room service.

"Why don't you take off your shoes and climb into bed while we wait?" Annie suggested. "You still look cold to me."

The girl kicked off her shoes and Annie couldn't help noticing how white and pinched her feet looked. "While we're waiting, I'm going to go get a pair of socks and one of my nightgowns for you."

"I don't want you to go to any more trouble."

"It's no trouble at all." She pulled some money from her pocket and handed it to her mother. "Is it enough?"

Jenny glanced at it. "Should be. If not, we'll charge it to the room. Oh, and get the cell from your father, would you?"

Annie gave Melissa a reassuring glance and slipped out of the room. She knew her mother wouldn't lecture her or make her feel uncomfortable, but Melissa didn't know that. She'd just met her.

So she practically ran upstairs, grabbed the socks, nightgown, and cell phone, and raced back downstairs.

The food had already arrived by the time she returned. Melissa had a tray balanced on her knees and was devouring the soup, which made Annie glad they'd made her stay. She didn't like that Melissa was so thin and had only had a breakfast biscuit and doughnut.

After she put the socks and nightgown at the end of the bed, Annie took a seat at the little table with her mother.

"Would either of you like some of this?" Melissa asked, pointing to her sandwich.

"I couldn't eat another bite," Annie told her. "We had a big dinner at an Italian place near where my mother used to live."

"We don't see many Amish in the city." Melissa picked up her sandwich and bit into it.

"We're from Lancaster County," Annie told her. "A little town called Paradise."

Melissa stopped eating. "You're kidding? The town's name is Paradise?"

Jenny nodded. "It's a pretty special place. I went to stay with my grandmother after I was hurt in an accident and the community welcomed me."

"Melissa, do you have any other family? An older brother or sister? Grandparents? Anyone who could help you?"

She shook her head. "My brother's in the service in Afghanistan. And Nana died last year."

Annie and her mother exchanged a glance as Melissa's lips began trembling. She put the sandwich down on the plate. Then her eyes went wide and she looked at Jenny. "Why didn't I think of Aunt Lou?" she breathed.

"Aunt Lou?" Jenny prompted carefully.

"She and my mother don't get along. She said once she didn't want to talk bad about my mom because, well, you know, she's my mom. But she said Mom needed to take better care of us, that she neglected us and only thought of herself." Melissa gave a short laugh. "She's right. Anyway, I didn't even think about calling her. What time is it?"

"Nine-fifteen."

"D'you suppose I can use the phone to call her? She lives upstate."

Jenny walked over and handed her the cell phone. "Here, why don't you use this? Annie and I will step outside to give you some privacy."

Melissa waved her hand. "Privacy? You guys already know all my business. You stay here."

Then she just sat there and stared at the phone, not dialing it.

"If she doesn't want to help, you don't have to worry," Jenny told her quietly. "We'll all get a good night's sleep, and then in the morning I'll make some calls."

"My mom knows how to find help," Annie told her. "She knows people here. She used to be a reporter."

"I didn't think the Amish did stuff like that."

"She was a reporter before she was Amish."

Melissa picked up the phone and began punching in a number. Annie looked at her mother while they were waiting for the aunt to pick up and saw her looking down, her hands clasped in her lap. Her lips moved, and Annie realized she was praying. So she did the same, praying God would help this young, lost child.

"Aunt Lou?" Melissa said, her words halting and hopeful. "It's me, Melissa. I need your help."

13

The minute she walked into their suite, Annie went straight to her father. He sat on the sofa in the living room area, the newspaper lying unread on his lap.

He looked up with a little wariness when she walked toward him, and when she swooped down and hugged him she could feel him stiffen at first, then he relaxed and hugged her back. She straightened and enjoyed his look of surprise.

"What was that about?"

"For caring. I know I said I was an adult when you barged into Melissa's room, but you care. It doesn't sound like her parents do—maybe they never did."

Jenny slipped her arm around Annie's waist and squeezed. "It's not our place to judge."

"I know. I just feel sad about it all. This is when she needs her parents."

"God's plan isn't always clear to us."

"Can we watch the movie now?" Johnny asked.

Jenny looked at the clock on the wall. "It's too late to start it now. We'll watch it tomorrow. Finish your game with Aaron and then it's time for bed."

"So how is the girl doing?" Matthew asked her.

"She called an aunt and the woman is coming to pick her up in the morning."

"That's good news."

The game finished, Johnny went to bed.

Matthew folded the paper. "It's been a long day. I'm ready for bed. You?" he asked Jenny.

She nodded. "I'll be there in a few minutes."

Aaron put the game back in the box and set it on a shelf near the television. "You wanted to talk to us?"

"How did you know?" Jenny asked with a smile.

"I know that look," he said, looking sheepish.

"I feel like I should have warned the two of you more about what you might encounter in the city," Jenny began. "It's a big city with the kind of problems that exist in many places. It's never wrong to help someone. But please, come to me if you feel you must help someone here again, okay? It might not turn out as well next time."

Annie looked at Aaron and then at her mother. She nodded. "We will," Annie told her.

"Agreed," Aaron said.

Everyone went to bed, but Annie couldn't sleep, too wired at what had happened. She pulled out her journal and wrote about the visit to the network and the newspaper and, finally, about Melissa. What must it be like, she wrote, to be so young and so alone in a big city. And to be pregnant and be a teenager.

She couldn't imagine how she would feel, what she would do if her parents had judged her and told her she had to fend for herself. Would other people in her family come to her aid like Melissa's aunt was willing to do? The Amish weren't perfect. Sometimes a couple married outside the usual time after the harvest and the baby came before nine months after the wedding.

The phone rang. Annie looked at the time. Two a.m. Calls at that hour couldn't be good news . . . Who could be calling and not be using her father or mother's cell phone?

She pulled on her robe and went out to answer it, but her mother had already come out of her room and picked it up. After listening for a few moments, she told the caller she'd be right down.

"Who was that?" Annie asked when her mother set the phone down on its cradle.

"The front desk. There seems to be some problem in Melissa's room."

"Oh, no, is she okay?"

"Yes, but I need to go down there. I have to get dressed."

"I'm coming with you." Annie turned to go to her room.

"No—"

"I'm coming."

Matthew came out of his room, rubbing his eyes. "Is there a problem?"

"I have to go downstairs to Melissa's room."

He came alert. "Something wrong with her?"

"I'll know more after I go down there."

Aaron was sitting in the living room talking with Matthew when Annie emerged, dressed. She caught her mother at the door and they rode downstairs in the elevator.

A hotel staff member was waiting at the door of Melissa's room. "We got a call from a guest about a loud argument in the room. When we came to see what the problem was we found a very inebriated young man in the room. A young man who isn't registered as a guest in the room. We've sent him home in a taxi."

Jenny knocked at the door and Melissa let them in. Her eyes were reddened as if she'd been crying, and she was dressed in the clothes she'd worn earlier, not her nightgown.

"I'm sorry, I just keep causing problems," she said and she sat down on the bed and began crying. "I called my boyfriend. I just wanted to tell him where I was going, and I was leaving to stay with my aunt. When he showed up, I thought he'd come to say goodbye. But he just wanted to—to party—" she broke off, sobbing.

Annie sat down on the bed and patted her back. "I'm sorry."

"My life just sucks right now," Melissa said. She reached for a tissue from the box beside the bed and wiped her cheeks and nose. "Does the hotel want me to leave the room?"

"No," said Jenny. "They sent your boyfriend home in a taxi, just in case he'd come in a car. They didn't want him to drive."

"He doesn't own a car. He doesn't even have a job. I don't know how either of us is going to take care of a baby."

Then she started crying again, and suddenly, she stopped and her hand flew to her mouth. "Oh, I feel sick!"

She jumped up and ran to the bathroom, slamming the door behind her. Then they heard gagging noises.

Jenny knocked on the door and Melissa came out, looking pale and sick.

"I didn't throw up." She pressed a damp washcloth to her face and sat down again.

"Did you drink any alcohol?" Jenny asked.

Melissa shook her head violently. "I wouldn't do that to the baby. It's got enough against it with the parents it has, don't you think?" Her tone was bitter.

"I'm not here to judge you." Jenny's tone was brisk. "Let's get your things together and go upstairs to our suite. There are two beds in Annie's room."

"I don't want to bother your family any more than I have."

"You're not bothering us," Jenny said quietly. "But I don't want that young man to come back and bother you again."

"I don't think we need to worry about him," Melissa said. "I refuse to have anything to do with him anymore. He doesn't care about me or the baby. It's his loss."

❧

Annie woke and blinked at the weak sunlight coming in the window.

She heard faint snoring and turned her head to look over at the occupant of the next bed. Melissa had collapsed into bed and slept through the night.

Seeing her made Annie miss Mary. She wished her sister had been able to come on the trip.

The trip had been amazing and it wasn't over yet . . . but she'd never been away from her brother and sister for this length of time—ever, actually. And Phoebe. She missed the woman who'd been like a grandmother to her.

Annie thought it was so sad that Melissa was so alone, with her brother far away. And her grandmother was dead. Maybe she would have helped her now if she were alive. Annie hoped the aunt Melissa had called would show up.

The bedroom door opened quietly, and her mother stuck her head in. She put her finger to her lips, then tiptoed in to kneel on the bed beside Annie and gesture out the window.

Snow fell in great white drifts and spread a sparkling white blanket over the streets and cars parked on the street below. Few people ventured out.

"Snow day!" Jenny whispered. "I thought after Melissa's aunt comes for her we'd snuggle in and watch the Christmas movies. Take a break from sightseeing for a day."

Annie nodded. "Sounds like fun." She glanced behind her and saw that Melissa's eyes were open and she was watching them. "Hi. Did you sleep well?"

Melissa sat up and yawned. "Like a rock. I've been so tired since I got pregnant. People say get as much sleep as I can now because I won't sleep when the baby comes." She wrapped her arms around her knees. "I hope it'll be a good baby. I'll need to find some way to finish school so I can get a job to support us."

"Having a baby's never easy. But they're so precious." Jenny glanced at Annie and smiled. "Annie was a little girl when I married her father. I had Johnny years later."

"Wish you could have met my older brother and sister," Annie told Melissa. "Joshua got hurt by a horse and Mary's a teacher so she was still in school. Maybe if we ever come back here we can all get together."

"I think I hear people stirring," Jenny said. She got up. "Get dressed and we'll go to breakfast."

"It's okay, I don't have to eat again," Melissa began.

"Don't be silly. They have the most fabulous breakfast bar here. And you have to see how polite the waiters are even though the Bontrager men have these enormous appetites."

Annie held up her hand. "And one of the Bontrager women. Melissa, the waffles here are amazing."

"You sold me," Melissa said, smiling shyly. She gathered up her clothes and went into the bathroom.

"She still looks so tired."

Her mother hugged her. "Stop worrying. I imagine even though she slept, it wasn't a restful sleep with all that happened yesterday. But she's young. She'll be okay."

They all went downstairs and ate breakfast. Annie knew she worried, but she was relieved when she saw Melissa did justice to her breakfast. She even laughed—something Annie hadn't seen her do—when she saw the little strawberries topping a dollop of cream cheese on top of the waffle.

"Imagine making a snowman out of a strawberry," she said, shaking her head.

Annie just wished the poor girl didn't keep looking toward the door, an expression of concern on her face.

Annie glanced at her mother and Jenny nodded. She asked Melissa how far away her aunt lived and she looked thoughtful for a moment. "I figure she'll be here by lunchtime. I saw it was snowing, though. What if the roads are bad?"

"She'll be here."

Melissa sighed. "I hope you're right."

Jenny patted her hand. "I know it feels like everyone's let you down," she said quietly. "But everything's going to work out."

"Are all Amish this calm and this friendly?"

Annie pulled at the back of her brother's shirt to get him to sit still. "*Mamm?*"

"I'd like to think so," Jenny said. "But we're human, not perfect." She looked around the table, then up at the waiter as he appeared. "Have the Bontragers cleaned out the breakfast buffet?"

"We like to see our guests enjoy our food," the man said, his expression bland. But Annie saw his lips twitch and there was a twinkle in his eyes.

"I thought since it's a bad day to be outside we'd watch *Miracle on 34th Street*," Jenny told Melissa. "We visited the Macy's window display."

After they returned to their suite, Aaron and Matthew settled on the sofa. Annie and Melissa took seats in the comfortable armchairs while Jenny put the movie in. Johnny sprawled on the carpet in front of the television.

"Can we have popcorn?" Johnny asked, looking up at her.

"You just ate breakfast!" Jenny exclaimed. She turned to put her hands on hips and give him an exasperated look.

"But you said we'd have popcorn with the movie." He gave her a winsome smile.

"You can have some with the second movie if you're hungry then."

"Melissa, what's your favorite Christmas movie?" Annie asked as she sat in the armchair next to her.

"*Elf.* Or maybe *Home Alone 2.*"

"I haven't seen either of them."

"I thought the Amish didn't watch movies or television. I mean, you don't use electricity, right?"

"We don't. This is a special treat," Jenny told her as she sat down and used the remote control to start the movie.

"Why don't the Amish use electricity?" Melissa asked Annie as the movie began.

"It's something that brings in television and computer games and can keep a family from talking and doing things together. If everyone did something like this—watched a good family movie together—I don't think there'd be so many problems. But it's not what the church leaders have seen happen to *Englisch* families."

"Is this what they call a 'chick flick'?" Aaron asked.

Jenny laughed and shook her head. "No. I think you'll like it."

On the screen, a fashionable older man with a neatly trimmed beard was seen rapping his cane on the door of a shop. When the clerk inside opened it, he was told the display of the reindeer pulling Santa's sleigh was wrong. The deer weren't in the right order, he said. The clerk just stared at him, shook his head, and then locked the door again.

The dapper-looking man then walked down a line of parade floats, found a Santa drinking from a flask, and raised a fuss.

"Is he the same Santa we saw with an Army bucket?"

Jenny shook her head. "No, this movie was made a long time ago. And it's a Salvation Army bucket. They collect money to help people."

The movie played on. When the little girl said she didn't believe in Santa Claus, Johnny turned to look at Melissa. "We don't believe in Santa."

"Me neither," Melissa said, her face expressionless.

Annie cast a glance at the hotel window. Snow was coming down hard. "*Mamm*, do you think we should let Melissa call her aunt?"

"That's a good idea. Come, Melissa, we'll go into the other room and call her."

Melissa sprang up so quickly Annie was glad she'd asked. It was obvious the girl was worried her aunt might not be coming for her.

Annie hoped it was just the weather that had made the drive take longer. She closed her eyes and prayed.

When the two women emerged from the bedroom a few minutes later, Melissa had tears on her cheeks, but she was smiling. "She'll be here soon."

"I knew it," Annie told her.

"We should celebrate with some popcorn," Johnny said.

"What do you think, Melissa?" Jenny asked her. "Want to celebrate with some popcorn?"

She glanced around the room at the others, took a shaky breath, and let it out. "I think popcorn would be a great way to celebrate."

Jenny drew the box of microwave popcorn from the plastic shopping bag and handed it to her. "Maybe you can show Annie how to work the microwave. It's been years since I used one, and the one in the hotel kitchen looks like something from a rocket ship."

Melissa took the box. "I'd love to. I use the microwave to cook almost everything."

Annie followed her into the kitchen. This she had to see. She'd seen a microwave—she was Amish, but it didn't mean they didn't know what one was. It would be interesting seeing popcorn cooked in one.

❧

Aaron watched the tearful reunion of Melissa and her aunt, a woman who clutched her niece to her chest and hugged her tightly the minute she got into the room.

He was glad things had worked out so well. It didn't appear Melissa's aunt was going to lecture her about getting pregnant. Instead, she fussed over how thin the girl was, thanked the family for helping her, and pulled out her wallet to press money on Aaron when Melissa told her he'd paid for the hotel room.

When Annie smiled at him and nodded approvingly when he refused the money and told her to save it for Melissa's baby, he felt good that he'd spoken up last night and suggested he would pay for the room. Hadn't one of the ministers talked about how Jesus said to help others?

Melissa's jacket and purse were gathered up, Annie and Jenny hugged her and her aunt, and then with a flurry of goodbyes and promises to stay in touch, Melissa and her aunt were gone.

Some silent signal passed between Jenny and Matthew because it only took a look and he was following her into the kitchen. When they returned, Matthew was unwrapping the other movie Jenny had bought.

"Annie, let's go take a walk," Jenny said. "I want to show you something."

Aaron watched her get up and put on her jacket. Intrigued, he walked over to them where they were standing by the door. "Mind if I go with you? I'd like to stretch my legs."

When Jenny turned to look at him, not saying anything for a long moment, it occurred to him this could be some woman thing. Maybe they had some need to buy something personal. He could feel his ears growing red.

"Maybe the two of you want to talk."

"No," Jenny said after a moment. "You're welcome to come."

He slipped on his jacket, and they left the suite. Outside, he saw the snow had stopped. Snowplows had cleared the streets, but there were few cars on them and even fewer people.

"Where are we going?" Annie asked as the doorman hailed at taxi at Jenny's request.

"Annie's always wanted to see New York City as you know," Jenny told Aaron. "But after the situation with Melissa, I got to thinking maybe she was just getting a cleaned-up tourist view of it."

They climbed into the taxi and Jenny gave the driver the address. He raised his eyebrows. "You sure that's where you want to go?"

She nodded. "Don't worry. I have a friend who runs the place. He'll look out for us."

Aaron and Annie exchanged a look. She shook her head, letting him know she didn't know where they were going either.

"I wasn't home much once I started working for the network," Jenny said. "And certainly the income I earned meant I didn't come into contact with some of the grittier elements of the city. But one day a friend invited me to see the work he was doing. Back then, we did a feature on it for the news to help with contributions."

She looked out the window. "When I saw the snow today, I thought of him and the people he helps. I thought I'd show it to you."

They got out of the taxi and began making their way toward the building.

A long line of people stood on the sidewalk. The building bore a sign proclaiming it to be a rescue mission. Aaron had seen homeless people on the streets as they went sightseeing this week but never so many in one place. They looked tired and pinched with cold. Most of them carried possessions in backpacks and bags and carts.

He wanted to know about the people with children. How was it possible they were homeless when they had children? The city seemed to have such extremes, with some having so much money and some having so little. Sure, there were some differences in the Plain community—some were wealthy, some had a lot less. But there were no homeless. No one was without a place to sleep—especially on a cold day.

Annie was taking it all in with those enormous blue eyes of hers. He figured they'd be talking about this later, and she'd be scribbling in her notebook.

A tiny black woman with what looked like a thousand tiny braids stood with a clipboard, taking down names and directing them inside. She looked up and grinned when she saw Jenny approach.

"I didn't believe it when Jamar said you were coming!" she cried and wrapped Jenny in a warm hug.

"Looks like I picked a busy day."

"They're all busy these days, honey," the woman said. "But yeah, the snow days are the worst."

Jenny introduced Annie and Aaron, and then Wanda told her to go on inside. "He's in there serving. Split pea is the *soup du jour*, baby."

Chuckling at her own joke, she turned back to the next person in line. "Let's get your name and needs down here on my list so you can get inside and warm up."

Inside, they found even more people standing in line waiting for food and seated at the tables eating it. Mothers and fathers fed their children before themselves and old people helped each other with milk cartons that resisted cold, arthritic fingers.

Loaves of bread and boxes of baked goods were stacked along one wall. Workers served soup from big cauldrons and filled plates with chicken and dumplings. The place smelled even better than the fancy restaurant in the hotel they were staying in, Aaron couldn't help thinking. He found himself hoping they'd be eating here even though it seemed wrong of him to do so. They had so many needing help here, and he wondered if they could afford to feed all of them.

The tallest man Aaron had ever seen walked around with a coffeepot, and each time he stopped to fill a cup he'd touch a shoulder and say something to make most of the people smile. A helper followed him, ready to give him another filled pot and take away the empty one.

Then the man turned and saw Jenny. He smiled and held out his arms, and they hugged.

"Be honest. You heard it was split pea soup day and had to visit," he said as he stood back and grinned down at her.

"Best split pea soup you'll ever eat," Jenny told them.

"Better than my grandmother's?" Aaron asked him.

Jamar turned his grin on Aaron and shook his hand, then Annie's. "It's my grandmother's recipe. Maybe you should try it and see for yourself."

"Oh, no, I couldn't," Aaron shook his head. "I wouldn't want to have some and you run out. You have a lot of people who look hungry."

"We won't run out," Jamar said. "We've got lots of split peas and ham put away for the winter. Jenny? What about you and Annie?

"I wouldn't miss a bowl of your split pea soup," she said. "You have to try it, Annie."

So they sat at a table and ate soup and caught up. "I knew you'd be okay," he said quietly. "You're a survivor."

"I had it easy compared to a lot of people here," she told him. "I had some money saved. I had family."

"And you had God."

"Everyone has God," Annie blurted out.

Jamar nodded. "They do for sure. But they don't always believe it. So they walk around in despair."

"They can't believe that if they stay here for long," Jenny said.

"I hope not. And whoever I can't reach, why, I just set Wanda on them," he told them and his laugh boomed around the room, startling a few people nearby.

After they finished eating, he gave them a guided tour. They saw rooms filled with beds, a small clinic, and a lending closet with shelves and shelves of blankets, jackets, and clothing. Annie asked him endless questions about the mission. Where did it get its funding? How many people did it serve? Did the room with computers truly help people find jobs?

"I bet she could do a feature for the network as good as the one you did," Jamar told Jenny.

She was silent for a long moment and then she nodded seriously. "I believe you're right." She glanced at the clock on the wall. "We have to go."

"Got the big banquet tonight. Yeah, I heard about it." He hugged her again. "Don't let so many years go by again, Jenny Bontrager."

"You and Wanda come see us next time. We'll show you some fine Amish cooking when you do."

"We'll take you to a restaurant," Annie said with an impish smile. "*Mamm's* still practicing her cooking."

"Well!" Jenny pretended to be offended, then she laughed. "She's right."

Jamar escorted them to the front door. Aaron pulled a bill from his pocket and handed it to him.

"Why, thank you!" Jamar said, his eyes big as he eyed the hundred. "That's so generous."

"It's just money. It's more generous to give your life helping others as you do," Aaron said simply.

"Amen, brother," said a tattered-looking man as he passed.

Annie slipped her hand in his as they walked out into the cold. Aaron felt the warmth of her approval deep inside.

"It wasn't wrong what you two did for Melissa," Jenny said. "I was just worried about the consequences. Back home, we know the people in our community. In a big city, we don't have that luxury, and bad things can happen by getting too close to the wrong people."

The taxi pulled away from the curb and they waved at Jamar and Wanda. "Here, sometimes people look to organizations like this one to help the needy. People like my friends try to make the help personal."

Annie reached over and squeezed her hand. "Thank you for showing me something about this place where you used to live."

14

When Annie walked into the grand ballroom and saw dozens of people looking at her and her family, her palms started to sweat.

And she wasn't even the one who had to give a speech. She sat down at the table reserved for them and turned to her mother. "I've never seen so many people."

"I know." Her mother took a sip of water. "I wish I'd gone over my notes one more time."

The water trembled in the glass as Jenny set it down.

"Are you . . ." Annie trailed off.

"Am I what?"

"You can't be nervous. You used to talk to millions of people."

"I used to talk to a camera," Jenny corrected her. "Not the same thing as a big room full of people."

She pulled out her note cards and surreptitiously studied them. Then she shuffled her cards together, put a rubber band around them, and tucked them into her purse.

"But you gave speeches sometimes, didn't you? I thought I remembered you saying something about it once."

"A long time ago. A very long time ago."

"You can do anything," Matthew said quietly. "Anything you put your mind to."

"What a sweet thing to say," she said quietly.

The two of them exchanged a look that warmed Annie's heart as it always did. She turned and saw Aaron had seen it too and was looking back at her as if he shouldn't witness such a private intimacy. He smiled at her and reached for her hand under the table.

"Thanks for inviting me."

"You've already thanked me. And them."

He shrugged. "I don't think you can say thank you too much, do you?"

"You're welcome, sir," said the waiter who was setting a glass of ice water before him.

Aaron looked up and grinned.

Annie watched the room fill. The *Englischers* had come dressed in such finery: the women in beautiful long dresses of satin and fancy fabrics decorated with glittering stones and such. The men wore formal suits. She and her mother had worn their Sunday best and her mother looked beautiful and calm and at ease. Annie felt a little uncomfortable compared to the rest of the guests.

Her mother, perceptive as always, noted her uneasiness. "What's wrong?" she whispered.

"We're underdressed."

She saw her mother struggling to keep her lips from twitching. "We're Plain, remember?"

Annie laughed. "I know I'm being silly. It's not that I want to dress like that. It just feels a little strange, is all."

"I felt that way when I traveled in some countries overseas," Jenny told her. "Feels like you stick out like a sore thumb sometimes. But it's just the way it is sometimes."

"It doesn't matter anyway," Annie assured her. "We're here for you tonight."

"Sorry, we ran late," David said as he joined them. "Joy and the kids are right behind me."

Sure enough, they rushed in a few minutes later. "One of those days, you know? And traffic was bad." Joy looked up gratefully as David held out her seat.

"Great turnout," David said as his eyes roamed the room. "People paid big bucks for these seats, you know. It's all going to the foundation to help the kids." He slanted a look at Jenny. "Like I told you when I called you. You don't have to worry that it's about ego here."

He met Jenny's gaze. "She's making faces, isn't she?"

Jenny laughed.

"I love to tease him," Joy admitted. "There's so much ego in network news."

A flurry of movement at the door caught their attention.

"Speaking of ego," Joy murmured.

"Here are our honorees! David, Jenny, everyone, good to see you," said Gordon. "This is the wife, Wendy."

Interesting, thought Annie. The woman looked half his age. She'd read how some men married much younger women, but it didn't happen often back home. They were dressed like so many of the other people in the room, but Wendy wore big glittery diamonds at her ears, neck, and wrists. Annie wondered how she lifted her hand with a ring so big. She'd never seen diamonds so large, but from what she knew she doubted they were rhinestones or something man-made. She also knew Aaron was probably trying not to look at Wendy as she bent to sit down, her bosom nearly spilling out of her low-cut neckline.

Waiters began serving salads. The plates consisted of lettuces, tomatoes, and other vegetables Annie was used to seeing in summer but not in winter. Then they ate more canned vegetables than fresh.

David saw her studying her plate. "A lot of produce is flown here from other countries. A lot of the flowers you see on the table too."

He turned to Matthew and began asking him about the farm. Joy rolled her eyes. "Matthew, can I send him to your place so he can see how hard you work?"

"I'm not afraid of hard work," David said.

"David thinks we should grow our own vegetables," Joy explained. "I asked him when he thought he had time for that."

Jenny looked at the empty seat next to her. "Is someone else coming?"

Gordon looked at David. "I don't know of anyone else coming, do you?

"Nope," said David. "Must just be an extra seat."

Wendy perked up. "But I thought you said—"

Gordon leaned over to her. "Did you see who just walked in? That guy on the soap you like."

"Which one?"

"I don't know, the one you're always talking about."

Wendy turned in her chair and looked. "I don't see him."

"Maybe I was wrong." Gordon ate with an enthusiasm Annie usually saw in a farmhand during harvest. "You could get a gardener, David. Have him do all the manual labor."

"Sort of defeats the whole do it yourself thing I'm after."

Gordon shrugged.

A man hurried up to the table. He stood there by the chair waiting for her mother to look up from her food, and when she did, a grin spread across his weathered face.

"You came!"

She sprang up and hurried around the table to throw her arms around him. They hugged for a long moment, and when they stepped back, Annie saw both of them had tears in their eyes.

"Everyone, this is one of the people I was hoping to see when I came here. Ross, meet my family." She smiled at him. "He was my boss at the network."

～❧～

Aaron had never felt more like a fish out of water.

All around him were *Englischers* all dressed up, many of them talking to each other like they knew each other.

And the food . . . Little snacks were passed around, called a fancy name he barely caught. The little fish eggs—caviar?— weren't bad, but the waiter passing them around frowned when he took several. Jenny whispered they were expensive and so he gathered you were supposed to make sure everyone had some. The salad had greens he recognized in it, but the dainty looking flowers were unexpected.

A tray of "lamb lollipops" was next. Even though people were using nice table manners, it was apparently okay to hold one of the lamb lollipops by the bone and nibble on the meat.

Oh, and the steak. Aaron would have come here just for the steak. It wasn't something eaten often by the Amish who were frugal by nature and had many mouths to feed. Many people back home bought a side of beef, had it wrapped and used it until it was gone. But there was only a certain amount of steak on that side and the rest was used as roasts or ground into hamburger.

When he eyed the steak Annie left on her plate, she smiled and pushed it toward him.

"You need to eat more," he whispered.

The girl talked entirely too much and was too engrossed in what was going on around her to do more than pick at her food.

"I can't eat as much as you or I'll turn into a little heifer," she whispered back.

Aaron glanced over and saw Matthew was helping Jenny finish her steak as well.

"Besides, I figure if the food is this good, dessert's going to be amazing. I want to have room for it."

And it was amazing. Everyone looked up when the lights were dimmed and waiters began streaming in a line down the aisles, each carrying a tray aloft with a flaming dessert. Their waiter stopped at their table, set his tray on the table, and extinguished the flames with a wave of his hand. He cut slices of the dessert, revealing a base of cake topped by ice cream and swirls of meringue browned by the showy flames.

"Bet you don't see a show like this back home," Gordon said, elbowing Aaron.

He turned and looked at the man. "No, sir."

"I know what you're thinking," David whispered to Jenny. "But people who are attending tonight paid a lot of money for their tickets. The hotel and some other vendors donated the food. It's our biggest fundraiser to date. We're going to be able to feed and care for more children than ever before."

"I know you wouldn't do something to spend money that could go to the children," she assured him.

Dessert disappeared, coffee was served, and people began looking toward the podium.

The man who had been Jenny's boss excused himself and went to the podium. He talked about feeling nervous sending a rookie reporter like Jenny overseas. And how she had hounded him for the opportunity.

Aaron saw Annie look at her mother then, appearing surprised to hear her mother described this way.

"Jenny was right about why she should be the one I sent there to see what was happening," Ross said. "She had fresh eyes, a way of seeing things without a cynic's view. She was the one who made us look into the eyes of the children, and when we did, we couldn't look away. We had to care."

A big television screen came to life, showing Jenny dressed in *Englisch* clothes and standing in a bleak-looking place with bombed-out buildings and people and children wandering around injured, their expressions hopeless. Jenny talked with a mother who held a child in her arms. An off-camera voice interpreted the woman's words as a plea for food, medicine, and shelter.

The child's eyes caught Aaron, so compelling he couldn't look away. Until today, he had never seen a child in need of food, a family without a home. He'd never seen war or devastation, not just because it didn't happen in his community but because his religious beliefs prevented serving in an army.

He had never seen suffering like this.

Annie was mesmerized, Matthew as well. He didn't often show his emotions in public, and though Aaron had seen how deeply he loved his wife, he had never seen the man display his affection in public. Tonight, he slipped his arm around her and held her close to him, comforting her as tears slid down her cheeks while she watched the footage.

The image on the screen faded, making the child's eyes linger before the screen finally became dark.

Ross's voice sounded suspiciously husky, as if emotion gripped his throat. So much for his saying many news people were cynical after seeing years of war. He began talking about how Jenny had been wounded and brought back to the States.

Instead of being worried she'd never be able to go back to doing the work she'd loved, he said, Jenny had been worried about the children she'd seen in war-torn areas. David had stepped in, doing a story about her and her concern, and the network's big contribution was the beginning of the foundation David now oversaw.

"When we contacted Jenny to tell her we wanted to honor her and David for their work, she refused at first," Ross said. "Jenny was a private person, a humble person, long before she became Amish. She feels she's done no more than anyone else who has called attention to someone in need. But we convinced her we would all be celebrating the work we share when we come together like this, raising money for good, not just the people who started it."

He leaned on the podium. "So join me in saying thank you to the two people who started a wonderful foundation and helped you contribute many dollars tonight."

"What he's saying is these people got their pockets plucked like a chicken tonight," Gordon chuckled in Aaron's ear.

There was laughter and applause as Jenny and David rose, and together they walked to the podium.

Aaron turned to watch Annie. He'd thought she'd grown from a cute little girl he went to school with into a beautiful woman but never more than at the moment she rose to applaud her mother. She glowed with pride as she watched her mother honored along with David.

Then Annie looked at Aaron, and she smiled at him. The world fell away in that moment, as if they stood alone staring at each other and only when Jenny began speaking did Aaron come back to reality.

"I want to thank you for coming tonight and for your generosity of spirit," Jenny said. "You've proven when you know there's a need, you want to help. And I want to thank David for all he's done to make the foundation an advocate for children victimized by war."

David talked for a few minutes, spelling out where the money was spent that year and inviting the audience to refer to handouts about it on their way out. There was applause again as Jenny and David made their way back to the table.

People began leaving then, some of them stopping by the table to say hello to Jenny, David, Gordon, and Ross. Matthew spoke quietly to the waiter and fresh coffee was brought for Jenny and David since they hadn't been able to finish theirs before they were called up front to speak.

"Well, we're going to be hitting the road," Gordon said, getting up. He stopped at Annie's chair and bent down to look her in the eyes. "You've got some big shoes to fill there, Annie Bontrager."

Annie thanked him but looked puzzled as she watched him walk around the table saying goodbye to the others before collecting his wife and leaving.

❧

The evening had been amazing. The whole day had been. Such a study in contrasts—from an inner-city soup kitchen to a big charity function attended by the rich and famous.

Annie had never imagined either world back in her Plain community. She wasn't sure what she'd imagined would happen on the trip, but it sure hadn't been anything as exciting as this day had been.

Her mother groaned as she leaned back in her seat in the limo.

"Tired?"

Jenny nodded. "But happy. It was a good night. Did you hear what David said? It was their best fundraiser." She sighed. "I don't think I've ever met so many people at one time."

Turning to Matthew, she searched his face. "Did you have a good time?"

"It was different. Not bad."

"I don't have to ask Johnny. He had a great time."

Annie stroked the silky blond hair that fell over her younger brother's forehead as he slept cuddled against their father.

It still felt strange to travel in a limo through the city. Streetlights threw their light into the vehicle as they passed by. People moved on the sidewalks even though it was getting late. It seemed the city never slept.

Annie yawned. She wasn't used to staying up this late, and neither was her family.

"It was so special to see my old boss," Jenny said with a sigh as she looked at Matthew. "He gave me such a chance when he hired me."

"He knew he had someone special," Matthew told her.

"Did you hear what Gordon said?" Aaron spoke up.

"It was nothing," Annie said.

"I don't think it was nothing. He was obviously trying to say something. When people as important as him talk, they have a reason."

"What did he say?" Matthew asked as he looked at both of them.

Annie shrugged. "I don't know, something about I had big shoes to fill."

"What did he mean?" Aaron asked Jenny. "You'd know. You're *Englisch*."

"She's Amish," Matthew said quietly.

"I'm sorry, I meant to say you were *Englisch* before you became Amish. You'd know what he meant."

"It's an expression not unique to the *Englisch*," she said slowly, looking at Annie. "People talk about a child stepping into the shoes of a parent, into the footprints they've made. Taking on the type of work or goal of their parent."

"So he thinks she's going to do what you did?" Aaron asked.

"You know I want to be a writer," Annie said, looking confused.

"Maybe he thinks you want to be more."

She leaned forward and put her hands on her knees. "It doesn't matter what he thinks. I decide."

"But he must think you're interested in—" he stopped, looking to her parents. "I don't know, in doing something like Jenny did. You went to the network. Did he ask you if you wanted to work there?"

"No!" Annie found her temper rising. Why was he suddenly interrogating her like this? "Do you think a man as important as him takes the time to ask a person like me what they want to do?"

"If you're the daughter of Jenny Bontrager, maybe."

It was as if someone had just used a big vacuum to suck all the air out of the car. No one spoke.

Before Annie could figure out what to do, summon up something to say, the limo was pulling up to the hotel. The driver turned off the engine and got out to open the door.

Annie stepped out and walked ahead of Aaron. When they entered the elevator, she stared straight ahead.

"We home?" Johnny asked sleepily as he leaned against his father.

"We're at the hotel, remember?"

He rubbed his eyes and nodded. "I want to go home. It's almos' Christmas."

"We go home day after tomorrow. We still have some fun things to do, remember?"

"Annie, listen, I—" Aaron began, but she shook her head.

The doors slid open, and they walked to their suite.

"Go get your pajamas on and brush your teeth," Matthew told Johnny. "We'll come tuck you in."

"No reading tonight?"

"Not tonight. It's late."

Annie hugged her mother. "I had a good time tonight. I'm so glad we came."

Her mother hugged her back. "Me too."

She stood on tiptoes and hugged her father. "Thank you again for making the trip possible, *Daed*."

His hug was warm and comforting, but when she pulled away she saw worry in his eyes.

She gave Aaron a quick glance, avoiding looking at him. "'Night, Aaron. See you all in the morning."

Going into her room, she shut the door and bit her lip. Something didn't feel right. It felt like he thought she had some . . . ulterior motive. Like she was . . . looking for a job or something.

She sank down onto the bed, stunned at the thought. He couldn't possibly think so, could he?

There was a knock on the door, and then her mother poked her head in. "May I come in for a minute?"

Annie nodded, and her mother shut the door behind her and sat down on the bed. She'd taken off her bonnet and coat but hadn't changed yet.

"What was that about in the limo?"

"I have no idea." Annie lifted her hands and let them fall into her lap. "I just had this thought. Did it seem to you Aaron thought I was looking for a job here?"

Her mother nodded. "I sort of got that impression. Where did it come from?"

Annie stood, took off her jacket and bonnet, and laid them on a chair. She began taking the pins from her *kapp* and unwinding her bun. "For sure and for certain not from me."

"I didn't think so. But—"

"But what?"

"Your father just asked me the same thing, if I thought you had talked to Gordon about a job."

Annie rolled her eyes. "Where do men get these ideas?"

Jenny patted the bed. "Come, sit down. Let me tell you something about your father.

"Hand me your brush," she said, and Annie gave it to her and sat beside her.

"I remember sitting at the kitchen table one night while you and your brother and sister were in the living room," Jenny began as she began to brush Annie's waist-length hair. "We were talking about you—not just you but them too—and he began telling me he worried his children might not want to be baptized when they were old enough. That they might not want to join the church and stay in the community."

She paused a moment. "I think it might have been on his mind at that moment because I'd come back to the community my father had moved away from. And I remember Joshua was so interested in my cell phone and my life here in the city. All of you were. I was a bit of an oddity to you."

Annie reached to touch her mother's hand. "You weren't odd to me."

"Well, let's say *different* than what you were used to. And kids are always fascinated with the unusual. I think your father's still a little worried about you."

"I know. We talked about it the other day. But my wanting to come here wasn't to get a job. I've just always wanted to come here and see it for myself—especially at the holidays."

Jenny leaned over and looked out the window. "And what do you think now? There's this song, an old song. It goes something like, 'How do you keep them down on the farm after they've seen Paree?'"

Annie turned and laughed. "Funny."

"I think it had something to do with soldiers going to fight the war, men who'd never been off their farms and outside their county, let alone the country. France and Paris fascinated them. They were different after they went."

"It's all been wonderful here, such an adventure," Annie began, looking for the right words. "And it's been so interesting to see where you came from, what shaped you."

She tilted her head and studied her mother. "When we're children, we think our mothers are just there for us, revolving around us like the sun. But I got to see you as your own person here, someone who had a life and a job and friends. Who had goals and dreams. And who chose to give it all up to be my father's wife and my mother."

"I gave nothing important up," her mother said firmly. "But I got so much when I became your father's wife and your mother. I truly became the person I was meant to be."

She looked down at the scar on the hand holding the brush. "Even the bombing was a gift. I might never have started the foundation or written the books I love writing. I thought I knew what I wanted to do. Thought I knew what God planned for me. But he had something so much bigger and more wonderful than anything I could have dreamed of."

With a sigh, she got to her feet. "Let's get some sleep. We have a lot planned for tomorrow." She glanced at the clock, then bent to kiss Annie's cheek.

Impulsively, Annie reached up to hug her tight and then watched her mother pause at the door.

"You know, I wonder if Aaron isn't a little worried you'll want to stay here."

"You think so?"

Jenny nodded. "Maybe. Talk to him tomorrow."

"I will."

Annie thought about what her mother had said as she changed into a nightgown and brushed her teeth.

What *did* God have planned for her? She wondered about it as she slipped between the sheets and laid her head on the pillow. Would it be more than she could imagine?

Because she had *such* an imagination God had already given to her!

15

"What a beautiful day."

Aaron glanced around him. The previous day's snow had melted, making puddles, and revealing the trash still on the curbs. Exhaust fumes filled the air.

The holiday spirit that had prevailed during previous days seemed absent too. More than one person walked around him and glared.

"Wish tourists would stay in bed until we get to work," he heard one woman mutter.

"Oh, sorry!" Aaron said, quickly stepping out of the way.

"She's right, not everyone's a tourist," Jenny said with a grin. "It's a busy time of year, especially if everyone's hoping they can get some time off to shop and see family for the holidays."

"Here we go," said the doorman. "Here's your limo. Where to today, folks?"

"I thought we'd go to Rockefeller Center."

"Great idea. Have fun!"

"I don't think I've ever seen you in such a good mood," Aaron said.

Annie slanted Aaron a look. "My *mamm's* always in a good mood."

"I am in such a good mood," Jenny said, giving Annie a warning look. "I think I was a little tense about the banquet last night, but it went so well."

She leaned forward and looked out the window. "Weatherman said no snow today."

Annie felt Aaron watching her. They needed to talk. But when would they find a time with her family around?

They joined other tourists milling around the Center. It had to be the biggest Christmas tree in the world, glistening with ornaments, the entire sight a thing of wonder. Annie thought it must be even more beautiful when it was night and the lights were turned on.

Johnny was fascinated by the enormous golden statue over-looking the skating rink. He looked back and forth from the brochure Jenny had found to the statue and back to the brochure again.

"Prom—Prom—what's his name?"

"Prometheus. He's mythical—meaning he's from an old story. No one is sure if he was a real person or not." She paused. "He looks like he's flying, doesn't he?"

"Like a superhero."

"Sort of," Jenny said. "He's supposed to be stealing fire from the gods to give to man."

"Gods? There's just one God." Johnny frowned as he tried to read the brochure.

"True. Back a long time ago, some people believed there were many."

"Were the people big back then?"

She laughed. "No. The man who made this just wanted to make a great big sculpture."

"Eighteen feet tall and eight tons," he read. He looked up at his father. "The basketball player at the party last night—how tall was he?"

"Seven feet, one inch," Matthew told him.

They walked closer to the rink. People were skating along on its surface. Some were obviously just learning. A few, though, spun around like they were experts. Annie watched one jump into the air and spin around, land on one foot, and then go into a fast spiral that made her skates spit little pieces of ice around.

"So who's going to join me?" asked Jenny.

Johnny jumped up and down. "Me! Me!"

"What about you, Matthew?"

Matthew gave Jenny a cool stare. "I told you, I'm not getting on the ice. I had enough of falling when I was younger."

"I will," Annie spoke up. "It'll be fun. The ice looks smoother than the pond back home."

"I think I'll sit this one out with Matthew." Aaron jerked his head to stare at Annie. "Did you just cluck? Jenny, Matthew, your daughter just clucked at me."

Jenny clucked at him.

Aaron turned to Matthew. "Can you believe this?"

"Don't look at me," Matthew said. "It's every man for himself."

"Fine," Aaron said. "I know how to skate. I've done it back home."

He had. They'd gone with other young people from church. But Aaron had often sat it out, talking with the other young men.

They went to get their skates, and Annie guessed they didn't get many Amish here for they were stared at a lot. Some people pulled out their cell phones to take a picture, but no one bothered them as they sat and put on their skates.

Johnny had received a pair of skates two Christmases ago, but when he stepped out onto the ice he wobbled and threw his arms out and struggled for his balance.

And then he skated away from them.

"Figures," said Jenny. "He picks things up like that." She tried to snap her fingers, but there was no sound since she wore gloves. "I have to be crazy. I haven't done this in years."

She stepped out onto the ice and swayed. Made it a few feet. And went down.

Annie prayed like she'd never prayed as she rushed out to help her. Aaron reached her before Annie could and fell. The two of them sat there staring at each other and then they laughed.

When Annie reached them, she stood with her hands on her hips and shook her head. "Well, I guess no one's hurt if you're laughing."

"I just hurt my pride," Jenny said. "At least, I think so. I can't feel a certain part of my body the ice is so cold."

Aaron struggled to get to his feet, and they kept sliding out from under him.

Several people stopped to help. A woman who'd been executing some dazzling jumps showed Jenny how to move forward then watched and waited to see if she needed more help. When Jenny made it a few feet and got the rhythm, the woman smiled and nodded, then skated off.

Aaron gained his feet and thanked the man who'd helped him. He continued to struggle for a few minutes and looked as ungainly as a bear who'd wandered out on the ice. But he shook his head when the man circled the rink and stopped on his way to ask if he needed any help.

"Men won't ask for help, will they?" she inquired with a bit of sarcasm.

"Don't need it," he maintained, flapping his arms like a scarecrow in a field. He stared at her. "Since when did you get so good?"

"I didn't sit on the sidelines with my buddies when we went skating," she told him, skating backward, a trick she'd learned last winter.

He made a face at her. They moved slowly around the rink, him awkward on the ice, Annie determined not to easily forgive what had happened the night before.

It was a few minutes later when Jenny skated up to them, her forehead puckered in concern.

"Johnny—have you seen Johnny? I can't find him anywhere."

❧

Jenny looked pale, and when Annie touched her mother's arm, she felt her trembling.

"Where did you see him last? Which direction was he going in?"

"That way!" she said, pointing to the right of the rink.

"Okay, I'm sure he's fine. Aaron, you go that way, we'll go this way."

They skated off, Annie's eyes sweeping right, then left, searching for one small boy in a sea of so many adults and children. Aaron met her on the first trip around the rink, then again.

"We have to get help." Jenny cast a frantic glance around. "Where's a cop when you want one?"

Annie had never seen her mother like this. "*Mamm*, I know it's a big city, but Johnny's a smart boy. He wouldn't go off with anyone."

"Bigger kids than him have disappeared. I'm going to take one more trip around the rink and then if I can't find him I'm going to go tell your father."

She skated away from them before they could say anything.

"He's got to be around here," Aaron said. "He's not the kind of kid who would just go off —"

"But he's never been in a place like this. Listen, I'm going to take my skates off and go looking for him outside the rink. You keep looking here."

Before she could turn to rush away, he pulled her into his arms and hugged her. "We're going to find him."

She was too shocked at the gesture to say anything.

"Go," he said, and he turned away first.

Annie rushed away. After she quickly exchanged her skates for her shoes, she started looking around on foot. The day was cold, but she felt a line of perspiration trickling down her back. It wasn't just from exertion. The panicked look in her mother's eyes had scared her. Her mother knew about a big city . . .

She tried calling his name, but it was too noisy in the area. Calling his name only got her curious looks.

Then she spotted a police officer. She rushed up to him, then saw by the way he looked wary and stepped back, it hadn't been a good idea.

"I'm sorry, my *bruder* is missing," she said, lapsing back into Pennsylvania *Dietsch* in her agitation.

"*Bruder*?"

She shook her head. "Brother. My brother. "

"You're Amish, right?"

She nodded.

"Here on vacation?"

"Yes."

"We don't get many Amish on vacation."

Annie was too worried to waste time explaining.

The officer pulled out a small notebook and began asking her questions: What was his name? How old was he? What was he wearing? Was he in the habit of wandering off?

Annie answered all his questions, but her agitation was growing. "When are you going to start looking for him?"

The officer gave her a level stare and remained unruffled. "Easy, miss. Just a few more questions. The more information we get, the better."

As soon as he got the answers to his last two questions he used his walkie-talkie to call in. Within minutes, two other officers appeared and there was a discussion of strategy.

Annie rubbed her forehead. She could feel a headache coming on.

The officers finished talking and took off in different directions, leaving the original one standing there with her.

"I need to find my parents," she told him.

"Is that them there?"

She turned and sure enough, they were walking quickly toward her. The officer filled them in on what they'd done so far.

"I don't suppose you have a photo?"

Matthew pulled out his cell phone, worked on it for a moment, and held it out to him.

"Great. Can you send it to me?"

The two men huddled over their phones.

The officer looked up with a grin. "This is good, this is real good. I'll get it out to every officer in the city in just a few minutes." He focused on the phone and then looked up. "There. Done. Say, I thought the Amish didn't take photos."

"Some do, some don't. Depends on the community. Mostly it's a matter of courtesy. No one needs someone taking pictures like we're part of a tourist experience or whatnot."

Annie's eyes widened. She couldn't remember the last time her father had said this much.

He wrapped his arm around her mother's waist, something he didn't do in public. But as Annie looked at her, she saw how frightened her mother looked.

If her brother had wandered off for some silly reason she was afraid she would shake him when they found him.

First Joshua and now Johnny . . . her brothers were making her crazy.

She determinedly shook away the dark thoughts. She needed to pray. God was here, with them, not outside the situation. She believed that. If it was God's will Johnny was to be taken from them she'd have to accept it, but she desperately hoped it wasn't what was going to happen.

The walkie-talkie crackled to life. Someone said something in a code—letters and numbers she didn't recognize. But the officer stood straighter and seemed to come to attention. "They checked the lower level and didn't find him."

Annie slumped.

A few minutes later, another voice spoke a code over the walkie-talkie.

"Would you mind coming with me?" the officer asked her parents.

"Did they find him?" Jenny cried. "Did they find Johnny?"

"A woman thought she recognized the photo one of the officers showed her."

Jenny clutched Matthew's sleeve. "They have to have seen him. How many Amish kids are running around here in one day?"

They walked with him about a block or so and found the woman talking with a female police officer.

"He was walking over in the direction of the restrooms," she was saying.

Suddenly everything made sense. Her brother was always drinking something and then having to find a restroom.

Annie broke away from the others and hurried on up to the restrooms for men. A woman stood near the door with a stroller. When a man approached, she shook her head and held up her hand. They argued for a moment and he turned away, frowning, then his expression cleared when he saw the officer.

The man rushed over. "Hey, she won't let me use the restroom. Can you talk to her?"

The woman pushed the stroller toward them. "A young kid went in there. I'm not letting some man go in there until he comes out. Too many perverts hanging around public restrooms."

The man turned and put his hands on his hips. "Lady, I'm not a pervert."

She lifted her chin and stared him down. "You never know these days," she said. "I watch the news. I know what goes on in this city. I saw the news about the little boy who was molested last week in a park restroom. This is an Amish kid. He wouldn't know about bad people."

"I have my rights! Officer, tell her—"

The man held up his hands. "Just give me a minute, I'll check it out."

Annie didn't wait. She began running toward the restroom, and it was a good thing the woman had kept the men out because she rushed inside.

"Johnny!"

He jumped as her voice echoed around him in the empty, tiled space. "Jeez! You scared me!"

"Do you know how you scared all of *us* by wandering off?"

"Sorry." He hung his head for a moment and then he looked up. "Did you ever see a sink like this? Watch how the water comes on when you put your hands under it."

"Johnny!"

"Found him?" the officer asked mildly as he entered.

The boy's eyes grew big. "Am I in trouble?"

The man grinned. "Not with me. But I don't know about your parents."

"*Daed's* sure going to have something to say to you," Annie warned.

Johnny shook the water from his hands and wiped them on his trousers. "Guess I better go say I'm sorry."

"Yeah, I'd say."

He walked out and she followed him. Her mother ran forward and wrapped her arms around him, hugging him, and crying over him. Her father looked stern, but then, when Jenny released the boy, he picked him up and hugged him hard.

"Thank you for your help," Matthew told the officer and shook his hand.

"Glad he's okay," the officer said, smiling. "Sometimes things don't work out this well."

Jenny wiped her tears away with her hands. "Yes, thank you so much." He strolled away, talking on his walkie-talkie.

She turned to the woman who'd played protector. "Thank you for looking out for him."

"Hey, it takes a village," the woman told her.

"Is it okay to go in now?" the man who'd argued about the restroom asked in a sarcastic tone.

The woman swept her hand in an exaggerated arc. "Be my guest."

As they walked away, Johnny looked up at his mother. "What did she mean by 'village,' *Mamm*?"

❧❧

Aaron wondered if he was ever going to get a chance to talk to Annie.

He'd hoped to talk to her as they skated, but maybe it had been a dumb thing to expect. There were so many people on the ice, and besides, it took some exertion to skate. Talking wasn't exactly easy to do at the same time.

Then they'd had the excitement of Johnny vanishing on them. He'd thought Jenny had overreacted. After all, boys wandered off sometimes. He'd done it to his own parents.

Then, when he saw the police react so quickly, he wondered if he'd been naïve. Look how the woman had reacted when she didn't want the man to go into the same restroom as Johnny . . .

He hadn't ventured outside his community much. Work had kept him busy, especially as he was building his business the past few years. He might not have even looked beyond the traditional avenues of sales for his work if he hadn't met Paul who suggested he expand his market by advertising his furniture on the Internet.

Work, church, visits with family and friends. An occasional trip into town for supplies. A man didn't need much else. Well, except a wife.

Annie stood talking with her parents a few feet away. She looked no different than she did at home, her dark blue dress, black bonnet, and black jacket were the same. But here she stood with the backdrop of the big golden sculpture overlooking the skating rink, steel and glass buildings towering all around them like manmade mountains, and seemed to fit into this world so naturally.

Watching her, remembering how excited she was to visit the network offices where her mother had worked and the newspaper, hearing what the network man had said last night—well, he couldn't be blamed for thinking she might be thinking this would be an exciting place to live.

But saying something to her had just caused problems between them.

She walked toward him. "*Mamm* and *Daed* are going to go get some coffee. We can go with them or we can stay here and talk."

"That's a good idea."

"The coffee or the talking?"

"Talking."

She shrugged. "It was *Mamm*'s idea."

He studied her, seeing the stiff posture, the way she avoided his eyes. It wasn't going to be easy to work this out.

Annie was a complicated woman. She was full of questions, liked to see beyond the restrictions and borders of the community she lived in. They were opposites.

"So are we going to talk?"

Her words were direct, but she was still not meeting his eyes. She crossed her arms over her chest. It was obvious she was still upset with him.

"I saw where they film television shows here," he began conversationally. "Are you and your mother going to go through some of them?"

She shook her head. "We were only interested in visiting the place she used to work." She watched some people walking past. "If you're interested, I'm sure no one would mind waiting while you went to look."

"Why would I want to tour a show about late-night television?" He pulled at the brace on his hand. "If the Amish could watch, it'd be on at what, nine p.m.?"

He watched her struggle not to smile.

"Guess this news and television stuff is interesting to writers, huh?"

She shrugged. "I guess."

"It all seems . . . make believe. Like it's not real."

"It's pretty real here."

He looked around, taking in a world as alien to him as if he'd stepped onto another planet. This was planet New York City, he thought.

"So I guess you really like it then? I mean, it's giving you ideas to write about or something?"

She turned to him. "You just don't understand, do you? A blade of grass, the scent of bread baking, a child's laugh. They're all interesting. They all inspire me. I don't need some exotic place like this to get ideas to write about. I see things to write about, places to explore in my imagination, God's touch everywhere in my own home, in my own life."

She got up to pace. "I wanted to come here because it always sounded so magical around Christmastime. But not *at* Christmas. Christmas is at home with everyone I love around me and us all giving gifts we made for each other. When the family leaves here on Friday, I'll be going with them, Aaron. I'll be going home."

A gust of wind blew the ties of her bonnet around her face. She caught them and held them in one hand.

He reached over and took her other hand in his, stroking it. "I'm glad, Annie Bontrager. I'm sorry if I over-reacted yesterday. I don't—" he stopped.

Say it! he told himself. *Just say it!*

"I don't want to lose you," he told her, and then he was glad he said it because her eyes shone.

Her hand tightened on his and it made him feel good . . . and then she squeezed it harder and released it. He didn't have to look to know Matthew had walked up.

Reluctantly, he released her hand.

"Matthew," she heard Jenny hiss.

"Got us some Country Christmas coffee," Jenny said, handing Annie a cup. "It has chestnut, graham cracker, and maple flavor." She took a sip of hers. "Sorry, the barista made this adorable design on top of yours, but it got jostled a bit as we walked."

"A Christmas tree!" Annie exclaimed. "Look, Aaron, isn't this fancy!"

Matthew handed Aaron a cup. "Plain coffee for us. Added sugar to yours."

"Thanks."

"Mine's hot chocolate with a candy cane," Johnny told Annie. "And lots of little marshmallows."

Annie smiled at the mustache on his lip. She pulled a tissue from her pocket and wiped at the sticky goo.

"So, who's ready to go up on the observation deck?" Jenny asked. "The view is amazing."

"Not me," Annie said firmly. "Aaron, you should go."

He shook his head. "I'll stay here with you."

"I want to go!" Johnny cried and promptly spilled some of his hot chocolate.

"We'll be back soon," Jenny promised, taking Johnny's hand.

"We're not going anywhere," Annie told her. She watched them walk away.

"Did you see the look on your father's face when you said you wanted to stay here?" Aaron asked her. "Bet he's sorry he couldn't find any arsenic to put in my coffee."

"Honestly, you have such an imagination," Annie told him. "My father likes you."

It wasn't a lie. Like she'd thought before, maybe there was only so much a father could like a man who was interested in his daughter.

16

The doorman tipped his hat to Annie when the family returned to the hotel.

"There's a message for you at the front desk, miss. I was taking a break and talking to the desk clerk when it came in."

Annie looked at her mother. "I hope it's not about Joshua?"

Jenny shook her head. "Grandmother would have called on the cell."

They stopped at the desk and got the message. Annie ripped it open while they rode upstairs on the elevator.

"Gordon wants to talk to me at the network office. Says he'll send a limo."

"What?"

Annie handed her the message. Jenny read it and her eyebrows went up.

"Well, wonder what this is about," her mother said.

"I'll call him."

She went to the phone in the suite and dialed the number listed on the message. A woman answered and said Mr. Manning wasn't available. When she offered to take a message and heard Annie's name, she asked her to hold on for a moment.

"Would you be able to come to the office at four today?"

"Sure," Annie said. "What is this about?"

"Mr. Manning didn't give me any information about it but told me if you called to ask you to come at four. I'll call now and arrange for the limo to pick you up."

Annie hung up. She looked up and saw Aaron standing there listening along with her mother and father.

"Well? Why does he want to see you?" Jenny asked.

"I have no idea. His assistant said he didn't tell her, just said to ask me to come in."

Her parents exchanged a look. "I don't like the idea of her talking to him," Matthew stated bluntly.

"I'm sure he isn't going to propose something illicit," she assured him wryly. She bit her lip. "But David let me know some time back he's not like our old boss."

She looked at Annie. "Do you want me to go with you?"

Annie bit her lip. Part of her wanted her mother with her when she went to the man's office, and part of her wanted to go alone. She was an adult. Her mother hadn't accompanied her anywhere in a very long time.

Jenny touched her hand. "Tell you what. I can go with you and wait in the lobby there. If you need me, all you have to do is ask me to come upstairs."

"That sounds great," Annie said, feeling relieved.

She looked at Aaron. He met her gaze, but he didn't say anything. Maybe he was afraid to say anything.

"What are we going to do?" Johnny asked them. "Can we go back to the zoo?"

"It's a little late," Matthew said. "We can play some games. Go for a walk." He looked at Aaron. "What would you like to do?"

It was almost comical how surprised Aaron looked, Annie thought. "How about we go for a walk first? Then we can beat Johnny at a game."

"You can try," Johnny told him.

Matthew glanced at the clock. "Let's go now." He kissed Jenny on the cheek. "See you later."

"You seem awfully eager to go for a walk after we've just spent much of the day walking around. What's going on?"

"It's almost Christmas," he said. "Don't go asking questions."

Annie went to her room and Jenny followed. "Shut the door."

Jenny did as she asked. "You're changing?"

"In a minute. I didn't want anyone to hear us."

"They already left. What is it?"

"You must know why Gordon wants to see me." Annie sank down on her bed and twisted the strap of her purse.

Shaking her head, Jenny took off her coat and laid it on the other bed. "I don't know any more than you do. I guess we'll just have to see."

Annie flopped back on the bed and stared at the ceiling. "Four o'clock is an hour away. I'm going to die of curiosity."

Jenny shook her head and laughed. "Get up and take your jacket off and we'll pick out what you should wear."

As agreed, her mother waited in the lobby for her. Annie checked in with the receptionist and took the elevator up to the executive's office.

"There you are!" he said, greeting her after his assistant opened the door to his office. "Glad you could make it on such short notice. Anything Lynn can get for you? Coffee? Perrier?"

"No, thank you."

He gestured at the chair before his desk. "Have a seat." He resumed his seat after she sat down.

"I'll get right to the point," he said. "I want to offer you an internship. Do you know what that is?"

She nodded. "It's a chance to work with people at a place where you'd like to learn, maybe get a job at afterward."

"Excellent. I could tell you were one bright young woman the minute I met you. Apple doesn't fall far from the tree."

Jenny was her stepmother, but she'd never treated Annie like a stepchild. Besides, what good was it explaining this to the man, she told herself. And since Jenny was the only mother Annie could remember, she knew she'd been shaped by her.

"I'm not interested in working here though."

"I thought you wanted to be a writer."

"I do, but I'm not interested in being on air."

"What about working as a writer?"

The idea of learning more about being a writer was so tempting. Her thoughts began racing.

"What sort of thing would I write about?"

"I'd like you to work with Tommy, that young news writer you liked on a show. People are fascinated with the Amish."

Annie could almost hear the screeching of brakes in her head. That wasn't the man's name. It was Tony. Yes, she'd thought about writing about her Amish life. In a good way. Would a television show be a good way? She'd heard such conflicting things about television shows and movies that were about the Amish.

"I don't know—" she began.

"Take some time, think about it," he said, waving his hand and smiling at her jovially. "But don't think about it too long. We don't want to see someone else jump on this."

She nodded and stood. "Thank you for asking me to talk about this."

"You Amish don't care about money and things, do you?"

Taken aback, she stared at him. "Um, no, we live simply."

Gordon made a steeple of his fingers and looked at her over them. "You didn't even ask about the pay."

He leaned forward and wrote on a piece of paper, then stood and handed it to her. "This is what the position will pay. We'll also give you an allowance for an apartment."

She took the paper. "Thank you. I'll let you know."

"So how was it?" her mother asked when she met her in the lobby.

"Interesting. Very interesting. He offered me an internship."

"What's that?" Jenny nodded at the paper in her hand.

Annie realized she was holding the piece of paper Gordon had handed her as if it were on fire. She unfolded it and looked at it. "What does it mean when there's a k after a number?"

"Thousand."

"*Mein Gott*," she whispered.

"What?" Her mother looked at the paper. "He offered you this? Wow."

·ᘿᘉᕲ·

Taking a walk with Matthew and Johnny wasn't helping Aaron with his restlessness. He just couldn't get his mind off what the network man wanted with his Annie.

His Annie. Well, it was the way he'd come to think of her. She was the one for him, the one God had made to be his wife.

He pulled out his cell phone and checked the time. Only five minutes had passed.

"Expecting a call?" Matthew asked him.

"Checking the time," he admitted, feeling sheepish.

"Can I have a hot dog?" Johnny asked as they neared a sidewalk stand.

Matthew hesitated, then nodded. "You'd better not say you're not hungry when we go to supper."

"You know he's never going to say that."

The minute the words were out, Aaron wondered if he'd been too forward. He and Matthew had a sort of uneasy truce lately that he didn't want to disturb.

"The kid has a hollow leg," he said quickly.

"Look who's talking. You're having a hot dog too, right?"

"To keep him company."

"Right. We'll need three," Matthew told the hot dog man. "We don't know when Jenny and Annie will be back. They wouldn't want us to sit around hungry."

Aaron liked the way he thought. "Let me pay," Aaron he said, pulling out his wallet. "You haven't let me pay for anything on this trip."

"Fine."

They stood out of the way of people walking past them and ate. People sure seemed to like hot dogs. Either that or they were finding it a quick way to get something to eat while they shopped for Christmas presents.

Standing here people watching reminded Aaron of the way he'd sat with Annie yesterday. No one liked studying people more than her.

"So what do you think Gordon wants to talk about? Do you think he wants to offer her a job?"

Matthew frowned and wiped his mouth with a napkin. "I don't know. If he's the man in charge of everything I wouldn't think he'd be doing the hiring. Jenny didn't seem to think so when we talked last night. But what else could it be?"

"Annie's really had a good time here." He stared at his hot dog. Suddenly it didn't taste so good.

"But she loves her home and her family. Her friends."

Aaron met Matthew's level stare. "So you're not worried?"

"I wish I could say I'm not. I'm trying to trust."

"Annie—or God?"

Matthew smiled slowly. "Both. You've known Phoebe for a long time. You know how she likes to say worry is arrogant—it's like saying God doesn't know what He's doing."

Aaron nodded and sighed. "I've heard her say so a time or two. Or a dozen."

"You gonna eat that?" Johnny asked him.

He took a healthy bite of his hot dog. "Yes."

They threw away their trash and continued walking down the street, looking in store windows here and there. Some of the *Englisch* looked a little anxious as they peered into windows before going inside the stores. Aaron guessed they hadn't done all of their shopping—especially the men.

He went over a list of family members he'd made gifts for: two wooden planters for his oldest sister for the flowers she liked to keep near her front door. A small cradle for sister who was expecting a baby. He went down the list in his head, going over the presents.

And for Annie, a long, narrow carved box to keep her pencils in. He hoped it would please the writer in her. And a small keepsake box to put her hair pins and covering pins in. He thought she'd like the pencil case the best.

There was this little niggling feeling, though, as if he'd forgotten someone. He'd been so busy with orders and then the unexpected trip here he hadn't had time to think about it.

So when they went back to the hotel he got out a piece of paper and began listing names and what he'd made for each of them. And then he knew: he'd forgotten a gift for his mother. Well, not forgotten, exactly. He'd made something for her—a hanging spice rack for her kitchen—but then gotten an order for one and decided to make his mother another. He stared down at the brace on his wrist. He hadn't planned on this . . .

He sighed.

"Something wrong?" Matthew looked up from the book Johnny was reading to him.

"I just realized I forgot a Christmas present."

Matthew glanced around him. "There are a lot of stores here, but they look expensive."

"The money doesn't matter." When Matthew gave him a dubious look, he shrugged. "It's for someone important. My mother," he hurried to explain when he realized the man might think he'd forgotten to make or buy a present for Annie.

"I'll still have time to make something when I get back." He picked at the brace. "If the hand and arm don't cooperate I'll get her something for her quilting at Stitches in Time."

The door opened and Annie and Jenny walked in. Aaron searched Annie's face for some sign of how things had gone, but he couldn't puzzle out her expression. It almost seemed . . . stunned.

"Well, how did it go?" Matthew asked. "What did Gordon want to talk about?"

Annie paused in the act of unbuttoning her jacket. "He offered me an internship at the network."

∾❧∾

Aaron and her father looked thunderstruck.

"An internship," Matthew repeated. "Here? In New York City?"

She removed her coat jacket and lay it over the back of the sofa, then took her mother's and did the same with it. "Yes."

"An internship doing what?" Aaron asked her.

"Writing."

Apprenticeships were part of the Amish way of life. He'd done one with his own father and many of his friends had done them with different businesses after they graduated from school. Old-timers said it was one of the reasons why years ago the federal government and the courts had decided the Amish could run their own schools and end formal education after the eighth grade.

But the apprenticeships the Amish did were mostly done in the community. The Amish community, not the *Englisch* one.

"*Mamm?* I'm hungry," Johnny said. "Can we go eat now?"

"Oh, look at the time!" Jenny exclaimed as she glanced at the clock. "Comb your hair and wash your hands. Then we'll go eat."

"What did you tell him?"

Annie was surprised at the time herself. She didn't think they'd been gone that long. Time had seemed to fly when she talked to the network head.

"He said to think about it. He didn't expect an answer right away." She turned to her mother. "Do you have some aspirin? I have a bit of a headache."

Jenny nodded and sat down on the sofa to rummage in her purse. She pulled out a bottle and handed it to her. "Here, it's not aspirin, it's ibuprofen."

Annie went into the kitchen to get a glass of water and Aaron followed her.

"So you left it at that?" he asked her. "You're supposed to think about it?"

Surprised he'd followed her, she nodded. "That's what he said. There's no need."

"Because you've already made up your mind," he said, sounding resigned.

"Yes." She looked askance at him.

"We're ready!" Jenny called.

"Come on, we have to go," she said to him. "We'll talk about it at supper."

"But everyone will be there."

"Yes. So?"

Aaron looked frustrated, but before she could say anything to him her mother appeared in the doorway. "Ready to go?" She looked at Annie, then Aaron.

"Coming."

"I called David. He's going to meet us at the restaurant."

"David? Why is David coming?" Aaron asked Annie.

"*Mamm* thinks it would be a good idea to talk to him about today." Annie picked up her jacket and slipped it on.

"Why? Seems you have your mind made up."

Annie stopped dead in her tracks. "What?"

"We have a driver waiting," Jenny said as she held open the door.

"We'll talk at supper," Annie told Aaron.

She heard his resigned sigh, but there was no time to stop now and talk. And besides, she was as hungry as Johnny. Maybe the excitement was making her hungry. She'd always thought she had a lot of imagination, but she'd never dreamed that something like Gordon offered was possible for someone like her.

Of course she couldn't take it. She had no intention of leaving her family and her home. Or Aaron.

She glanced at him and saw he was staring moodily out the window. Then, as if he sensed her gaze on him, he turned and looked at her.

"I'm happy for you," he said quietly. "I didn't say that to you earlier."

"Thank you." She frowned, then plunged ahead. "But you don't sound happy for me."

"Hamburgers?" Johnny bounced on his seat when the driver pulled up in front of a place whose sign advertised it as an "All-American Burger Joint." Annie doubted it was a joint. It looked expensive.

"I like hamburgers even more than hot dogs!"

"You do, do you?" Jenny looked at Matthew. "When's the last time you had a hot dog?"

"Oh, hours and hours ago," he said. "I'm hungry, just like I told *Daed* I'd be."

"Here, let me help you out," Matthew said quickly, getting out of the vehicle and holding out his hand to Jenny. "Did I tell you how lovely you look tonight?"

"Such flattery," Jenny murmured. "Look out when they start such talk, Annie. What did you three gentlemen get up to this afternoon?"

Matthew patted the crown of his son's hat. "We didn't get into any trouble, did we, Johnny?"

The boy looked up at his father. "No, we didn't. And I am hungry because I only ate one hot dog."

Matthew winced.

"Just as I figured." Jenny walked up to David and hugged him. "Thanks for coming on such short notice."

"Your kids didn't come?" Johnny asked him.

"Not tonight. They're at rehearsals for our church play."

They went inside and crowded into a big booth. Once they'd placed their orders for cheeseburgers and fries and milk shakes, David grinned at them.

"Well," he said, his eyes sparkling with mischief. "You'll never guess what I found out about the big boss."

Jenny leaned forward. "What?"

"I checked with my assistant after you called me. She should sign on with the CIA. Never saw anyone who could dig up information like her. Anyway, she says Gordon wants a series on the Amish. He's got Tony working on it."

"Gordon couldn't remember Tony's name when we talked. That bothered me. Here I'm getting this big fuss made over me, and he can't remember someone who already works there."

"It's all about the need," David said. "Young guy is taken for granted because big boss is chasing over someone he knows will bring him what he wants. Supply and demand."

The waitress set a basket with a cheeseburger and French fries down in front of him. He squirted ketchup liberally all over his fries, then picked one up. "Mmm. Can't eat like this as often as I want."

"So what exactly is it he wants?" Annie asked. She picked up a French fry and bit into it.

"You. And the figure he offered you? I'm pretty sure my agent can get twice as much for you."

"Agent?" Jenny asked, stopping with her cheeseburger half-way to her mouth. "You have an agent?"

"Hey, it's a different world since you worked here." David looked over at Matthew. "How's the steakburger?"

"*Gut*," Matthew said, using a napkin to wipe his mouth. "Very juicy."

"It's one of our favorite restaurants. Don't let me forget to place an order for Joy and the kids. If I go home without it I'll be in big trouble." He took another hefty bite of his own burger and chewed, then took a sip of his Coke. "Aaron, are you always this quiet?"

Annie watched him shrug. "I don't know much about what you're talking about."

"Can I play one of the pinball machines?" Johnny asked Jenny. "I ate all my supper."

"Even the parsley meant as a garnish," Annie said dryly.

"Huh?"

"The curly green stuff. You didn't have to eat it."

"Oh. Why would they put it on the plate if they didn't want you to eat it?"

"Very logical," David said, nodding.

"If you can give me a minute, I'll play with you," Aaron told him as he picked up his Coke. "I'll treat you."

"I've got money. I earned it."

"Then I'll let you treat me," Aaron told him as he got up.

Annie watched them walk over to the pinball machines. She liked the way Aaron got along with her younger brother. But it bothered her that Aaron had been withdrawn since they left the hotel suite.

David pushed aside his empty basket. "So would you like my agent to represent you, Annie?"

She shook her head. "There's no point in it. I don't want to work in New York City."

"Oh, is that all? Madeline can negotiate with Gordon so you can work from Paradise."

Annie put her cheeseburger down and stared at him. "Do you mean it?"

"Sure. You might have to come in now and then, but I think she can get you what you want."

Excitement began bubbling in her veins. She looked at her mother. "I didn't even think—can it be possible? I mean, you do it but with your books."

"If you're interested in the opportunity, it can't hurt to let David's agent talk to Gordon," Jenny said slowly.

"*Daed?* What do you think?"

He met her gaze but didn't respond for a long moment. "I think if this is something you want to try, you couldn't do better than to try it with David's help. And this agent of his."

David grinned at Annie. "Then it's settled. Madeline will be delighted to help you, and I'll be delighted to have made the big boss cough up some more bucks. He played hardball with us the last time we negotiated a contract."

He glanced around and stood. "Where did our waitress go? I want to give her my takeout order."

Annie sprang to her feet and hugged him. "Thank you so much for the advice!"

"The work is hard," he warned. "You might not thank me later."

"Of course I will," she said confidently. "It's a wonderful opportunity. An early Christmas present."

Then she saw Aaron watching her. The room was a little dim over by the machines, probably to make the flashing lights on the pinball machines seem more dramatic. But she thought his expression looked bleak, his shoulders slumped.

17

$\mathcal{A}$aron stood with Annie's family on the sidewalk in front of the Empire State Building. Everyone was excited about going inside.

Everyone but Annie.

"But everyone who comes to New York City visits the Empire State Building," Jenny was saying.

Annie shook her head. "I can't go up there."

Her mother stared at her. "You mean you won't."

"Can't. Sorry. I'll just stay down here. You all go on and take your time."

Her father took her mother's hand. "Come on. I told you she wouldn't go. She's been afraid of heights since she was a little girl."

Her mother rubbed Annie's arm. "You don't have to go up. But I did once years ago and the view of New York City is so amazing."

"I'll take your word for it."

"Aaron?"

"I'll be up in a minute."

He watched her parents and her brother join the crowd of people filing into the building. She hadn't been enthusiastic about coming here this morning and had looked up at the tall building with dread when they got out of the limo. He knew why she hated heights—she'd been stranded in the hayloft of the family barn when she was a little girl. She'd climbed up and then been too scared to climb down. Back then, she'd had some difficulty with her speech and her yells for help went unheard.

"You don't have to stay here with me," she told him.

"I want to."

She turned to look at him. "Are you sure? After the way you acted yesterday?"

He stared at the brace on his hand, then at her. "It's a lot to take in, that's all."

"I don't understand."

"We came here for a vacation, and I thought it would . . . I don't know what I thought it would be like. I mean, I'd never been in a place like this, never gave it a moment's thought."

"You haven't had fun?"

"I've had a great time." He hesitated.

"You obviously have something to say," she said quietly. "Why don't you just say it?"

"I thought we were growing closer, but now I don't know."

"Annie!"

They looked up to see Jenny rushing toward them, her cell phone in her hand. "David's on the phone. He says he has some news."

Annie took the phone and started talking to David. When she apparently had some trouble with reception, she got up and walked a few feet away.

"Did I interrupt something?"

"We were just talking." Aaron shrugged.

Jenny sighed. "This has been fun, but I'll be glad to be going home tomorrow. How about you?"

"I'll be glad to be home. This has been a great experience. I want to thank you and Matthew again for inviting me."

"My, so formal." Jenny smiled at him. "We loved having you."

"So . . . I guess Annie will be staying?"

Jenny had been watching people walking past, but she dragged her attention back to him. "Wow. I didn't think I could be surprised by anything people did here," Jenny said. "Look at the way—no, don't look." She glanced back at him. "I'm sorry, Aaron, what did you say?"

Annie walked back over and handed her mother the cell phone. "David said Madeline is optimistic about getting what she wants from Gordon."

"That's good news." Jenny looked up at the top of the building. "Change your mind about coming up?"

"No."

"Can't say I didn't try." Jenny looked at Aaron. "How about you?"

"I'll join you in a minute."

Aaron turned to Annie. "You're sure you don't want to? Seems like someone who's on her way up shouldn't be afraid of a little height."

"What's that supposed to mean?"

"It's a big step, taking on what you're taking on," he said. He picked at the brace, the annoying, useless brace. "Big dreams, big buildings. Seems they go together here."

"What is it you're trying to say, Aaron? Am I wrong to have big dreams? You're ambitious, too. I've never seen someone so ambitious about his business. I've barely seen you for the past two months because you've been working so hard."

Aaron rubbed at the back of his neck where tension was accumulating.

"If you hadn't stressed your hand you'd still be back home putting in eighteen-hour days instead of being here on vacation with us." She stood with her arms folded across her chest.

"At least I'd be home."

"What?"

A woman walked past and stared at them curiously. Aaron didn't blame her. The Amish were rarely in the city, and they rarely carried on a heated discussion in public.

"I shouldn't have come," he said. "All it's done is make me see there's too much distance between us. I must have been *ab im Kopp* to think you and I—"

"You and I what?"

"You and I were suited." He took a deep breath. "I'm going to go join your family."

"Suited?" She followed him. "What do you mean by suited?"

He turned so suddenly she ran into him. "I was going to ask you to marry me."

Then, just as quickly, he walked away.

❧

Aaron's words hung in the air.

He was going to ask her to marry him? *Was?*

"Was?" she asked, following him inside the building.

"What would be the point now?" he asked her. "Do you expect me to sit and wait for you for a year?"

"Wait for me? Will you stop and tell me what you're saying?"

"You said you weren't going to take the internship, and now it's obvious you are. What am I supposed to do, Annie? Sit back home wondering if you're ever going to become my wife?"

She stood there, speechless, for a long moment, and then she strode after him. "I didn't ask that. I didn't know you were going to ask me to marry you. But people wait for each other all the time."

"When they know they're both committed to the same thing."

"You can't say you're committed," she said flatly. "Why are you jumping to conclusions about this offer? The agent is trying to make it so I don't have to stay here for the internship, I could work from home and just come here occasionally."

They stood before the elevator, and Aaron stood staring at the doors, as if willing them to open. "I guess I have trouble believing that."

"Well, believe it. My mother does it—works at home and sends her work to her editor." She fumed for a moment. "Or did you forget?"

When he didn't answer, she huffed and turned away.

"*Ya*, I did," he said finally.

She didn't dare look at him. He sounded confused. Upset. And was it her imagination she thought he sounded just a little like he was sorry he'd made a fuss?

"Surely, you're not going to do this, are you?" he asked her as the elevator doors opened and she stepped inside with him and a number of other people. "You don't have to go up just because I was giving you a hard time earlier."

She stared forward. "I'm doing it. And not for you." It was time she dealt with this fear. She wasn't a little girl anymore, and she certainly didn't have any trouble expressing herself.

The ride up was swift. Annie felt her stomach sinking as fast as they ascended. She felt her palms beginning to sweat and perspiration break out on her upper lip. She was not afraid of an elevator. It was what she'd see when she got out of it.

When the elevator arrived at the top and the doors opened, she let the others step out first and prayed her knees would return. It felt like she had Jell-O in those joints right now.

"You okay?"

"What?" There was this mysterious beating noise, one so loud she couldn't hear him. Then she realized it was her heart beating.

"I said, are you all right?"

"Fine." She managed to step off the elevator and focused on Johnny running toward them.

"I thought you weren't coming!"

"I couldn't miss it," she managed through gritted teeth.

"Did you know they made a movie about this big ape called King Kong, and he climbed the building?" He held up a book. "*Mamm* bought me this from the gift shop."

"I didn't know that."

"Yeah. Do you know why he climbed the building?"

"No, why?"

"'Cause he was too big for the elevator!" Johnny guffawed and took her hand. "C'mon, I'll show you where I looked out through some binocular things."

Annie was thinking a slow approach to the view might be best, but Johnny was pulling her along. She sighed. Maybe it was like swimming—you just had to jump in and hope you remembered what to do. She walked forward with him a little faster.

"I thought you weren't going to come up here," her mother said.

Her voice sounded funny. Sort of tinny. Maybe it was the altitude.

"I didn't make her," Aaron said quickly.

Jenny laughed. "Of course you didn't. No one makes Annie do anything." She peered at her. "You look a little pale. Are you sure you're okay? You don't have to be up here. It should be fun."

"Oh, it's fun," she said, lifting her chin. "This is a place of big dreams and big buildings, and I should get used to it. I'm not a little girl anymore."

"Now, Annie—"

Matthew walked over. "What's going on?"

"Nothing," Annie said. "I'm fine. More than fine. See, I'm walking over to look out at the view."

"Matthew, I don't like this," she heard her mother say. "She doesn't look well."

"I didn't make her come up here."

Annie waved a hand without turning around. "He didn't. I'm fine."

The view from up here was everything she'd heard it was: rows and rows of skyscrapers stretching as far as the eye could see, a testament to man's imagination and hard work. The city just seemed more fantastical. Invincible. Worthy of the admiration and attention it received from so many.

Even so, she loved the landscape of home with its more natural setting and fewer people. She wanted to see the fields and farmhouses and live the slower pace of life.

She wanted to go home.

She turned. Later, she realized she'd probably moved too quickly after the adrenaline rush of marching out here in spite of her fear. Her mouth suddenly tasted of cotton, her vision turned yellow, and her knees became jelly and refused to support her.

Down she went. Or halfway down. Aaron reached out and caught her, and everyone made a big fuss about clearing a place for her to sit down.

"I'm fine," she insisted, but not before someone shoved something vile-smelling under her nose.

She coughed, sneezed, and tried to brush away the hand in front of her.

"What is *that*?!"

"Smelling salts," said the woman crouching near her. She gave Annie a big smile and with her free hand pushed back the scarf that blew in her face. "I keep them in my purse for when I get my chemo."

Annie realized then why the woman had the scarf wrapped around her head. "Thank you," she said quietly. "But what's worse? Feeling dizzy or smelling that?"

The woman, who looked in her late thirties, laughed. "Smelling this. But you do what you gotta do to stay here, right?"

Nodding, Annie looked up into the concerned faces of her family crowded around her. "Talk about embarrassing." She held up her hand to her father, and he helped her to her feet.

"Thank you," her mother said to the woman, who nodded and walked away.

She turned to Annie. "Let's go find a ladies' room and put a cold cloth on your face. And don't tell me you're fine," she said as she took Annie by the arm and led her away.

Jenny grabbed paper towels, wet them with cold water, and held them to the back of Annie's neck. "How's that?"

"Wet. Cold." But she put up with it because her mother looked so concerned . . . and because she could tell it was helping. She gazed at her reflection and winced. Her skin was bleached of color, her eyes too big and dark. Her lips trembled.

Her mother hugged her. "Feeling any better?"

"A little." She felt her lips tremble. "Oh, *Mamm*, everything's such a mess. Aaron and I had a fight, and right in the middle of it he said he was going to ask me to marry him on the trip."

"Whoa, what?" Jenny's eyes were huge. "I knew he was serious, but—?"

"You missed the 'was' here," Annie said miserably, wadding up the paper towels and throwing them in a trash bin. Tears threatened. She dug in her purse for a tissue but couldn't find one.

Jenny pulled some tissues from her purse and handed them to Annie. "Don't panic. Every couple fights."

"You and *Daed* never do."

"Guess you forgot overhearing us having a . . . discussion the other morning. Listen, if God wants the two of you together, nothing can keep you apart. I saw that with your father and me."

Annie took a deep breath. "I know."

"Dry your eyes, and we'll go back to the hotel."

"I don't want Aaron to see me like this."

Jenny tilted her head and studied Annie. "You know what? We've been so busy rushing around sightseeing, we haven't had time to shop. Let's go do some retail therapy. It's Christmas, and we're in one of the best cities in the world to Christmas shop."

Annie didn't think she'd ever heard her mother use the term "retail therapy," but she made shopping in the city sound like such fun. "Okay."

"We'll start with Macy's. The men might not ever see us again."

❧

"Getting things together a little early, aren't you?"

Aaron looked up at Matthew standing in the doorway.

"I'm going to go to the airport and get a flight back."

Matthew sat down on the other bed. "Why would you do that? We're going home in the morning."

"I think it'd be better for everyone if I did."

"The fight was bad, eh?"

"She told you we had a fight?" Aaron asked warily.

"It doesn't take much to figure it out. But there's no reason to be taking off like this."

Aaron took some shirts from the chest of drawers and put them in his suitcase. "I didn't figure you, of all people, would want me sticking around."

Matthew shrugged. "Maybe you've grown on me a little. In any case, couples fight, and they patch things up."

"I don't think we're going to be able to patch this up." Aaron pushed the shirts down in the suitcase. "Maybe we're just too different."

"How?"

"You know. She's smart and creative and so ambitious."

"Those words could be used to describe you."

Aaron's eyes widened. "I'm just a practical guy who works with his hands."

"Like me."

"*Ya.*" Aaron wondered what he was saying.

"How would you describe Jenny?"

Aaron sank down on the bed next to his suitcase. "Generous in spirit and talented . . ." he paused and thought, then looked at Matthew. "And smart and creative and ambitious."

"You know, Annie is the same girl she's always been. She's always been scribbling, always been curious and adventurous. Coming here hasn't changed her."

"But can you take the girl out of the city?"

Matthew gave him a stern look. "Home and family mean more to Annie than I think you give her credit for." He rose and started out of the room, then turned back at the door. "So. You still going to the airport?"

"Maybe not."

"Did you look up what a flight back will cost?"

"Uh, no, not yet. Why?"

Matthew pulled out his cell phone, tapped on it, then held it out to Aaron. "Here, this is what it'll cost you."

Aaron nearly swallowed his tongue. "Oh." He would be ab im Kopp if he did so.

"I'm going to go make some coffee. Want some?"

He nodded. "That would be great."

They had a cup of coffee, then another. Played a game with Johnny. Matthew read the newspaper. Johnny complained about being bored and then went into the bedroom and fell asleep.

Aaron paced and looked out the window.

"It's five minutes since you last looked at the clock," Matthew said without looking up from his newspaper. "I've found when women say they're going shopping it's best to just relax and enjoy some quiet time."

"They've been gone for hours."

Matthew looked up. "And?"

"And—I don't know. I guess I wasn't expecting them to be gone so long."

"Sounds like you might be missing someone you couldn't get away from fast enough earlier."

Aaron felt himself flush. "When you put it that way . . ."

Grinning, Matthew folded the paper and set it on the coffee table. "Why don't we go wake up Johnny and go for a hot dog? Jenny and Annie wouldn't want us passing out from hunger."

Aaron figured Annie was going to be mad at him for quite a while, but he didn't think it was a good idea to say so to Matthew. He kind of liked the way they were getting along right now.

"Sounds good. Let's go before they get back."

They woke Johnny and bundled up and walked to the hot dog vendor they'd patronized the day before. This time they didn't make Johnny promise to keep a secret because what was the point? The kid had proven he couldn't keep a secret.

After they ate, they did a little shopping of their own. Johnny spotted a small store featuring snow globes and insisted they had to go inside.

"This is what started it all," Matthew said thoughtfully as he held up a snow globe that featured the *New York Times* building with snow swirling around it. "Jenny brought one home for Annie for Christmas one year."

He looked at Johnny. "She brought home some news that year that made my Christmas as well."

"Huh?" Johnny stared at him.

"We found out we were going to have a *boppli,*" Matthew told him.

"Oh. You mean me?"

"Do you know of any other *boppli* your *mamm* and I have had?"

Johnny giggled. "No."

Aaron picked up a snow globe of the network building Annie and Jenny had visited. He couldn't help wishing she'd never visited it. That was selfish, of course. But it was the truth. Maybe he wouldn't wait to give it to her for Christmas. Maybe it would be a good peace offering.

"So where are you from?" the shop clerk asked them when Aaron took the snow globe to her to ring up.

"Paradise, Pennsylvania."

"Oh, if you flew here you need to know the airlines don't allow these as carry-on."

"It's all right," Matthew assured her. "A friend arranged for a private plane for us."

The clerk whistled. "Some friend."

"He works at the TV network," Johnny spoke up. "Do you watch him? His name is David."

"Oh, the anchorman! I watch him all the time." The clerk wrapped the globe in bubble wrap, then settled it in a sturdy box and put it in a small shopping bag. She took Aaron's money and gave him change. "You have a wonderful Christmas, okay?"

Aaron watched Johnny walk over to a display of snow globes featuring storybook characters.

"What was I thinking?" he asked Matthew. "You know Johnny's going to tell Annie the minute we get back to the hotel."

"I'm afraid you're right." Matthew watched his son. "Let me think what to do."

In the end, Matthew bought Johnny a snow globe with his favorite childhood storybook character inside—Thomas the Tank Engine—and struck a bargain with him. Matthew told him he'd take the snow globe back if he breathed a word to Annie about the one Aaron bought her . . .

"Wasn't that a bribe?" Aaron asked Matthew as soon as Johnny had walked away.

Matthew looked at him.

"Never mind."

They made it back to the hotel just a few minutes ahead of Annie and Jenny. Aaron had time to hide the snow globe in his suitcase and join Matthew and Johnny in the living room just as the two women walked in, their cheeks pink with the cold and their eyes sparkling with excitement.

"We had such fun! The stores were so crowded!" Jenny said, setting her shopping bags down on the coffee table and collapsing into an arm chair. "My feet are killing me!"

"Her feet are killing her? *Daed*, she dragged me into so many stores!" Annie sank into her own chair and pointedly avoided looking in Aaron's direction. "Johnny, what have you got there?"

"A snow globe. It has Thomas the Tank Engine inside. See?"

Annie admired it. "Very nice. I like snow globes."

"I know." Johnny slid a surreptitious look at Aaron.

Annie followed the direction of Johnny's look, and Aaron met it with a bland one of his own. She glared at him and turned her attention back to her family, chatting with them as if he wasn't in the room at all.

Fine with him. He didn't know what God had planned for them. Surely, it was going to take Him to heal this rift because he didn't see any way for the two of them to do it themselves. He didn't like waiting once he'd made up his mind he wanted to do something.

But what else could he do?

18

It was so good to be back.

The city might have been exciting, but Annie loved where she lived and felt her excitement growing with every mile they got closer to the farmhouse.

Phoebe and Joshua met them at the door with hugs. Joshua used a cane, but his color was improved.

They barely had time to drop their luggage in their rooms and eat the supper of pot roast and vegetables Phoebe had prepared when family and friends started arriving.

Mary and her husband, Ben, came bearing two loaves of pumpkin bread still warm from the oven. And questions—Mary had so many of them. What had they done? Where had they gone? The banquet . . . what had it been like?

"You should have gone with us," Annie told her after she'd asked all the questions. "*Mamm* and I went shopping."

"I don't suppose you brought me something home," Mary said with a trace of wistfulness.

Jenny laughed and hugged her. "You'll have to wait for Christmas."

Joshua listened to the chatter for a few minutes and then he, Matthew, and Johnny put on their jackets and went to the barn.

"I never let him have the horse in the house," Phoebe said as she poured coffee for Jenny. "But I had trouble keeping him out of the barn while you were gone."

Hannah and Chris were next. It wasn't long before Chris joined the men in the barn.

"We got the postcards you sent," Hannah told Jenny and Annie. "The kids loved them. We'd have brought the kids over, but they're with their grandmother making Christmas presents."

Mary and Hannah caught them up on all the happenings while they'd been gone. A lot had happened. Several babies had been born. Leah from Stitches in Time had returned from visiting Pinecraft, Florida, with her husband.

Annie found herself tuning out as she wondered what Aaron was doing right now. She shook her head. Oh, why did she care?

"So are you going to tell us what happened with you and Aaron in New York City?" Hannah asked with a sly tone in her voice. "Did you get engaged?"

Annie felt a blush stealing up her cheeks. "Nothing happened," she said flatly.

"No?" Mary leaned forward and gave Ben a pointed look. "We thought the two of you would get engaged when you went to the city."

Ben held his hands up. "Hey, don't pull me into this. You asked me if I thought Annie and Aaron would get engaged and I said I didn't know." He stood. "I think I'll go see what they're doing out in the barn and leave you ladies to your talk."

"He's as big a gossip as any woman," Mary said.

"Speak for yourself," Annie said. She stood, picked up her mug, and put it in the sink. Leaning down, she hugged Phoebe. "I need to make a quick call to my boss before she goes to bed. I'll be right back to do the dishes."

"You don't need to do dishes on your first night back," Phoebe told her.

"I want to."

Annie didn't need to call her boss, but it was a good excuse to slip away from the questions about her and Aaron. She unlocked the phone shanty and made the call, then, when she went back to the house, she started washing the dishes.

"So you had a good time?" Phoebe asked her, joining her at the sink with a dish towel in hand.

She handed Phoebe a clean dish and nodded. "It was so much more than I thought it would be."

"But you seem sad."

"I'm just tired. We were on the go every minute."

Johnny came back into the house, bringing a gust of cold wind with him. He looked like he was pouting. "*Daed* said it was time for me to come in and get ready for bed."

"I'll be up in a few minutes to say good night," Jenny told him.

Johnny went up the stairs, seeming to make the trip take as long as he could. Annie grinned as she handed Phoebe another dish.

Phoebe dried the dish and put it in the cupboard. "You know my generation kept our relationships with the person we were courting private. So I'm not going to ask you questions like your sister. But if you want to talk, you know I'm here."

"I know. Thank you."

Mary brought the mugs she and Hannah had been drinking from to Annie to wash. "Phoebe, why don't you sit down and I'll help Annie."

Phoebe straightened and gave her a look. "I don't need to sit down."

"I know. I want a chance to hear some more about New York City."

Annie looked at Phoebe. "She means Aaron."

Phoebe grinned and handed the dish towel to Mary.

There was a flash of movement outside of the room. Annie looked out the window and saw her father standing outside the barn talking to her brother and Chris.

"It was so nice seeing *Mamm* and *Daed* getting a chance to relax and have some fun in the city," she told Mary. "They're always working so hard here. And you should have seen them at the banquet. She was very surprised to be remembered by so many people, and I think it floored her when they raised so much money for the foundation.

"And *Daed*! You should have seen how he looked so proud of her."

She smiled as she washed a mug, rinsed it, and handed it to Mary to dry. "And one night, they went for a walk, just the two of them, and they came back holding hands and looking so happy."

"What's this? Are you talking about me?" Jenny asked as she came up behind them.

"Guilty," Annie said with a laugh. "I was telling Mary how you and *Daed* looked so romantic when you came back from a walk one night."

Jenny rolled her eyes and shook her head. "We're not exactly elderly you know."

She leaned forward and looked out the window. "This reminds me so much of when I first came here. The time of year, I mean. Remember, Grandmother? The trees were bare, it was snowing, and I felt like everything was over for me. But it wasn't."

They heard a thump overhead. Jenny sighed. "I better go see what Johnny's up to. It sure doesn't sound like he's in bed reading, does it?"

"I wish you'd gone," Annie told Phoebe, glancing back at her. "The banquet was like nothing I'd ever seen, so fancy and with so many people all dressed up. All of them there to see *Mamm* and David and help raise money for the foundation." She looked at Mary. "I can finish the pots."

"Good. I had a long day." She went to sit at the table with Hannah.

Phoebe walked over to hang the wet dish towel to dry.

"I think it was the first time I realized *Mamm's* not just my mother," Annie mused. "She's a person of her own. Do you know what I mean?"

"*Ya*, I do. Sounds like you did some growing up while you were away."

"Aaron sure didn't act happy with me at the end," Annie blurted out before she could stop herself.

She glanced behind her and was relieved to see Hannah and Mary were talking and hadn't heard her. "Something happened there at the network, the place where *Mamm* worked before she came here. I'll tell you about it later, when they're gone. I don't want to share it, in case it doesn't work out."

Annie shook her head and sighed. "I don't know. Things have been changing so much. I don't know what's going to happen."

"Delight thyself also in the LORD: and he shall give thee the desires of thine heart," Phoebe murmured. "Commit thy way unto the LORD; trust also in him; and he shall bring it to pass." She smiled. "Psalm 37:4-5."

She handed the pot to Phoebe and let the water drain from the sink. "You know, I was always so curious about her life before she came here. *Mamm*'s I mean. She had this job that sounded so interesting, an apartment in the city she gave up."

"I gave up nothing," Jenny said quietly.

Annie jumped. "I didn't realize you were standing there."

Jenny handed her a coffee mug. "Just walked up. You know, I told Phoebe once I fell in love with Matthew's children before I fell in love with the man."

Smiling, Annie turned and hugged her mother. "I was so lonely, so needy after my mother died. I was hoping I'd get a new mother some day. I had this waiting heart. And then you came and all our lives were different."

"Wow," said Jenny, and Annie saw tears welling up in her eyes. "I didn't know it was Christmas yet."

∼⌒∽

Days passed without Aaron catching a glimpse of Annie.

It used to be he'd occasionally see her as she walked to work or they ran into each other. Or he went to her house for supper.

But he didn't do that—go to her house for supper. He figured they both needed some time to figure things out.

Trouble was, he'd been to see his doctor, who told him the brace had to stay on for at least another two weeks. So he had too much time to think. One day he'd gone by Stitches in Time and bought his mother a gift. Well, he hadn't bought a gift—he'd gotten her a gift certificate. Then she could buy whatever fabric or thread or whatever she wanted. He'd done it for her once for a birthday and she'd liked it.

Paul called his name and entered the workroom. "Good to see you back."

"It's good to be back."

Paul pulled up a chair. "Wife sent me into town for some last-minute things. I thought I'd see how you're doing. How was New York City?"

Aaron shrugged. "It was okay."

"But not a place you'd care to go back to."

"No. Annie, though . . ." he trailed off.

"Annie what?"

"I think she liked it. It's the kind of place writers like to go, I guess."

He didn't say more. It wasn't the way things were done. If Annie was going to take the internship, it was her news to share as she wanted.

At the thought, he frowned.

"Things didn't go the way you hoped?"

Aaron tossed down the pencil he'd been doodling with. "We spent a lot of time sightseeing. We didn't get to spend as much time together, just the two of us, as I'd hoped."

"Too bad." He said nothing for a moment. "How's the wrist?"

"Doctor said I need to wear the brace for another week or two." He turned the paper around. "I thought I'd make a couple of these and see how they go."

Paul nodded. "Dressers are one of our top sellers. Just let me know when you get one done and I'll put it up on the website. Oh, I have these for you."

He reached into his pocket, pulled out some papers, and handed them to Aaron. "You let me know when you can deliver them. We don't want to stress your wrist."

"Aaron?"

He straightened and his eyes widened when Annie stepped into the room.

"Oh, I'm sorry. I'm interrupting," she said when she saw Paul.

"Not at all," Paul got to his feet. "I came into town to pick up some things for my wife. I better get going." He turned to Aaron. "Let me know when you get the dresser done. No hurry. You have a merry Christmas and a happy New Year, both of you."

"You too," said Aaron, and Annie echoed him.

Aaron gestured at the chair Paul had vacated. "Please, sit down. Can I get you something to drink?"

Annie shook her head.

He couldn't take his eyes off her. It was so unexpected that she had suddenly appeared. And there wasn't a prettier girl in the world.

"How—?" they said at the same time and stopped.

"Ladies first."

"How have you been?"

"Good. You?"

"Good." She looked over at his sketch. "So you're already back to work. I thought you were supposed to give your wrist a rest."

"I am. This is just a sketch."

"What kind of wood are you going to use?"

"I'm not sure yet. I have to look at some, get a feel for what's best."

He shrugged. It wasn't something he'd ever talked about with anyone. To his own ears it sounded a little strange. A man who worked with his hands didn't have fancy words for the heart of the wood, what thing he could craft out of it that would be the best use of the living tree it had once been.

She paused and looked at it some more. "I read about Michelangelo. The sculptor. He said he could see the statue in the marble and had to chip away the marble so others could see it too."

"I'm hardly some artist."

"You should stop doing so many small projects and concentrate on things where you can use your creativity," she said. "I like this. It's the kind of thing you should do more often. It's . . . I don't know how to describe it. You're better than the other carpenters here. More creative."

Aaron felt his throat close up. How was it this woman who had aggravated him so much recently could know him so well? It was the kind of knowing that was more than the two of them growing up together, growing closer as they got older.

She just understood him. And he'd thought he understood her. *So how was it they'd come to feeling so awkward with each other?* he asked himself as silence stretched between them.

"Annie, why did you come here today?"

She sat straighter in her chair and looked at him. "I thought I'd see if you wanted to come to our house for Christmas."

Aaron found himself holding his breath. Was this an olive branch she was extending?

"I would like that very much," he said carefully.

Needing to do something with his hands, he picked up the measuring tape on his desk, turning it around and around. He knew a relationship meant compromise . . . meeting halfway. He just didn't see how they could work it out.

"Have you heard anything more about the internship?"

She shook her head. "David's agent said not to expect anything until after the first of the year. You know, because of the holidays."

"I see."

Annie stood. "I have to get back to work. I'll see you at Christmas."

Aaron got to his feet and watched her hesitate. He found himself moving toward her, reaching to touch her arm. "Annie?"

Her eyes flew to his, and she stared up at him with wide, startled eyes. "Yes?"

"I've missed you."

"I missed you too."

Aaron's cell phone rang.

Annie glanced at it, then at him. "You need to get that, and I need to get back to work."

Reluctantly, Aaron dropped his hand. "Have a good afternoon."

"You too."

She left and Aaron looked at the display on the cell. There was only one person he wanted to talk to, and she was walking out of the room. He let the call go to voicemail.

❧

Annie stood in the middle of the living room and gazed around. There was no place like home for Christmas.

The evergreen boughs she'd arranged on the fireplace mantel were simple, not at all like the Christmas decorations she'd seen in New York City—especially the big Christmas trees with lights and glittering ornaments.

But she loved the simplicity of the fresh boughs and smiled as she breathed in the scent. Votive candles in little glass jars cast a nice glow. Her father had lit a fire, and the flames danced merrily, warming the room.

Her mother had placed bright red poinsettias around the room. It seemed she couldn't get enough of them.

Annie smiled as she placed her father's worn leather-bound Bible on his favorite chair near the fireplace. It wouldn't be long before he'd be surrounded by friends and family as he sat there reading the story of the birth of Christ. The greatest story ever told.

Satisfied there was nothing else she could do, Annie started toward the kitchen to help with the food.

But first, she walked to the front room of the house and looked out the window by the door.

"Wonder who you're looking for?"

Annie rolled her eyes. "Don't tease."

Mary grinned and followed her into the kitchen. She opened a plastic container she'd brought and began arranging cookies on a plate.

Their mother and Phoebe set out cups for coffee and tea for the adults. Several percolators bubbled on top of the stove, filling the air with the welcoming scent of coffee. Milk warmed in a pan for hot chocolate for the *kinner*.

Hannah and Chris and their children arrived and then a nonstop stream of family and friends. Each time the door opened Annie felt a sense of anticipation, and each time she tried to look happy at the sight of the visitor.

"You *did* ask him to come, didn't you?"

Annie picked up a cookie and shoved it into her sister's mouth. Mary just chewed and after she swallowed, she laughed and hugged her. "I can't help it. I just want you to be as happy as Ben and I are."

Everyone came but Aaron.

She tried not to be disappointed but guessed she must not have done a good job of it. Her mother slid her arm around her waist and hugged her, and she caught her father watching her several times when she looked up.

As the evening dwindled to a close, people began drifting out, some of them carrying drowsy children in their arms. Annie wrapped her shawl around her shoulders, walked outside, and gazed up at the stars. It was a night to think about how the wise men had been guided by the one star to the baby Jesus on that special night so many years ago. She wished a certain man had been guided here tonight. Maybe, in spite of what she'd thought, Aaron wasn't the man God had intended for her.

Sighing, she turned and then heard something. A buggy approached, pulled into the drive. Aaron's buggy.

He got out and walked up to the porch. "I'm sorry. My grandmother fell ill. I tried to call your father's cell."

Annie's heart, battered though it felt, began beating again. "It was so noisy in there he must not have heard it. How is she doing?"

"Better. Annie, why are you standing out here? Aren't you cold?"

She lifted her face to look at the stars again. "It seems like a night to think about the star—the one on that special night."

He climbed the stairs and came to stand beside her.

The front door opened, and her mother stuck her head out. She took in Aaron's presence and went back inside. A moment later, she reappeared holding out Annie's jacket.

Annie walked over and took it from her.

"As long as you keep talking, you can work anything out," Jenny said quietly.

"You sure?" Annie asked and she could hear the trace of wistfulness in her voice.

"Just don't freeze to death out here. Come inside, and I'll make sure your father and I go upstairs, okay?"

Annie nodded. "Thanks."

"Merry Christmas, Aaron."

"Merry Christmas, Jenny."

The door closed again.

"Annie, I want to apologize for the way I acted in New York City."

She stopped in the act of putting on her jacket and stared at him.

"I was selfish. I was only thinking of myself."

A brisk wind blew across the porch. Annie shivered and drew her jacket on and began buttoning it with fingers stiff from the cold. She wondered if they should go inside, but she didn't want anything to interrupt what he seemed intent on saying.

"I don't want you to go back there," he said, moving closer.

"That doesn't sound like an apology," she said, stepping back.

"I don't want you to go, but I want you to do what makes you happy."

"Really?"

"Yes, I mean it." He reached for her hands and winced. "You're freezing. We should go inside."

"In a minute. What do you expect me to say?"

"Yes."

"Yes?"

"Marry me, Annie. We'll work it out. It might not be a traditional Amish marriage, but I figure being a little different has worked for some people I know."

She grinned. "Like my parents?"

"And a few others I know." He rubbed at her hands to warm them. "I want you to be happy, and if doing an internship there will make you happy, then that's what you'll do."

"You're such a hardhead," she told him, shaking her own head.

Shocked, he dropped her hands. "I'm trying to be a better man here, and you tell me I'm a hardhead?" he asked, exasperated.

"'Oh, ye of little faith,'" she said, and she surprised him by reaching up to kiss his cheek. "I tried to tell you David's agent thinks we have a good chance of me staying here and working long distance for the network on their project."

"If it was something that could be done, why didn't he mention it at the beginning?"

"I suspect Gordon thought I'd jump at the opportunity," she said. "I'm sure he's used to getting what he wants. David said to 'hang tough.'"

She tilted her head and looked at him. "My mother said as long as people keep talking, they can work things out."

"So she figures Gordon will let you do what you want?"

Annie laughed. "Actually, she said it just now when she handed out my jacket. She meant you and me."

Aaron bent his head and kissed her, and though his lips were cool when they first touched hers, they quickly warmed as passion built between them.

When they finally parted, Annie felt breathless, and for a moment, the stars spun overhead. She clung to him until the stairs stopped and simply hung there, sparkling in the black night sky.

"Let's go inside and get you warm."

She laughed and slipped her arm in his. "I'm already warm. But let's go in and tell my parents."

"This time next year, we'll be celebrating our first Christmas as man and wife," he said as they walked arm in arm across the porch.

Annie sighed happily. This was turning out to be the best Christmas ever.

Amish Recipes

Pumpkin Whoopie Pies

For the Pumpkin Cookies

3 cups all-purpose flour
1 teaspoon salt
1 teaspoon baking powder
1 teaspoon baking soda
2 tablespoons ground cinnamon
1 tablespoon ground ginger
1 tablespoon ground cloves
2 cups firmly packed dark-brown sugar
1 cup vegetable oil
3 cups pumpkin purée, chilled
2 large eggs
1 teaspoon pure vanilla extract

For the Cream Cheese Filling

3 cups confectioners' sugar
1/2 cup (1 stick) unsalted butter, softened
8 ounces cream cheese, softened
1 teaspoon pure vanilla extract

Directions

Preheat oven to 350 degrees. Line two baking sheets with parchment paper or a nonstick baking mat; set aside.

In a large bowl, whisk together flour, salt, baking powder, baking soda, cinnamon, ginger, and cloves; set aside. In another large bowl, whisk together brown sugar and oil until well combined. Add pumpkin purée and whisk until combined. Add eggs and vanilla and whisk until well combined. Stir flour mixture into pumpkin mixture and whisk until fully incorporated.

Using a small ice cream scoop, drop heaping tablespoons of dough onto prepared baking sheets, about 1 inch apart. Bake until cookies are just starting to crack on top and a toothpick inserted into the center of each cookie comes out clean, about 15 minutes. Let cool completely on pan.

For the filling: Sift confectioner's sugar into a medium bowl; set aside. Beat butter until smooth. Add cream cheese and beat until well combined. Add confectioners' sugar and vanilla, beat just until smooth. (Filling can be made up to a day in advance. Cover and refrigerate; let stand at room temperature to soften before using.)

Assemble the Whoopie Pies: Line a baking sheet with parchment paper and set aside. Transfer filling to a disposable pastry bag and snip the end. When cookies have cooled completely, spread filling on the flat side of half of the cookies. Sandwich with remaining cookies, pressing down slightly so that the filling spreads to the edges of the cookies. Transfer to prepared baking sheet and cover with plastic wrap. Refrigerate cookies at least 30 minutes before serving and up to 3 days.

Frrrozen Hot Chocolate

3 ounces chocolate—use a variety if you wish
2 teaspoons store-bought hot chocolate mix
1 ½ tablespoons sugar
1 ½ cups milk
3 cups ice
Whipped cream
Chocolate shavings

Directions

Chop the chocolate into small pieces. Place it in the top of a double boiler over simmering water. Stir occasionally until melted. Add the hot chocolate mix and sugar. Stir until completely melted. Remove from heat and slowly add ½ cup of milk until smooth. Cool to room temperature.

In a blender, place the remaining cup of milk, the room-temperature chocolate mixture, and the ice. Blend on high speed until smooth and slushy. Pour into a giant goblet and top with whipped cream and chocolate shavings.

Glossary

ab im Kopp—off in the head. Crazy.

aenti—aunt

allrecht—all right

boppli—baby

bruder—brother

dat—father

daed—dad

danki—thank you

Der Hochmut kummt vor dem Fall—Pride goeth before the fall.

grossmudder—grandmother

haus—house

guder mariye—good morning

gut-n-owed—good evening

kaffi—coffee

kapp—prayer covering or cap worn by girls and women

kichli—cookies

kind, kinner—child, children

kumm—come

lieb—love

liebschen—dearest or dear one

maedel—girl, unmarried young woman

mamm—mother

mann—husband

Mein Gott—my God

nee—no

onkel—uncle

Ordnung—The rules of the Amish, both written and unwritten. Certain behavior has been expected within the Amish community for many, many years. These rules vary from community to community, but the most common are to not have electricity in the home, to not own or drive an automobile, and to dress a certain way.

Pennsylvania Deitsch—Pennsylvania German

redd-up—clean up

rumschpringe—time period when teenagers are allowed to experience the *Englisch* world while deciding if they should join the church

schul—school

schurr—sure

schweschder—sister

sohn—son

verdraue—trust

wilkumm—welcome

wunderbaar—wonderful

ya—yes

Discussion Questions

(Spoiler alert! Don't read before you read the book!)

1. Annie has a special wish for Christmas. Have you ever had a special wish for Christmas? What was it? Did you get it?

2. What is your favorite Christmas memory? What traditions do you follow?

3. The place Annie hopes to go at Christmastime is so different for her. Have you ever taken an adventure to a new and different place? What did you hope to get from that adventure?

4. Annie wants to become a writer like her mother. Her interest in writing began when Jenny married her widowed father. Do you believe environment plays a role in who we become—in what we do? Or do you feel that people have a predisposition, a gene that determines their talents?

5. Do you believe opposites attract? Why or why not?

6. Do you think there is one perfect person for each of us? Or do you think there can be more than one?

7. The Amish believe that God "sets aside" a mate for us. Do you believe this?

8. When Annie meets someone in need, she reaches out to her, and there are unexpected consequences. Have you ever helped someone and had things turn out differently than you expected?

9. Annie has a very special dream—a goal. Conflict arises when the man who is interested in her doesn't understand. Does your significant other or your family understand and support a dream or goal of yours?

10. Annie's Christmas trip takes a disappointing turn. What do you do when you face disappointment?

11. When Annie complains that so much change is going on in her life, Phoebe tells her, "Delight thyself also in the Lord: and he shall give thee the desires of thine heart. Commit thy way unto the Lord; trust also in him; and he shall bring it to pass" (Psalm 37:3 KJV). What psalm or verse helps you when you are feeling distressed by change?

12. Phoebe, Jenny's grandmother, likes to say that she doesn't worry about someone, because if she worries she's saying that God doesn't know what He's doing. Do you agree or disagree?

13. When Aaron comes to talk to Annie, her mother advises her that if people just keep talking, they can work most things out. Do you agree?

*If you liked **Annie's Christmas Wish**, here's a look at how it all began, when Jenny King returns to Paradise, Pennsylvania, to stay with her Amish grandmother and recuperate from injuries from a car bombing. There, she is reunited with Matthew Bontrager, "the boy next door" she fell in love with years ago.*

A Time to Love

ﾟ

Book 1 of the Quilts of Lancaster County Series

1

Jenny woke from a half-doze as the SUV slowed to approach a four-way stop.

"No!" she cried. "Don't stop!"

"I have to stop."

"No!" she yelled as she lunged to grab at the steering wheel.

David smacked her hands away with one hand and steered with the other. The vehicle swerved and horns blared as he fought to stop. "We're in the States!" he shouted. "Stop it!"

Jenny covered her head and waited for the explosion. When it didn't come, she cautiously brought her arms down to look over at David.

"We're in the U.S.," he repeated quietly. "Calm down. You're safe."

"I'm sorry, I'm so sorry," she whispered. Covering her face, she turned away from him and wished she could crawl into a hole somewhere and hide.

He touched her shoulder. "It's okay. I understand."

Before he could move the SUV forward, they heard a siren. The sound brought Jenny's head up, and she glanced back fearfully to see a police car.

"Pull over!" a voice commanded through the vehicle's loudspeaker.

Cursing beneath his breath, David guided the SUV to the side of the road. He reached for his wallet, pulling out his driver's license.

A police officer appeared at David's window and looked in. Jenny tried not to flinch as he looked at David, then her. "Driver's license and registration, please."

David handed them over. "Officer, I'd like to explain—"

"Stay in your vehicle. I'll be right back," he was told brusquely.

When the officer returned, he handed back the identification. "Okay, so you want to explain what that was all about— how you started to run the stop sign and nearly caused an accident?"

"It's my fault," Jenny spoke up.

"Jenny! I—"

"Let her talk."

"You can't stop at a four-way," she told him in a dull voice. "You could get killed." She drew a quilt more tightly around her shoulders.

"You look familiar," the officer said, studying her face for a long moment. "Now I got it. You're that TV reporter, the one who was reporting from overseas, in the war zone—" he stopped. "Oh."

He glanced at David. "And you're that network news anchor. What are you doing in these parts?"

"Taking her to recuperate at her family's house."

The officer glanced back at Jenny. "Didn't know you were Amish. Thought they didn't believe in television."

Jenny fingered the quilt. "It's my grandmother," she said, staring ahead. "She's the one who's Amish."

She met the officer's gaze. "Please don't give David a ticket. It was my fault. I freaked and grabbed the steering wheel. I didn't want him to stop. But it won't happen again."

The officer hesitated then nodded as he touched the brim of his hat. "I have friends who've been through the same thing. Be careful. You've been through enough without getting into a car accident."

She nodded. "Thank you."

After returning to his patrol car, the officer pulled out on the road and waved as he passed them.

Jenny looked at David. "I'm sorry. I just had a flashback as I woke up, I guess."

"It's okay," he told her patiently. "I understand."

She sighed and felt herself retreating into her cocoon.

He glanced in his rearview mirror and got back onto the road. They drove for a few minutes.

"Hungry yet?"

She shook her head and then winced at the pain. "No."

"You need to eat."

"Not hungry." Then she glanced at him. "I'm sorry. You must be."

He grinned. "Are you remembering that you used to tease me about being hungry all the time?"

"Not really," she said. "Lucky guess, since we've been on the road for hours."

He frowned but said nothing as he drove. A little while later, he pulled into a restaurant parking lot, shut off the engine, and undid his seat belt. "It'll be good to stretch my legs. C'mon, let's go in and get us a hot meal and some coffee."

"I don't—"

"Please?" he asked quietly.

"I look awful."

"You look fine." He put his hand on hers. "Really. Let's go in."

Pulling down the visor, she stared into the mirror, and her eyes immediately went to the long scar near her left ear. It still looked red and raw against her too-pale skin. The doctor had said it would fade with time until she'd barely notice it. Later she could wear extra-concealing makeup, but not now, he'd cautioned. The skin needed to heal without makeup being rubbed into it.

"Jenny?"

She looked at him, really looked at him. Though he was smiling at her, there were lines of strain around his mouth, worry in his eyes. He looked so tired.

"Okay." With a sigh, she loosened her hold on the quilt and rewrapped her muffler higher and tighter around her neck. Buttoning her coat, she drew her hat down and turned to reach for the door handle.

David was already there, offering Jenny her cane and a helping hand. When she tried to let go of his hand, he tightened his.

"The pavement's icy. Let me help," he said. "Remember, 'Pride goeth before a fall.'"

Her eyes widened with amusement as she grinned. "You're quoting Scripture? What is the world coming to?"

"Must be the environment," he said, glancing around. Then his gaze focused on her. "It's good to see you smile."

"I haven't had a lot to smile about lately."

His eyes were kind. "No. But you're here. And if I said 'thank God,' you wouldn't make a smart remark, would you?"

She thought about waking up in the hospital wrapped in her grandmother's quilt and the long days of physical therapy since then. Leaning on the cane, her other hand in David's, she started walking slowly, and her hip screamed in pain with every step. Days like today she felt like she was a hundred instead of in her early thirties.

"No," she said, sighing again. "I think the days of smart remarks are over."

The diner was warm, and Jenny was grateful to see that there were few customers. A sign invited them to seat themselves, and she sank into the padded booth just far enough from the front door that the cold wind wouldn't blow on them.

"Coffee for you folks?" asked the waitress who appeared almost immediately with menus. She turned over their cups and filled them when they nodded. "Looks like we're gonna get some snow tonight."

"What are you going to have?" David asked.

Jenny lifted her coffee cup but her hand trembled, spilling hot coffee on it. Wincing, she set the cup down quickly and grabbed a napkin to wipe her hand dry.

David got up and returned with a glass of ice water. He dipped his napkin in it and wrapped the cold, wet cloth around her reddened hand. "Better?"

Near tears, she nodded.

"She filled it too full," he reassured her.

Reaching for an extra cup on the table, he poured half of her coffee into it. "Try it now."

Jenny didn't want the coffee now, but he was trying so hard to help, she felt ungrateful not to drink it.

"Better?"

She nodded, wincing again.

"Time for some more meds, don't you think?"

"The pain killers make me fuzzy. I don't like to take them."

"You still need them."

Sighing, she took out the bottle, shook out the dosage, and swallowed the capsules with a sip of water.

"So, what would you like to eat?" asked the waitress.

Jenny looked at David.

"She'll have two eggs over easy, bacon, waffles, and a large glass of orange juice," he said. "I'll have the three-egg omelet, country ham, hash browns, and biscuits. Oh, and don't forget the honey, honey."

The waitress grinned. Then she cocked her head to one side. "Say, you look like that guy on TV."

David just returned her grin. "Yeah, so I'm told. That and a dollar'll get me a cup of coffee."

She laughed and went to place their order.

Growing warm, Jenny shed her coat and the muffler. She sipped at the coffee and felt warmer. When the food came, she bent her head and said a silent prayer of thanks. Then she watched David begin shoveling in food as if he hadn't eaten in days, rather than hours.

She lifted her fork and tried to eat. "I like my eggs over easy?"

He frowned and stopped eating "Yeah. Do you want me to send them back, get them scrambled or something?"

"No. This is okay."

"How did you eat them at the hospital?"

She shrugged. "However they brought them."

Deciding she might have liked eggs over easy in the past but now they looked kind of disgusting, half raw and runny on the plate, she looked at the waffle.

"I like waffles?"

"Love them."

Butter oozed over the top and the syrup was warm. She took a bite. It was heaven, crispy on the outside, warm and fluffy on the inside. The maple syrup was sweet and thick. Bliss. She ate the whole thing and a piece of bacon too.

"Good girl," David said approvingly.

"Don't talk to me like I'm a kid," she told him, frowning. "Even if I feel like it."

He reached over and took her free hand. "I'm so proud of you. You've learned to walk again, talk again."

"I'm not all the way back yet," she said. "I still have memory holes and problems getting the right word out and headaches and double vision now and then. I have a long road ahead of me."

David looked out the window. "Speaking of roads . . . as much as I hate to say it, I guess we should get back on it as soon as we can."

Jenny turned to where David was looking and watched as an Amish horse-drawn buggy passed by slowly. The man who held the reins glanced over just then and their eyes met. Then he was looking ahead as a car passed in the other lane and the contact was broken.

He looks familiar, she thought . . . *so familiar.* She struggled to remember.

David turned and got the waitress's attention. As she handed him the check, she noticed Jenny, who immediately looked down at her hands in her lap.

"Why, you're that reporter, the one who—"

"Has to get going," David interjected. "She needs to get some rest."

"Oh, sure. Sorry."

She tore a sheet from her order pad and handed it to Jenny with a pen. "Could you give me an autograph while I go ring this up?"

She hurried off, sure that her request would be honored.

"Could you sign it for me?" Jenny asked David.

Nodding, he took the paper and quickly scrawled her signature, then added his in a bold flourish.

"Here you go, two for one," he told the waitress when she returned. He tucked a bill under his plate and got up to help Jenny with her coat.

The SUV seemed a million miles away, but she made it with his help. Once inside, she sank into the seat, pulled the quilt around her again, and fastened her seat belt.

"It'll take just a minute to get warm in here," David told her.

Jenny stroked her hand over the quilt. "I'm not cold. . . . I hate those pills," she muttered and felt her eyelids drooping. "Making me sleepy. The waffles . . . lots of carbons."

She opened her eyes when he chuckled. Blinking, she tried to think what could be so funny.

"Carbs," she corrected herself carefully after a moment, frustrated at the way the brain injury had affected her speech. "Lots of carbs. Don't think I used to eat lots of carbs."

"So take a nap," he told her. "You talk too much anyway." He grinned to prove he was teasing.

Smiling, she tried to think of a snappy comeback. They were always so easy for her, especially with David. But then she was falling into a dreamless sleep.

Sometime later, she woke when she felt the vehicle stop. "Are we there?"

"Stay here," she heard David say, then she heard his door open and felt the brief influx of cold air before it closed. She couldn't seem to wake up, as if her eyes were stuck shut. The door on her side opened, and she heard the click of her seat belt, felt arms lift her.

"I can walk," she muttered.

He said something she couldn't quite grasp, but his voice was warm and deep and so soothing that she relaxed and let him carry her. And then she was being laid on a soft bed, covers tucked around her.

Home, she thought, I'm home. She smiled and sank deeper in dreamless sleep.

⁓◖⁓

Jenny woke to find herself in a bed, the quilt spread over her. Bright sunlight was pouring in through the window.

The walls of the room were whitewashed and plain. There were few furnishings: an ancient, well-polished chest of drawers was set against one wall, a wooden chair beside the bed. A bookcase held well-worn volumes and a Bible.

She sat up and saw someone had propped her cane on the wall near the bed. Grasping it, she walked carefully to the chest of drawers. When she caught a glimpse of herself in its small mirror, she grimaced. Reaching into her purse on top of the chest, she pulled out her hairbrush and drew it through her short ash-blonde hair. Her face was too thin, the circles beneath her eyes so pronounced she felt she must look like a scarecrow. Even her eyes looked a faded gray.

Leaning heavily on her cane, huffing from exertion, she moved back to the bed and climbed into it. Pulling the quilt over her, she waited for her breathing to level.

It was so quiet here, so different from her apartment in New York City, which overlooked a busy street.

There was a knock on the door. "Come in," she called.

The door opened and her grandmother peeked around it. "I heard you moving about."

She smiled. "Yes. *Guder mariye, Grossmudder.*"

Phoebe's austere face brightened. "You remember some of the language?"

"Some."

Jenny found it interesting she could remember even though she struggled to find the right word in English right now. She held out her arms and her grandmother rushed to embrace her. They sat on the bed, wiping away tears.

"You got it," Phoebe said, looking at the quilt that covered Jenny.

Jenny's fingers stroked it. "I woke up in the hospital and it was tucked around me," she said quietly. "I said your name before I could say mine."

Phoebe's lined face crumpled, and she bent her head, searching in the pocket of her dark dress for a handkerchief.

"God brought you through it." She wiped at her tears and straightened her shoulders. "There is no place He is not."

I'd been in the valley of death, thought Jenny. She knew how close she had come. Maybe one day she could tell her grandmother how she had seen her grandfather and her parents shortly after she'd been injured. Jenny hadn't been particularly religious before, but she had to admit that her near-death experience had made her look at her life—what was left of what had been her life—in a new way.

A note had arrived with the quilt, a nurse had told her. She gave it to Jenny and then had had to read it because the head injury had left a lingering problem with double vision.

The words inside had been simple and direct: "Come. Heal." It had been signed "Your *grossmudder*, Phoebe."

Jenny studied her now. Phoebe's face was more lined and the strands of hair that escaped her *kapp* had more silver. But somehow she didn't seem any older than the last time Jenny had visited.

"You didn't come for so long after I wrote that I didn't think you would."

"I was doing physical therapy."

"David told me. He's a good man."

Jenny smiled briefly and then looked at the window. It was starting to snow. "I should get up and say good-bye so he can get on the road. I don't want him to get caught in a snowstorm."

"It's time to get up," Phoebe agreed, standing and lifting the quilt away from Jenny. "But he left last night."

"Left? Without saying good-bye?"

"There's a note for you. He spoke of something called 'e-mail' that's in a computer?"

Her lined face lit briefly with a smile. "I asked him if the machine he brought with your things ran on sunlight. He'd forgotten we have no electricity."

Jenny's lips curved. "A solar battery, hmm? Good idea, but mine doesn't have one. And that would still leave the problem of how to access the Internet."

"Internet?"

"Don't ask me to explain how it works," Jenny told her. "I interviewed someone about it once, but it's still a mystery to me."

She sighed. "I haven't had time to get a new phone. Maybe that should be first on my to-do list."

Phoebe handed her the cane. "First let's get you up and ready for this day we were given."

A sharp pain shot through Jenny's hip as she got to her feet, and she had to bite her lip to keep from moaning. She stood still for a moment to gear up for her next move. Phoebe held out her hand, work-worn, dry, and warm.

Jenny shook her head. "I don't want to hurt you."

"I'm stronger than I look. I lead a simple life, but I work hard. You remember from the two summers you came to visit."

Jenny nodded. It had been one reason she had told her father she didn't want to go back. She wanted to stay home, be with her friends and have fun, not work so hard harvesting summer crops and baking bread and scrubbing the kitchen.

And laundry. It was bad enough to have to scoop dirty clothes up and throw them into the washer and dryer back home. At her grandmother's house, laundry was a daylong chore. Who wanted that?

Instead of television there had been singing, and the songs weren't the latest pop hits—no, these were church hymns! It was such a drag, too, to hitch up a buggy instead of jumping into the car and having Dad drive her someplace.

Later, as she'd grown older, she'd regretted her youthful laziness, but it was too late then to visit. She was immersed in college, an internship at a TV station, and then her demanding job that took her everywhere but Lancaster County, Pennsylvania.

Her grandmother was older, a little more bent, but the bright light in her eyes was still there, reminding Jenny of the bird she was named after. And her spare frame looked strong beneath the simple dress and black apron she wore.

The medication had worn off long ago. Jenny wanted to just sink back into bed, but she couldn't. She needed to get moving. She saw Phoebe glance down and a quiet gasp escaped from her lips.

The pant leg of her sweats had ridden up as she moved to the edge of the bed and stood. The light faded from Phoebe's eyes as she glimpsed the scars that ran down the length of one leg.

Bending, Jenny pulled the leg of her sweats down to cover them.

"I didn't want to move you too much when we put you to bed," she told Jenny. "So I left your clothes on you." She cocked her head to one side. "Is that what the *Englisch* are wearing these days?"

"When they want something comfortable to relax in," Jenny told her with a grin.

With one hand, she pulled the tunic down over her hips and smoothed its wrinkles.

"Let's get you some breakfast and then you can take a bath and get fresh clothes on."

"Sounds wonderful."

Walking to the kitchen was a major challenge. Jenny insisted that she needed to walk without her grandmother's help and took the short journey slowly.

"I can't believe David carried me into the house."

"He didn't," said Phoebe, following a step behind.

Jenny stopped and turned to look at Phoebe. "You didn't."

Again there was a ghost of a smile on Phoebe's face. "*Nee.* It was Matthew."

Images flitted through Jenny's mind as she started to navigate the way again. She remembered strong male arms, a deep voice that had sounded comforting when she'd sleepily insisted she could walk.

"Matthew?" she repeated. There was something about that name, but she couldn't quite remember . . . one of the lingering effects of the head injury.

"He lives on the farm next to mine. He came to see if I needed any help."

"And I'm sure David was grateful for his help." She laughed. "David is a nice man, but he doesn't lift anything heavier than his wallet."

Wallet. Jenny frowned as she thought about what was going to happen to hers. The network was covering her salary, but how long would it do that? Disability payments would be less whenever they started. She didn't want to dip into her savings, but she knew it might be months before she could go back to work.

And who knew if she'd ever be able to do the overseas reporting she'd become known for?

Her grandmother's kitchen hadn't changed. There were simple counters and wooden cupboards, practical pottery bowls set on a shelf. A propane stove filled the room with warmth, and the scent coming from its oven promised something delicious would emerge soon. A hand-carved wooden table was big enough to seat an army. Jenny sank into one of its wooden chairs.

Jenny hadn't had much appetite for a long time, but her mouth watered when she smelled the bread baking and the coffee brewing. Oh, the scent of the coffee!

Her grandmother sliced a loaf that had just been pulled from the oven a few minutes before. She placed it on a plate, setting out a bowl of churned butter, a jar of wild blueberry preserves, and a dish of hard-boiled eggs.

Jenny bent her head and gave thanks for the meal. When she looked up, Phoebe was smiling.

"I'm glad that you still say your prayers."

"Dad left the Amish, but he didn't forget God," Jenny told her. "We visited a lot of churches until he found the one he liked, but having a spiritual relationship with God was always important in our home."

Phoebe patted her hand. "I know. He wrote me once that he did a year of missionary work in Haiti while you were in college. I just wasn't sure if you remembered God after you left home."

"Oh, I surely did."

As her grandmother turned to stir the soup pot already simmering on the stove, Jenny felt a pang of guilt, remembering how often lately she'd questioned God about what had happened to her—questioned Him about how He could let innocent children suffer as she'd witnessed so often in her work.

There was a knock at the door. Phoebe crossed the room to answer it and greeted a tall man who looked about Jenny's age. The morning light coming in the kitchen window caught at his blond hair when he took off his wide-brimmed black hat and hung it on a wooden peg.

When he removed his winter coat, Jenny saw his plain shirt and pants that showed off his muscular physique. His blue eyes sparkled as he greeted her grandmother and then glanced over at Jenny.

She stared at him, searching her mind for his name when he continued to stare hard at her. He knew her. She could tell it from the way his expression looked hopeful, then disconcerted when she didn't immediately respond. *Why can't I remember his name?*

"Jenny, this is Matthew," said Phoebe as she poured his coffee.

She felt so awkward sitting there, painfully aware of the scar on her cheek, of her rumpled sweats.

He pulled out a chair and sat at the table with the air of a guest who was frequent and welcome. His eyes were filled with a quiet, thoughtful intensity. "I thought you might need help this morning," he told Jenny.

"My grandmother said you carried me inside last night. Thank you. But I could have walked."

He smiled. "Perhaps. But you were sleeping so soundly."

Jenny found herself staring at his large, strong hands as he cupped his mug and drank the coffee her grandmother had poured. When Phoebe pushed the plate of bread and preserves toward him, he grinned and took a slice, spreading it thickly with preserves. He bit into the bread with relish.

"Nothing like your bread," he told her.

"I have a loaf in the oven for you," she said.

"*Wunderbaar.* I'm going into town. Annie has her appointment. Do you need anything?"

When she shook her head, Matthew turned to Jenny. "You?"

"A new back and hip," she wanted to say. But she didn't want to call attention to herself, didn't want to make her grandmother worry. She shifted in her chair, wishing she'd taken her detested pain pills to the kitchen with her. So she shook her head and thanked him again.

"Ah, Matthew, I've thought of something," Phoebe said suddenly. "I'll get the money."

"No need to give me money—"

But with her usual spryness, she'd already hurried upstairs for it.

Jenny liked the sound of Matthew's voice. She watched as he took another slice of bread and spread it with more preserves.

"You should try some," he said, pushing the jar toward her.

There was something on the edge of her consciousness, something that tugged and tugged at her memory. The preserves . . . what was it about them that made her think there was a link between the man and her?

She looked up and found him watching her with unusual intensity. It was almost as if he were trying to use telepathy to make her search her memory.

But for what? she asked herself. *For what?*

2

"Raspberries," said Jenny, then she stopped, shaking her head. "No, strawberries." Frustrated, she rubbed her temples. "No, that's not the word."

Tears sprang to her eyes, and her lips trembled. Unable to look at him, she stared at her plate, feeling humiliated. Days like this, she wondered if she would ever get better.

"It'll come," he said quietly. "Don't force it. Give yourself time to heal."

She looked up at him, saw the kindness in his eyes, then looked away. "It's like wires get crossed in my brain and I can't get the right word out."

"Give yourself time to heal," he repeated.

"Easy for you to say," she muttered.

He smiled. "Do you know what my Annie calls them? Boo berries."

"Annie?"

"My youngest. She's had some trouble talking."

"It's taking forever." Frustration warred with despair. "I can't go on camera looking like this, talking like this. Having trouble with my memory."

Matthew got up to get more coffee for them. She caught the scent of hay, of horses, of the outdoors. It was a pleasant, familiar smell of man and work.

"You look fine to me," he told her.

Her hand went to her cheek before she could stop herself. She shook her head. "You're just being nice."

"Eat," he said. "You're as tiny as a sparrow. Frail too."

I've never been described that way, she thought, stirring her coffee. A memory came to her, a cloudy one, of being carried through the cold and dark night. There had been movement and a voice she couldn't quite place and yet she had felt safe.

Looking up, she found he was watching her. "I'm sure I was heavier than a little bird when you carried me in."

He shook his head. "You don't weigh much more than my older daughter, Mary."

"David could have helped me."

"The *Englischer* wanted to, but he had on city shoes. The walkway was slippery. I feared he'd take a fall and hurt you both."

"You should have woken me. I could have walked," she repeated. Then she bit her lip. "I'm sorry. I must sound ungrateful. Thank you for helping last night."

Matthew nodded. "Sometimes we need to let someone care for us."

He glanced in the direction of her grandmother's bedroom, hesitated, then looked at Jenny. "Phoebe has faith that God is watching over you, but it's good that you came. I think she needs to take care of you."

Her grandmother hurried back then and gave Matthew a list and some money. She insisted on filling a metal Thermos with hot chocolate for him and Annie, saying it was a cold morning and they might want a hot drink.

He got to his feet and put on his outdoor things. As he opened the door to leave, he glanced back at Jenny. And then he was gone.

"You haven't eaten much," Phoebe said when she came to sit at the table again.

"Oh, it's not your cooking," Jenny said quickly. "I just haven't had much of an appetite."

Making an effort, Jenny spooned some of the preserves on her bread and bit in. The sweet taste of blueberries flooded her mouth, flooded her memory.

A hot summer day. Her fingers stained blue and dripping juice from picking the bucket of berries in her hand. A young blond man, his eyes as blue as the berries, standing there looking at her and laughing.

Matthew.

And her first kiss, so innocent and so sweet.

No wonder he had looked at her the way he had, as if he wanted her to remember something. She hoped she hadn't hurt his feelings.

Her grandmother was speaking. Jenny pulled herself back from the memories that, once started, wouldn't stop. "I'm sorry. What did you say?"

"You're looking pale. Maybe after breakfast you should lie down on the sofa before the fire."

Her back was aching, and the headache was beginning to be one she couldn't ignore. "I just hate being like this. I want to get back to normal."

"Patience, Jenny. This will take time."

"I wish I had your faith that everything is going to be all right," Jenny said as she walked slowly toward the sofa in the living room.

With a grateful sigh she sank down onto it and smiled as Phoebe pulled a new quilt over her.

"Warm enough?"

Jenny covered her yawn and nodded drowsily. "Wonderful. Thank you. For—for anything." She opened her eyes. "Everything."

Phoebe's smile was grave. "I knew what you meant. Rest, *Grossdochder*. Rest, dear one."

Exhaustion weighed down on Jenny like a soft, warm quilt. She slept.

⁘

Their eyes.

This was the first thing Jenny noticed on her first visit to the war-torn country. The children were so thin, so listless, their eyes vacant and staring. Mothers held them, their eyes desperate. No words were needed to communicate their fear that they'd lose their children before they got them food.

She could barely keep the tears from her voice as she spoke on camera of the plight of the children, the innocent victims of warfare.

Then there was a movement, the cameraman catching her eye as he looked past her, over her shoulder. As the camera moved she glanced in the direction he looked and saw the car hurtling toward them.

Turning back, she screamed a warning and the mothers and children scattered. Then, miraculously, the car stopped just feet from her. A man burst from it and ran.

Instinct made Jenny spin on her heel and run, but she wasn't fast enough. There was a deafening explosion, and she felt herself lifted, thrown, and slammed into the ground.

Jenny screamed and woke. Terrified, her heart pounding, she sat up and stared around her.

A man rushed into the room, and she nearly screamed again before she realized it was Matthew.

"Jenny?"

Tears rushed out of her eyes as her fingers clutched at the quilt. She was shaking, shaking so hard she felt she'd fall apart at any moment.

"Bomb!" she whispered.

Matthew knelt beside the sofa and took her hands in his. "Jenny, you're safe. Look at me, Jenny. You are safe. I promise."

Her breath hitching on a sob, she stared at him, her eyes wide with fear.

Her grandmother appeared in the doorway. "Jenny?"

"She's all right," Matthew told her, not taking his eyes from Jenny. "She must have had a bad dream." He pulled the quilt up around her shoulders. "You're here, at your *grossmudder*'s. You're safe."

"*Daedi?* Is the lady *allrecht?*"

Jenny turned her head at the sound of the childish voice. Phoebe held the hand of a little girl of about four who wore a simple long navy dress. Her eyes were the same blue as her father's, full of concern like his. Her pink cheeks were rounded, the picture of health and well-being, her blonde hair carefully brushed and drawn into two pigtails. She looked nothing like the children in Jenny's dream.

Gradually, Jenny's racing heart settled down and her breathing evened. "Bad—bad dream."

Her doctors called it post-traumatic stress disorder. But Jenny doubted either Matthew or Phoebe knew the term or what it meant.

The child watching her with big eyes didn't look like she even knew what a bad dream was. She put her hands on Jenny's cheeks and frowned. "*Fiewer.* Lady has a *fiewer.*"

Phoebe stepped forward and placed the back of her hand on Jenny's forehead. She frowned. "Jenny, you're awfully warm. Maybe I should get the thermometer."

"I'm just warm from the fire," Jenny said, but she knew it wasn't true. She'd experienced fevers several times since she'd been injured, but they always went away.

Phoebe looked doubtful, but she didn't insist. She turned to Matthew's little girl and took her hand. "Annie, come with me. I baked cookies today."

"I hope I didn't scare her," Jenny said as Phoebe left the room with Annie.

He shook his head and stared at her, his expression sober. "Do they come often, these bad dreams?"

She shrugged. "Less often these days. It must have been because I was so tired from traveling."

Annie came back into the room, carefully holding a glass of water. She held it out to Jenny. "*Wasser.*"

Jenny searched for how to say thank you. "*Danki,*" she pronounced carefully and the little girl smiled.

"Annie? Will you come help me put some cookies in a bag for your brother and sister?" Phoebe called from the kitchen.

The child looked at Matthew, and when he nodded, she ran from the room.

"You'll be all right now?" he asked her.

She nodded, avoiding his gaze, and drank some water.

"Jenny? There is no need to be embarrassed."

Lifting her eyes to his, she looked for pity and found none.

"From what your friend said, you have been through a lot."

"David talks too much."

Matthew grinned. "He's a good friend. When you were hurt, he came all the way here to tell Phoebe what had happened."

Wrapped, cocoon-like, in the quilt, Jenny stared at him. "He never told me that."

She'd wondered how he'd seemed to know how to get to her grandmother's last night with nothing more than the address. He hadn't used the GPS in the SUV. But David was a terrific investigative reporter. She'd assumed he'd looked it up somehow.

"We'll be going, then," Matthew said.

She nodded. "Thank you."

"*Du bischt willkumm.*"

Getting stiffly to her feet, she walked into the kitchen behind him. He carried his little girl out to the buggy, set her on a seat, then climbed inside. *The Amish love children, and Matthew obviously adores his little girl*, thought Jenny. She smiled as he kissed Annie on the forehead before he tucked a blanket around her.

Jenny stood at the window, watching the buggy roll down the road until she couldn't see it anymore.

When she turned, she saw that her grandmother was watching her.

"What is troubling you, Jenny?"

"I was remembering the last time I saw Matthew. I had a crush on him."

Jenny gazed at the winter-bare landscape, the trees void of leaves, their branches black against the gray sky. *Barren*, she thought, *like me*. She wrapped her arms around her waist, suddenly cold.

Her grandmother touched her shoulder. "Why are you so sad?"

"His little girl is so beautiful."

Phoebe pulled a clean handkerchief from her pocket and gave it to Jenny. She stared at the snowy square, not sure when she'd last seen such a thing. For a moment she didn't know why her grandmother had handed it to her, then realized that she had tears on her cheeks.

"Talk to me, tell me what's wrong, *liebschen*."

"I don't want to burden you."

"Why should talking burden me?"

Her legs were shaking from standing so long. Jenny walked slowly to a kitchen chair and sat. "You've been so kind to have me stay—"

"I haven't been kind, Jenny. You are my *grossdochder*."

"One who hasn't been the best at keeping in touch."

Phoebe's eyes were kind as she spoke. "Sometimes there is distance in families."

Jenny knew she meant more than the physical miles. Once her father had decided not to be baptized when he turned sixteen, he'd left the Amish community and never looked back. He'd only visited after his father died, and then he let Jenny come during those two summers years ago.

"I loved your letters, especially the ones from overseas. You described everything so that I could see it."

Not everything, thought Jenny. There had been a desire to protect this woman who lived the Plain life, as the Amish called it, from the terrible things she saw over there.

And yet, from the brief time she had visited here, she knew that life in an Amish community wasn't idyllic. Life was still life. Bad things happened, like when a farmer's tractor overturned and crushed him or a hit-and-run driver had killed a little boy walking a country road to school. Matthew's wife had died young; she remembered that Phoebe had written to her that the woman had been a victim of cancer. Not even the best treatment from the local *Englisch* hospital had been able to save her.

Life was life, after all, wherever it was lived.

"Jenny?" Her grandmother's voice was gentle but determined.

"The doctors say I might not have children. I had infernal—" she stopped, searching for the right word—"internal injuries."

Actually, she thought bitterly, *I might have gotten the word right the first time.*

Phoebe took her hand. "If it's God's will, you'll have them," she said simply.

"You say that a lot." Jenny wiped her eyes. "God's will."

Phoebe squeezed the hand she held. "It's simple but true. Now, eating something warm on this cold day will make you feel better."

"It's lunch already?" Glancing at her watch, Jenny saw that she'd slept nearly four hours.

"*Ya.* Hungry?"

"Not really."

She hadn't thought she was, but when Phoebe lifted the lid of the pot simmering on the stove, she discovered that the smell of the vegetable soup was enticing.

"Well, maybe a little."

"A good bowl of hot soup on a cold day," her grandmother said, serving it up with slices of bread.

Comfort food, thought Jenny. She needed it.

❧

Matthew walked into his house, letting in a blast of cold air. He stamped his feet on the doormat and pulled off his gloves, tucking them into his coat pockets. Shrugging off the coat, he hung it and his hat on the pegs on the wall by the door. He rubbed his hands together. "Cold out there."

His sister Hannah hurried over to take Annie's hat and coat off. She picked her up and gave her a big kiss on her cheek. "Your cheeks are cold, Annie. Go wash your hands, and we'll eat."

Obediently, Annie ran from the room. Hannah turned to Matthew. "How did her session go?"

"The therapist feels her speech is coming along fine," Matthew told her, washing his hands at the kitchen sink.

As he dried his hands, he watched her move about the kitchen, stirring the pot of hearty split-pea soup with chunks of ham, then getting out soup bowls and setting the table. She'd been sixteen when his wife had died three years ago and had moved in to help him take care of his *kinner*. The two of them were separated by twelve years, but they agreed on most things as a rule, so the arrangement had worked out well.

"You took longer than usual."

"I stopped by Phoebe's with some things she needed from town."

"Ah, I see."

Matthew settled into a seat at the kitchen table and Hannah put a bowl of soup before him. "You see what?"

"I heard that Phoebe's *grossdochder* is visiting."

Matthew nodded. He smiled when Annie ran back into the room and held out her hands for his approval. Smiling, he patted the seat of the chair beside him. "Your *Aenti* Hannah has prepared some nice warm soup for us."

Hannah set a bowl of soup at her own place, then a smaller one at Annie's. "That should warm you right up. Then it's time for a nap before Joshua and Mary come home from school."

The three of them bent their heads to ask a blessing for the meal before they began eating. Hannah buttered a piece of bread for Annie, took one for herself, and passed the plate to Matthew.

"The lady had a bad dream," Annie said suddenly.

"Lady?" Hannah looked curiously at Matthew.

"Jenny, Phoebe's *grossdochder*."

Hannah waited but Matthew didn't say more. *Men!* she thought. Well, there was more than one way to get information. She smiled at Annie. "What happened?"

"She was taking a nap, and she had a bad dream." Annie stirred her soup. "And *Daedi* held her hand."

Her eyes wide, Hannah turned to her brother. He looked a little embarrassed but said nothing as he reached for a slice of bread and buttered it with unusual care.

"He told her she was safe," Annie told Hannah.

"Annie, eat your soup."

"*Ya, Daedi.*" She put a spoonful into her mouth, then swallowed. "She says some words funny, like me."

"Matthew?"

He looked up from his soup.

"Do I have to pull it out of you?" she asked, exasperated.

"The Amish grapevine isn't working well enough to get information about Jenny?"

She frowned. "It's not wrong to be curious."

"If you say so."

"I remember how you felt about—" she stopped as she caught Matthew's warning look.

Glancing over, he saw Annie drooping over her empty bowl. "Time for a nap, Annie. Sweet dreams."

Annie slid down from the chair and stood by her father. She stared up at him with big blue eyes. "*Daedi*, you should have told the lady to have sweet dreams."

He nodded solemnly. "You're right. Next time I will."

When she held out her arms, he reached down and hugged her.

Hannah smiled as she got a hug too. "She is such a loving child." Getting up, she poured her brother a cup of coffee and set it before him. "Pie?"

"Of course."

She cut him a piece and smiled as he forked up a bite and sighed as he chewed it. He loved her baking. "It's time you thought about getting married again."

Matthew choked on the pie and took a gulp of coffee. "Where did that come from?"

"It's been three years. You need a wife. Your children need a mother." She sat again at the table. "Amelia would want you to be happy, for the children to have a mother. You know that."

Leaning back in his chair, Matthew regarded his sister thoughtfully. "You've been a wonderful sister, coming here to help—"

She waved away his words. "Family helps family."

"But you've put aside your own life. It's time you did what you wanted. Time you got married."

Standing, she gathered the bowls to wash them. "I have been doing what I wanted. And you're trying to change the subject."

He hid his grin by taking another sip of coffee. She knew him well. "How is Jacob?"

"I'm sure he's fine," Hannah told him. "But he's not the right one for me." She sat again. "I remember how you felt about Jenny."

"That was years ago."

"And now she's back."

"She's back to heal, Hannah, not to look in my direction again."

"But it could happen."

Taking a last sip of coffee, Matthew stood. "I have work to do."

She swatted at him as he passed her to reach for his coat. "Think about it," she told him.

"Did you forget she's *Englisch*?" he asked her gravely, settling his hat on his head. "She's not part of our world."

"No? Then why did she return?" Hannah wanted to know.

Matthew stared at her for a long moment. "Because Phoebe is her family. Jenny needs to recover, to have someone watch out for her. That is the only reason."

Hannah tilted her head as she watched him pull on his gloves. "Maybe. Maybe not. All I'm saying is you should think about it."

"I have work," he repeated. "And so do you. No more romantic daydreaming, Hannah. Idle hands, remember?"

Exasperated, she threw a kitchen towel at him, but she missed, and he walked out the door, laughing. Another blast of cold air, then he shut the door.

✍

Matthew thought about what Hannah had said as he moved about doing his chores. She'd shocked him when she'd said it was time for him to get married again. He hadn't thought about such a thing since Amelia died.

And he hadn't thought enough about what her living at his house, caring for it and his *kinner*, had done to her own life. He'd been selfish.

It was true that he'd been in shock from the day his Amelia had died after six months of desperate attempts to save her. He'd walked and talked and taken care of his children and his farm, but he'd been lost in his grief.

Then one day he woke up and realized that for two years he'd just existed.

Now he realized his children were his responsibility and it was time to see that Hannah found a life beyond his home. Time she found the happiness she deserved so much.

As he forked up hay for his horses, he thought about Jenny too. If Hannah had seen Jenny as he had today, she'd have known that Jenny hadn't returned hoping to rekindle their relationship. She'd come at her grandmother's invitation to heal here.

Jenny. She was so fragile, reminding him of a bird with a broken wing, a broken voice. Her eyes had looked so lifeless. The long blonde hair he remembered had obviously been shorn for her surgery. And the scar on her face. . . .

His hand tightened on the bucket of feed for his horses. How his heart ached at the way she'd been so self-conscious about it. She was still beautiful, but it was obvious that she didn't feel that way. She was so different from the bright, happy, carefree teenage girl he remembered and not just because she was older and she was struggling to talk and to move. No, it was obvious that Jenny was experiencing so much inner pain. He'd been getting a box from his buggy when he'd heard her scream as if monsters were chasing her. She'd been shaking so hard her teeth chattered when he reached her.

He hadn't told Hannah that Jenny didn't remember him. Shame came over him again now as he thought of how his pride had been hurt. Then he'd realized how badly Jenny was injured and he knew it would be very small of him to tell her about his hurt feelings.

Their worlds were so different and so much time had stretched between them, so many experiences. Once, they'd been friends. Once, they'd almost been more.

Then Matthew and her father had talked. The older man had shown up several weeks before the time Jenny was due to leave. He found Matthew out in the field and insisted they had to talk. Somehow the man had found out that his daughter was seeing Matthew. He said the relationship was over, that he'd left the Amish community behind, and he wouldn't allow her to be married to someone from it. He insisted she deserved a chance to go to college. He'd wanted her to have more than she'd have in the Amish community.

And that was that. Matthew was forced to agree there was no future for him with Jenny. It was all he could do. He had to respect her father. Respect for the head of the household came first in the community.

He never got a chance to talk to Jenny again before her father took her away later that day. He never knew if her father told her they'd talked. But she never answered the two notes he sent to her—even sent them back unopened.

Matthew tried to force away the painful memories. God hadn't meant for them to marry, he told himself, and he'd worked hard to forget her and he had married another.

He'd be a friend to Jenny now if she wanted one. He'd help her in any way that he could, for he'd discovered that he still cared so much for her.

And he'd pray that God would keep His gentle hand on this child of His and help her heal.

Want to learn more about author
Barbara Cameron and check out other great
fiction from Abingdon Press?

Sign up for our fiction newsletter at
www.AbingdonPress.com
to read interviews with your favorite authors, find tips
for starting a reading group, and stay posted on what
new titles are on the horizon. It's a place to connect
with other fiction readers or post a
comment about this book.

Be sure to visit Barbara online!

www.BarbaraCameron.com
www.AmishLiving.com

Look for a new Amish series beginning in 2014
by Barbara Cameron.

AMISH ROADS

**Some say that if you look at a map to see where Goshen,
Indiana, is that you'll see that all almost all Amish
Country roads lead to this charming community.
But all those roads lead out of Goshen too.**

For three young Amish women, the roads leading out of this
Amish community were the most tempting. They left during
their *rumschpringe*, wanting freedom from family and the
rules of the church, and shared an apartment in Indianapolis.
Now in their twenties, they are questioning their decision.

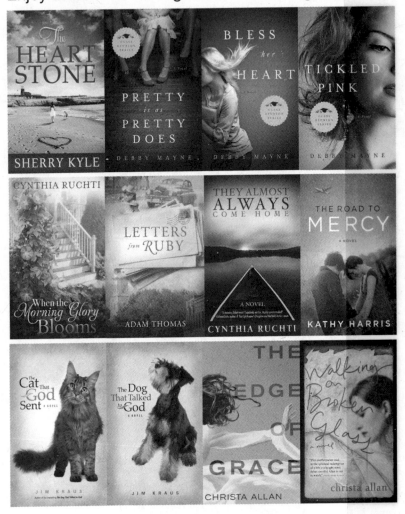